KARIM,

KING OF ENGLAND

KARIM,
KING OF ENGLAND

Baz Wade

— Matador
9 Priory Business Park,
Wistow Road, Kibworth Beauchamp,
Leicestershire. LE8 0RX
Tel: 0116 279 2299
Email: books@troubador.co.uk
Web: www.troubador.co.uk/matador
Twitter: @matadorbooks

ISBN 978 1789015 782

British Library Cataloguing in Publication Data.
A catalogue record for this book is available from the British Library.

Printed and bound in Great Britain by 4edge Limited
Typeset in 12pt Minion Pro by Troubador Publishing Ltd, Leicester, UK

Matador is an imprint of Troubador Publishing Ltd

For C.R.

Glossary

A & R. Artists & Repertoire. The division of a record label responsible for talent scouting.

BALFOUR DECLARATION. A statement contained in a 1917 letter from Balfour, the UK Foreign Secretary, to Lord Rothschild saying that HMG (see post) favoured "the establishment in Palestine" of a "national home for the Jewish people" provided that the rights of existing Arab communities were not prejudiced. The statement was essentially a fudge and has since been relied on by Israel and the Palestinians to justify conflicting standpoints.

*****BRITISH FREE STATE.** New name of RUK (see post) following declaration of Republic after abdication of the Monarch.

CHURCHILL, WINSTON. British politician instrumental in promoting disastrous Gallipoli campaign in 1915 as First Lord of the Admiralty. Wartime Prime Minister 1940-1945.

COLLINS, MICHAEL. Irish revolutionary, who was a leading figure in the early 20th century Irish struggle for independence. Active in Sinn Fein, the Irish Nationalist organisation. Negotiated with the UK Government, the 1921 Treaty creating the Irish Free State (later the Irish Republic). Killed by the IRA in 1922 for agreeing compromise allowing Northern Ireland to remain part of the UK.

CORTINA D'AMPEZZO. Italian ski resort in the Dolomites.

DISH DASH. Ankle length one-piece garment worn by men in Arab countries, including Dubai.

DYLAN, BOB. North American singer songwriter.

EEA. European Economic Area established 1994. Comprises the 28 member states of the EU (see post) plus the member states of EFTA (see post) excluding Switzerland. The member states are expected to comply with the 4 freedoms of the European Single Market comprising the free movement of labour, goods, services and capital.

EFTA. European Free Trade Association. A regional trade organisation and free trade area established in 1960 which comprises Norway, Switzerland, Iceland and Liechtenstein.

EU. European Union. A political and economic union of 28 member States.

FASLANE. Her (or His) Majesty's Naval Base, Clyde. Naval HQ in Scotland and home base to Britain's fleet of nuclear-armed submarines.

FCO. Foreign and Commonwealth Office is a department of HMG responsible for promoting British interests worldwide.

*__FREE DEMOCRATS.__ The political party formed when the Labour Party amalgamates with the MDP (see post).

GAZA STRIP. A small self-governing Palestinian territory on the Mediterranean coast, bordered by Israel and Egypt. Comprises 140 square miles and is inhabited by around 1,100,000 Palestinians. Currently administered by Hamas (see post). Tends to be more politically militant than the West Bank (see post).

HABIBI. Arabic word for darling or sweetheart.

HAMAS. Palestinian Islamic Fundamentalist Organisation.

HMG. His (or Her) Majesty's Government (of the UK).

HMRC. His (or Her) Majesty's Revenue & Customs. The tax man (or woman).

HOORAY HENRIETTA. Female version of Hooray Henry. A member of the English upper or upper middle class, usually keen on horses, with tendency to speak loudly in public. Aka Sloane Ranger.

IDF. Israeli Defence Force, aka the Israeli military.

IRA. Irish Republican Army – paramilitary wing of Irish Nationalism.

KIF. Arabic word for cannabis.

LSE. London School of Economics and Political Science – part of London University.

MACMILLAN, HAROLD. Conservative Prime Minister of UK 1957-63.

MANDELA, NELSON. Leader of African National Congress (ANC), the anti-apartheid organisation. First black President of South Africa (1994-99) and Nobel Peace Prize winner.

*****MUSLIM PARTY.** Left of centre political party formed to protect and promote Islamic religion, culture and law. Precursor of MDP. (see post)

*****MDP.** Muslim Democratic Party – mainly moderate Muslim political party – left of centre – seeks to defend Islam but leaders strongly critical of violent jihadis.

MI5. The UK domestic counter-intelligence and security Agency (aka "Spooks").

MI6. Military Intelligence. The foreign intelligence service of the UK (aka "Spies").

NIQAB. Veil worn over face by Muslim women.

OPEC. Organisation of Petroleum Exporting Countries.

PPE. Politics, Philosophy and Economics. Respected Oxford University degree course.

POST COITUS TRISTIS. Feeling of sadness after making love.

*QUILMOD FOUNDATION. Reformist Muslim think tank. Opposes jihadi politics and violence.

*RAINBOW CRESCENT ALLIANCE (AKA RAINBOW CRESCENT OR RAINBOW ALLIANCE). Electoral and Political Alliance between Muslim Party, Labour and Green Parties to oppose Conservative government and promote alternatives to capitalism and the Consumer Society.

*RUK. Remainder of United Kingdom after Scotland has become independent.

SAS. Special Air Service – Special Forces unit of the British Army.

*SCOTTISH INDEPENDENCE. Occurs when Scottish Government declares UDI (see post) after EU referendum.

SOAS. School of Oriental & African Studies – part of London University.

UDI. Unilateral Declaration of Independence.

VAL D'ISERE. Ski resort in the French Alps.

WEST BANK. Area to the east of Israel comprising part of west bank of Jordan River, currently partially occupied by Israel and partially administered by the Palestinian Authority. Israel has continued to allow Jewish settlements to expand on the West Bank and such policy has been condemned by the United Nations as the area has been earmarked primarily for occupation by Palestinians.

Denotes fictional organisation or event.

1

Karim knew this was the fiercest solo he had yet played live. He played hard, wailing above the din of a crowded pub, hating the reek of beer that seeped up from the out-dated carpet. As Kirsty leapt to the microphone to belt out the next verse, he took his left hand off the guitar to wipe his sweaty fingers on his trousers before adding more to the driving rhythm of the song. Sweat was flying off her face as she roared her passion into Sarah Joy's lines, like a lioness tearing into its prey.

"War is his game and he's playing for kicks
He has them all fooled with his cheap little tricks
They're feeling guilty but don't know what for
Begging like dogs for scraps at his door
He's Everybody's Bully"

As the song crunched toward its finale, a tide of cheers and whistles was rising up toward them from the standing crowd that was already spilling out of the door onto the street. The band took a bow and waved to their growing army of fans before disappearing off to the backstage area where they could cool off over chilled drinks, and earnestly discuss the impact of their performance. This was a top venue for unsigned bands, and A&R people from some big labels could be here tonight. It was the first time the Rainbow Warriors had played such an overtly political song for an encore. Consensus among the band members was that it seemed to have worked.

Sometime after 1 a.m, Karim was sitting on Kirsty's sofa in her Kilburn flat, still strumming his guitar to cement the chord sequences for a new song. He paused momentarily to determine the scent, wild fig or passion fruit, as Kirsty emerged in her dressing gown from the shower and sat beside him to resume their earlier conversation. "Please don't do it now," she said, putting her hand on his cheek. "Your 21st birthday is just a few months away." She leaned over the side of the sofa to plug in her hair dryer. "Let Andy Sheikh finish putting things in place to protect you against the tidal wave of publicity that will come."

He fixed his eyes on hers, static blue points taut with concern amid the maelstrom of wild red hair being blown about her head.

"The people of Gaza need action now," he replied. "Our Government is full of words but refuse to use the word 'disproportionate response' and so won't take action against the bully. Why should its victims have to wait till someone privileged like me has been manoeuvred into place by the media?"

"Because you don't realise what hell is going to break loose in our lives if you don't wait till your next birthday." Karim stayed silent as he carried on strumming his chord sequences. "This place will be besieged by journalists," Kirsty continued. "Don't just think of yourself. It will affect everyone you share your life with; me, my flatmates, everyone at SOAS. You can forget being able to finish your degree, life will never be the same again." Still Karim was watching his fingers move through the chords. "Your mother would have urged you to think twice."

Karim stopped and looked up. "It is because of her I want to act now. Don't forget UN action against land mines was accelerated by the effort she put into drawing the matter to the world's attention. She would expect me to take the same opportunity to make the most of my position."

Kirsty put the hair-dryer down and removed the guitar from Karim's lap. She took his hands between hers and squeezed them. "And what about the band? How are they expected to endure the pestering that your royal connections will bring? Think of the security implications for our tour next month."

"I have, my flame-headed temptress," he grinned, stroking her half-dried hair away from her eyes, "but the publicity it will bring the band will far outweigh that." Karim got up and went across the room to open the chipboard wall unit that passed for a drinks cabinet and took out a bottle. "There's no chance of Martin cancelling the tour. He'll use the contrast of my rock-'n'-roll lifestyle with my royal half-brother's to our advantage."

"Well you're probably right about that." Kirsty took the glass of dark rum that her boyfriend had poured for her. "But look, Karim, nobody is going to believe your claim to royalty for at least a few weeks. You'll be hounded mercilessly when you're least prepared for it. This is the worst possible time to announce to the world that Caroline was your mother."

Karim sat down next to her again. "Since she died, Kirsty, I've lived my life according to somebody else's agenda. Now I'm coming of age I want to take control of it." He leaned forward and pulled her face towards him. The taste of her tongue was sweet from the rum but he recoiled at the alcohol. "My question is – can I rely on you to hold steady with me as I set off on the rocky road ahead?"

2

The chairlift was a 4-seater. Ali and Caroline were sandwiched between Fiona, Caroline's old school friend, and Roderick, Caroline's bodyguard, aka Rod, aka Mr Plod (by Caroline). As the mother of the second in line to the British throne, Caroline was entitled to a bodyguard financed by the UK taxpayer.

Caroline had been divorced from Prince James for 2 years and partners with Ali for 18 months.

Ali had all the boy's toys he could ever want – helicopter, an executive jet, yacht and a ski chalet in Cortina. He was also generous, thoughtful and intelligent, and Caroline could not have been happier.

The drawback from the viewpoint of the stuffier elements of the British establishment was that Ali was an Arab, Moroccan to be precise, and a Muslim.

"Surprise surprise," said Caroline, "there's our friend Jim from the Sun."

Caroline waved at Jim, hoping that would be enough to satisfy him for 48 hours or so. Jim took a couple of snaps and waved back – the physical co-ordination involved in taking a photo, and waving, combined with Jim's only mediocre ability on skis, caused him to fall over, much to Caroline's amusement.

"Careful – don't break your camera," shouted Caroline – "or your leg!"

"And a happy Christmas to you ma'am," grinned back Jim – at this stage red-faced from mild embarrassment and physical exertion.

By this time the party had disembarked from the chairlift and decided to make for the nearest mountain hut for some lunch and a drink or two.

"Not quite so many paps around today – must be due to the holiday," observed Ali. He spoke too soon, as just at that moment Luigi and Franco, two of the more resourceful and ruthless paparazzi, appeared and took a seat nearby, waiting for Caroline's party to make a move, presumably.

Both the hunters and the hunted decided to sit it out for the time being.

After about an hour, Caroline said "I think it's time we made a move."

"Time for Plan B, I guess," announced Ali.

Plan B had been talked about and rehearsed in the

past. It involved the girls swopping jackets, hats and ski goggles in the toilets and the men doing likewise.

This manoeuvre was accomplished in a couple of minutes and a minute after that Rod and Fiona, in Ali's and Caroline's jackets, sped off down the slope pursued by most, if not all, of the Press pack.

Ali and Caroline exited a different door, hung back momentarily and then skied off in a different direction, pursued by no-one, or so they hoped. Caroline found the whole episode hilarious like some kind of school prank. Now she knew what it must be like to be a fox throwing a pack of hounds off the scent by pure animal cunning.

"We'll go off piste to the top of Col Druscie and then go back to the chalet via the black and that run through the trees you like."

Ali was an expert skier and knew the mountain as well as any ski instructor.

Caroline too was a highly competent skier, though perhaps not quite as fast as Ali.

"Fine, darling, whatever you say," replied Caroline.

As they got lower down the mountain, they were mainly in its shadow – but as the slope was north facing, the snow was still powdery and the couple found the skiing exhilarating, even if demanding, physically.

Eventually, they reached the tree line. Ali noticed a cul-de-sac, which he skied into, apparently to take a rest.

Caroline skied after him and skied to a halt, their skis nearly touching, he leaned forward to kiss her.

"Darling – I have an early Christmas present for you–"

"I thought you, as a Muslim, didn't celebrate Christmas," she said.

"When in Rome do as the Romans," he replied.

"Besides, you might say it's more than just a Christmas present."

By that time he'd produced out of nowhere a neatly wrapped package which he handed to her.

"Have you been naughty?" she said.

"Oh yes, extremely naughty – this is to compensate you for putting up with me."

By that time it was dawning on her that the present had very little to do with Christmas. She was excited but tried not to show it. She felt like tearing off the paper like a child. Instead, she carefully undid the package to uncover an exquisite Cartier box which she slowly opened.

Inside was a ring incorporating the largest diamond she had ever seen. Her mother might have described it tactfully as "overstated" – her grandmother, less tactfully, might have called it "vulgar" – but she, Caroline, thought it was truly wonderful.

"You can keep it on one condition," smiled Ali, "that you marry me!"

"But that's bribery…"

"It's okay, I was only joking, you can keep it anyway, whether you marry me or not – however I'd still like you to marry me – so will you marry me, please?"

"Well I'll have to think about it," said Caroline, pocketing the ring. Ali looked disappointed.

"Okay, I've thought about it, and the answer is… yes!"

The couple just about managed to embrace in a tangle of skis and poles.

Two hundred metres away, Luigi had managed to record this happy event by a series of maybe thirty snaps on his Nikon.

He, too, was an expert skier and had not been fooled by the pantomime at the mountain restaurant.

As he put the Nikon back in its case, he reflected on what the snaps might fetch on the market. He reckoned he could get Closer magazine to pay him well into five figures for a selection of the photos plus something similar for the photos plus a briefing to his contact in the British Secret Service – MI6.

For some reason he felt like an assassin – but put that thought behind him. Besides, he had a sick wife and two children to look after – as well as a recreational drug habit that needed funding…

CHRISTMAS DAY 1993:
MI6 HQ, LONDON

Ray Watkins was perusing a full set of the photos Luigi had faxed across. Ray was not especially bothered about working on Christmas Day – he tended as a bachelor to find Christmas somewhat lonely and boring. When asked by colleagues why he wasn't married, he would respond by saying he was a member of the "Misogynist Community."

This did not stop some of the secretaries smiling and fluttering their eyelids at him encouragingly, but to no avail. Ray reckoned they did not know what "Misogynist" meant and decided not to make an issue of it by telling them. Maybe they thought "Misogynist Community" was some kind of religious Order of quasi-monks. Maybe they weren't far wrong, he reflected!

Ray had paid Luigi only $6000 for the photos and nothing extra for the briefing, which was really more valuable. Ray knew that Luigi would try his luck also on the magazine market where he might get ten times as much – there was nothing Ray could do to stop that.

Be that as it may, from what Luigi said, the couple's body language and the expensive package, it looked like Ali was proposing to Caroline and in those circumstances Ray had orders to contact the appropriate MI6 rep in the field with a message. Ray had originally jokingly suggested "the eagle has landed", but his boss settled on "the bird has flown."

Ray had no concern about what would happen then – as a mere mid-ranking spook, he operated only on a need to know basis and did not enquire too deeply into political, ethical and diplomatic niceties.

Ray duly faxed the coded message to the MI6 rep, in this case Tony Scarman, care of the British Consulate, Venice.

CORTINA

Meanwhile at his chalet, Ali and Caroline were busy with festivities and with breaking the news of their engagement to his family, including his father, Hassan.

"I'm delighted for you, but also worried – in a way," said Hassan on hearing the news – "James and the other British royals won't be keen on Richard having a Muslim stepfather, in my view."

"But I get on just fine with Richard, we both like fast cars and yachting and so on – we need never discuss politics or religion – why would we?" responded Ali.

"I think it goes deeper than that – they will worry more about security and who Richard might meet unofficially."

"I'm sure we can handle that kind of thing. We don't want to endanger him any more than they do."

"If you have a child, Richard will have a Muslim half-brother or sister, they won't want that either."

Before dinner that evening, when they were alone, Caroline made an announcement. "Darling, I think I've got another Christmas present for you."

"What do you mean, think?"

"I think I'm pregnant."

Ali hesitated, then smiled – "I'm delighted but kind of worried as well – I think there's some truth in what my dad said earlier. We will have to tread carefully."

"I'm sure it will all be fine – so long as the baby's got my looks and your brains and not the other way round," joked Caroline. Ali smiled "I will tell dad, but no-one else – for the time being. By the way, you're lucky I understand your sense of humour, otherwise it would be Burka time for you!"

VENICE AND CORTINA
28 DECEMBER 1993

Scarman verified the message from Watkins, discovered it was genuine and put in a call to his "appropriate contact", an individual called Cesare Navarra.

Scarman gave Navarra the password and said "It's

over to you now, better get on with it sooner rather than later – you know where to find them."

Navarra had been warned by Scarman that there might be a call and many of the necessary arrangements were already in place. The former made his living employing, financing and organising mainly Mafia hitmen.

Navarra prided himself on being the consummate professional – discreet, efficient and clinical in regard to the execution of his orders – hence his nickname – the "Surgeon." The Police knew of him by his nickname only – they might have had their suspicions regarding the identity of the Surgeon, but Navarra was too clever covering his tracks to leave any hard evidence – besides his brother, Alberto, the Lawyer, would always look after him. Alberto was a Mafia money launderer and fixer. The Surgeon and the Lawyer, both as clever and cunning as foxes, were a formidable team. Importantly, all payments for the Surgeon's services were made by way of cash to Alberto's firm. The latter had sufficient contacts in the Banks, including those in Switzerland and the United States, to make the laundering of cash payments routine, even though seriously illegal. Law firms were the ideal recipients of such cash, which could be used to make loans, buy property and other investments and create plausible paper trails in the event of anyone asking awkward questions.

Today Navarra had got up early. His team of four operatives in Cortina had been fully briefed as to the targets and their vehicle – a silver Mercedes Estate, registration number MO-7 7322, but he might be called upon to make a decision in the event of something unforeseen arising.

The chosen vehicle to take care of the Merc was a black Range Rover with false number plates.

There would be two operatives in the Range Rover and the other two would be in the back-up vehicle – a recovery truck with four-wheel drive and a turbo charged engine.

Back in Cortina, Ali had also risen early. He had planned with the others to ski the Sella Ronda, a forty kilometre ski trek round the principal Dolomite, starting at Selva, a thirty-minute drive away.

The party of five comprised Ali, Fiona, Marco (the driver), Eva, a Czech chalet girl who had volunteered to join the party instead of Caroline, who had dropped out at the last minute due to feeling ill, plus Jan, Eva's Czech boyfriend.

Rod had wanted to join the party but felt duty bound to remain at the chalet with Caroline.

Marco would not be skiing, so the party climbed aboard the Merc Estate with 4 sets of skis and poles. Everyone was jovial and looking forward to the New Year celebrations which Hassan in particular usually celebrated with great generosity and enthusiasm.

They did not notice the Range Rover parked nearby which proceeded to follow them down the valley, at a discreet distance. The slush on the road had frozen overnight and Marco was driving slowly and carefully, causing Ali to remark "No need to overdo the caution, Marco, we haven't got all day!" Marco increased his speed by a few kph to please his boss – the Range Rover increased speed also, and 15 seconds later the Range Rover had drawn level with the Merc, to Marco's justified consternation. He had time to shout "Maniac!", at which point the Range Rover rammed the side of the Merc causing the girls to start screaming. The Range Rover's first attempt caused Marco to lose control of the Merc. The Range Rover's second ramming attempt saw the Merc pushed through what was left of a crash barrier following an accident a few days earlier, over the precipice, and the car cartwheeling down the near vertical cliff face, coming to rest upside down on the rocky valley floor below. Everyone in the car was rendered unconscious. Ninety seconds later, leaking fuel ignited, causing what was left of the car to catch fire. There were no survivors.

The Range Rover stopped and the recovery truck ground to a halt in front of the Range Rover, which was then quickly loaded onto the truck – the 4 mobsters hastily embarked and drove off with hardly a glance back at the carnage they'd caused.

As it was still only around 7.30 am, the road had not been at all busy and, apart from the 2 perpetrators and their 2 accomplices, there was only one witness, a taxi driver called Matteo who managed to call the Police to raise the alarm, but had the presence of mind to refer to the event as an accident rather than criminally intentional. He knew if he made accusations he might be called upon to appear endlessly in Court, which was not a welcome prospect. Besides, if the culprits were the Mob, where would it end? He had to think about his wife and family.

There was something else bothering him and he put in a call.

"Signor Khaled?"

"Speaking."

"It's Matteo, your taxi driver, I think I may have some bad news. Your son's car – I think it's a silver Merc Estate?"

"Yes – go on."

"There's been an accident – it went through the crash barrier on the Selva road and caught fire—"

There was several seconds silence while Hassan tried to recover from the initial shock and think straight.

"Signor? Signor?"

"Yes – are you sure it was an accident?"

There was a pause –

"No, maybe not, but I don't want to give evidence…"

"It's okay, you can trust me."

"I saw a Range Rover force the Merc off the road – it was then driven away on the back of a recovery truck. Who was on board, Signor?"

"Ali and various friends."

"I'm very sorry Signor, if it is as we think it is."

"Thank you for letting me know, Matteo. Please keep in touch and don't speak to anyone about this without conferring with me."

"The Police have my number – I will just say it was an accident."

"Ok."

Hassan had taken the call in his study – he decided to break the bad news without delay and went into the living room where Rod and Caroline were playing backgammon.

"How are you feeling Caroline?"

"Better, but not 100%."

"I am afraid I may have some bad news –"

"Why do you say may have?"

"There's been a car crash involving what I believe to be Ali's Merc and it looks like it wasn't an accident. I think Ali and the others didn't survive."

There was a few seconds silence followed by Caroline bursting into tears.

"How did you hear about this?" asked Rod.

"From Matteo, a taxi driver I often use – he witnessed the Merc being forced off the road. The point is we need to act fast before the Press and the Police get here, and we should give the impression that you two were in the car so the culprits don't try again to finish you off."

Rod's Army training had by now kicked in and he immediately saw the sense in what Hassan was saying.

"Okay, we'll lie low on the top floor and you can deal with the Press and Police."

"You may need to make a run for it overnight," said Hassan.

"Where to?"

"I've got contacts in Morocco who owe me a favour or two. My plane could pick up both of you at Treviso Airport."

"I'm not going anywhere," sobbed Caroline.

"I'm sorry sweetheart, it could be a question of life or death," said Rod.

"… and there's the baby to consider" added Hassan.

At Cortina Police Station, Captain Gino Lucetti was nursing a severe hangover. The last thing he felt like dealing with just now was a car crash involving celebrities and British Royalty, or ex-Royalty. He had listened twice to the recording of Matteo reporting the accident and had brought to bear his 28 years of experience on the case. Something about Matteo's somewhat faltering diction had persuaded him that Matteo was not disclosing the full story. But if it wasn't an accident, then it was a highly professional and well organised hit so the likely culprits were the Mafia, or a government agency – either way, he would incur their extreme displeasure if he were to ask awkward questions.

He lit another Camel cigarette, studiously ignoring the "VIETATO FUMARI" sign, and sipped again at the mug of black coffee which rested on a beer mat near the front of his desk.

The immediate problem was to establish precisely who had been on board the Merc Estate which had crashed and caught fire. He had discovered the registration number of the car and he would have to visit Chalet Torlarin, which was the address of Ali Khaled, the registered keeper of the car.

Meanwhile, back at the chalet, Hassan and Rod were planning Caroline and Rod's escape from their hiding place on the top floor. Hassan had already put in calls to his friend, Zaid, in Morocco who owned a secluded Camel Ranch west of Marrakesh and also to Francois, the pilot of his executive jet – Hassan had taken both into his confidence about the matter and he knew he could rely on them. Zaid said the couple could stay on his ranch incognito for as long as they liked – some of his family and employees were based at the ranch but all would be 100% discreet if he asked them.

Francois mentioned a potential problem with Passport Control at Marrakesh Airport but thought he could get round that with a well placed bribe – he would think $5000 would probably do it, but would check.

Francois confirmed the plane would be waiting for them at Treviso Airport at 4.00 am the following morning. It was agreed that Caroline would wear a niqab for the journey and if anyone asked questions, she was an Arab princess with her European lover on the run from her furious family.

It was around 1.00 pm when Captain Lucetti rang the doorbell of Chalet Torlarin. He was accompanied by an assistant and a driver – the latter remained in the car during the duration of the meeting. Anna, Hassan's housekeeper, opened the door and ushered the visitors in to Hassan's study.

"It's a terrible business, Captain – I've been expecting you – it looks like half my family have been wiped out."

Hassan was having trouble controlling his emotions but managed to remain coherent.

"Can I offer you some lunch? We have paninis and soup if you like."

"That would be very kind, Signor –"

"Please take a chair – both of you – Anna will arrange the food."

Lucetti said "I need to ask you a few questions but I realise this must have been a terrible shock so I could delay this process if you prefer…?"

"No carry on, let's get it over with –"

"Grazie, Signor – firstly, may I ask how you first found out about the crash?"

"Yes, the taxi driver, Matteo, who was a witness, phoned me and told me he'd raised the alarm with you."

"Yes, that's right – Matteo said he reckoned it was an accident – do you agree with that?"

"What do you mean?"

"Did your son have any enemies?"

"Some members of the British Royal Family did not like Caroline consorting with an Arab Muslim, otherwise none that I am aware of…"

Lucetti sighed.

"… But if Matteo was the only witness and he says it looked like an accident then I suppose we must accept his word for it – I've known him for many years and regard him as trustworthy."

"Quite so," said Lucetti.

"My next question is who was travelling in the Merc at the time?"

"Marco, the chauffeur, Ali…"

At that moment Lucetti's cell phone rang and Lucetti, observing the number, took the call.

"Si – Lucetti here" – after several seconds of Lucetti saying "si" and sighing again – the call ended.

"My team have recovered various personal possessions from the car including a ski jacket containing Caroline's ski pass."

Lucetti carefully refrained from mentioning that the ski jacket was partially burnt.

Hassan looked surprised for a split second then took refuge in burying his head in his hands to mask the surprise and the despair he undoubtedly felt.

Lucetti let Hassan recover his composure and then said "Shall we return later or can you go on…?"

"You can go on, Captain – if you like – but please let's get this over with…"

"Grazie Signor – just to recap, it looks like we can place Marco, Ali and Caroline in the Merc – who else?"

"That would be Rod – Caroline's bodyguard – and Fiona, Caroline's friend," replied Hassan, almost in a whisper.

"We will have to hold a news conference – I would suggest at 7.00 pm tonight in the School gymnasium – there's no obligation for you to attend – but it may be in your interest to do so to stop the Press hounding you so much... Okay, let's leave it there for the time being – thank you again Signor for your co-operation."

On the top floor of the Chalet, Caroline and Rod had both packed rucksacks with survival kits, to use Rod's terminology. Anna had told them Lucetti and his assistant were in the building and they were keeping a very low profile – Rod's expression again.

With Rod's approval, Caroline had decided to send one text to her son's nanny, Marigold Smith, aka "Smiffy", as follows:

Dear Smiffy – I was not in the car that crashed and neither was Rod. I have gone to ground as I've been told my life is in danger. Keep this to yourself and Richard – don't tell anyone else – let James think I'm dead. Do not try to contact me. I will be in touch again asap. Love to R and you. Caro

Although Richard was now 17, Smiffy was still on the payroll at St James Palace as an "admin assistant" – she was completely trustworthy, motherly towards Richard and respected by both James and Caroline. Richard loved her dearly – probably more than he loved either of his parents. Smiffy would know what to do and could be relied on not to rock the boat by telling James.

The Press conference was held at 6.00 pm in the Gymnasium and was chaired by Lucetti, who confirmed the time of the accident, the names of the victims and the existence but not the name of the witness.

Hassan was present but did not speak – Lucetti read out a short statement on behalf of Hassan's family saying how devastated they all were and asking for privacy at this difficult time. Someone from the Press asked if it was true that Ali and Caroline had recently got engaged, but Hassan declined to comment. To confirm they had would merely provide fodder for the conspiracy theorists and attract even more unwanted attention than was already the case.

The paparazzi were there in force, including Luigi, who had already formed his own opinion as to who was to blame for the "accident." He decided to keep quiet for now, partly because his own role in the matter was mercenary, to put it mildly, and also out of fear. If MI6 got to hear he was being indiscreet, they could easily eliminate him if they decided it was expedient so to do.

A shortened version of the Press conference was televised on the Italian national news and most other

TV networks around the world within the next few hours – it was billed as "Death of a Princess."

Among the many millions who watched this was Navarra – the Surgeon – who had already decided his fee was well earned and shortly informed Scarman, the MI6 rep, to consider himself invoiced.

Luckily for Caroline and Rod, the Czech girl, Eva, and her boyfriend were rolling stone types without family ties and hardly any friends apart from each other – so – for now – no-one asked awkward questions about their whereabouts.

Sensing there might be further photo opportunities and information to be had by following Hassan back to his chalet, Luigi did just that, and was rewarded with a "no comment" when he broached the subject of Ali and Caroline's relationship when Hassan approached the front door of the chalet.

Luigi was considering staging an all night vigil outside the chalet to keep track of goings on generally but was summoned by an urgent call from his wife with a shopping list and request that he fix the broken down washing machine.

Luigi decided to return to the chalet the following day...

After they had watched the Press conference on the news, Hassan remarked "I guess I'm in your hands now – if or when it gets out you weren't in the crash the Police will clobber me with a wasting Police time charge or whatever…"

"We're all in this together – what we're doing is for the best and to protect the unborn kiddie, in particular," said Rod.

"One thing I need to ask you Caroline," said Hassan. "How did your ski pass end up in the Merc? The Police found it in a ski jacket they retrieved."

"That's easy. I lent Fiona my ski jacket just before they left as hers was torn. She even said she liked the celebrity status wearing the jacket conferred. I said she was welcome to the jacket and the celebrity status! I just didn't get around to removing the ski pass from the jacket."

"That was lucky." Hassan continued "I've checked the Jeep and it's got easily enough fuel to get you to Treviso – I'll get the hire company to collect it from the airport. I've parked it about 30 metres from the back entrance out of sight of the front. I suggest you leave around 1.30 am – that will give you easily enough time to get to Treviso where Francois will meet you at the crew's entrance. That airport is half baked at the best of times so it's very unlikely anyone will question you, and if they do, just say you have a rendezvous with Francois, captain of a private jet."

At the allotted time and after supper and a short sleep, Rod, in a cashmere coat, and Caroline, in a niqab, jeans and fake fur jacket, located the Jeep and drove to Treviso Airport, arriving at about 3.20 am. They were able to rendezvous without difficulty with Francois – Rod did most of the talking, briefly introducing Caroline to Francois and thanking Francois in advance for his discretion and efforts in rescuing them.

Francois led them past a sleeping Customs Officer and onto the Lear jet, where he introduced them to Marcel, his co-pilot.

"Okay, guys, it's next stop Marrakesh," said Francois breezily – "I trust Rod you have the $5000 we need to get past Passport Control?"

"Yes, no problem," replied Rod.

Fifteen minutes after take off the aircraft was levelling off to cruise at 25000 feet and Rod and Caroline were raiding the drinks cabinet and were disappointed to discover there was no alcohol – only orange juice and tea.

About 80 minutes later the plane started its descent towards Marrakesh and landed 15 minutes after that at 5.45 am local time.

The Souk traders and kif dealers of Marrakesh had mainly not yet risen from their beds or, in some cases, emerged from their tents.

Francois made 2 calls on his mobile, one to his contact in Passport Control and the other to Zaid to confirm arrival. The handing over of the bribe took place during the next 25 minutes, following which Francois led the couple to Zaid's white Honda 4x4 which they located close to the crew's exit.

Zaid could not have been more charming – he was keen to help, as requested by his old friend, Hassan. He also felt privileged to be the host of Caroline, having regard to her celebrity and ex-royal status.

"I think you must be the most important British visitor to Marrakesh since Winston Churchill in 1943," he ventured.

"I believe he also travelled incognito in the war to avoid German agents and so on."

"How fascinating" said Caroline, "What attracted him to Marrakesh?"

"Apparently he told Roosevelt, the US President, that Marrakesh was the loveliest place in the world – he used to paint the mountains and reddish buildings in the sunset."

"Did he try the kif?" asked Rod.

Zaid laughed – "No, I think he stuck to whisky and cigars."

"Where are we heading?" asked Rod.

"My ranch – it's about 50 kms north east of Essaouira, which is on the coast. It's very secluded

– it's called Menara Stables – I have about 30 camels and the same number of horses. It's a stud farm so we have good security and so on as the animals are worth a lot of money. When you are tired of riding horses and camels you can swim in the pool or there's surfing about 10 kms away."

"I can't imagine I'll be surfing," said Caroline.

"Maybe not, but Rod could as he's unlikely to be recognised as there are so few people around," suggested Zaid.

"I'll wear goggles if necessary," joked Rod.

Caroline hardly managed a smile – she was on Valium to tide her over the deep grief she was feeling.

BUCKINGHAM PALACE, LONDON SW1

Her Majesty the Queen was very far from being amused. Her troublesome ex-daughter-in-law may have been removed from the scene, but was that removal temporary or permanent?

It appeared that confusion reigned supreme. How were they to be certain Caroline was dead without any trace of a body? The British media, particularly the red top papers, were in a state of hysteria, with accusations being hurled around about the likelihood of MI6's involvement in the car crash.

For the time being, Her Majesty had been advised to

wait for the Italian Police to complete their preliminary investigations.

Smithson, the Prime Minister, in particular was advising against a rush to judgment – apart from anything else there were rumours swirling around that Caroline might still be alive – then again the Police had found Caroline's ski pass in a charred ski jacket. It was messy and likely to get messier.

Her Majesty's main concern at the moment was the welfare of her grandson, Prince Richard, but he appeared to be quite calm and was often to be found in the company of his former nanny, Miss Smith.

As for her son, Prince James, he appeared to be relieved, up to a point, that his ex-wife, Caroline, might at last have been neutralised – she had in the last few years since their divorce used every opportunity to rubbish him and he was sick of it.

Although he dare not say it publicly, as far as he was concerned, if MI6 had been involved in Caroline's death, they all deserved medals and gold plated pensions and he might just make it happen on the quiet, when he eventually became King.

Back at the Menara Stables, Rod and Caroline were inspecting their new quarters which were comfortable, spacious, private and, most importantly, air conditioned. The accommodation consisted of a large flat above some stabling, including 2 double bedrooms, 2 bathrooms, kitchen and living room.

Zaid had allocated a married couple from among his staff, Umar and Zainab, to look after the visitors and had left strict instructions to the effect that Rod and Caroline's privacy was to be respected at all times and no information was to be leaked to other staff members or, even worse, to anyone beyond the boundaries of the ranch.

Over the next few months, Caroline and Rod's main enemy was boredom. They rode plenty of camels and horses, swam in the pool, socialised with Zaid, his wife and 2 grown-up daughters, but had virtually no contact with the outside world apart from via TV and radio.

About 3 months after they first arrived, Hassan paid them a visit during which he insisted on taking photos of Rod and Caroline holding the current issue of Paris Match, and discreetly including two or three photos of Caroline in her bikini with a bulge obviously apparent – he told them he might need proof one day they had survived the crash in Italy. In return, Caroline extracted a promise from Hassan that he would give a letter to Prince Richard from her – the letter read as follows:-

Darling R

I have been advised my life is in danger, which is why I have gone to ground, ably protected by Rod, who has been very attentive and understanding – a hero in fact.

I am now 3 months pregnant and have a strong feeling the baby will be a boy, in which case my greatest wish is that you and he should be friends, particularly if anything happens to me. I intend to call him Karim, which was Ali's grandfather's name – they were very close.

I realise your father will probably try and prevent this, particularly as Karim will have been brought up a Muslim.

I hope and pray that you do not end up enemies – blood is thicker than water, as they say.

I will try and write again soon –
God bless
Fondest love – Mummy

On her handing the letter to Hassan, he said "I promise you I will get this to Richard." What he did not say was how and when.

Two months' later, following the issue of a formal statement by the Police in Venice and Cortina that Caroline had perished in a road accident and a similar verdict in an Italian Coroner's Court, a low key private memorial service was held in London attended by Princes James, Richard and various members of Caroline's family. Selected members of the Press were invited to the service but TV cameras were barred at the request of Caroline's next-of-kin.

Back in Morocco, Caroline was beginning to ask questions relating to how and where she would give birth. Zaid assured her that Hassan's private Doctor and a midwife would look after her on the ranch, all paid for by Hassan.

No expense was to be spared and nothing was to be left to chance.

A preliminary visit by Caroline to a maternity clinic in the Hospital in Essaouira was arranged. Caroline wore a niqab for the journey for the sake of anonymity, and was accompanied by Rod in the role of expectant father. Zaid was the driver.

No problems were detected in the clinic in relation to the pregnancy.

Zaid, on Hassan's instructions, arranged for an air ambulance to be on standby in the event of any emergency arising while Caroline was at the ranch.

Caroline had been advised not to ride camels or horses from 4 months into her pregnancy so she passed the time helping one of the ranch hands with the breaking in of the yearling colts and fillies.

At the end of the eighth month of her pregnancy, Caroline was watching a young horse being led round the compound, which was enclosed by wooden gates and fencing, when the animal was spooked by a barking dog. The colt then reared up, shook off his handler and barged into Caroline, causing her to fall, jumped the gate and proceeded to bolt up the drive towards the ranch house.

Caroline, after dusting herself down, was more concerned about the welfare of the horse than herself, but started to experience severe labour pains a couple of hours later, causing Zaid to phone for the air ambulance.

At the time of the call the helicopter was away on another mission and it was 90 minutes later that it arrived at Menara to take Caroline to the maternity unit.

By the time Caroline reached the maternity unit she was slipping in and out of consciousness and it was decided to deliver the baby by way of a caesarean section without delay as there was no likelihood of Caroline being able to cope with a conventional birth, and she appeared to be bleeding profusely.

Karim Ali Stuart Khaled was born on 15 July 1994 at 6.15 pm local time.

Sadly, Karim only co-existed with his mother for 90 minutes, during which time Caroline managed to whisper his name and smile, but expired shortly afterwards.

Subsequently Caroline's Death Certificate recorded the cause of death as post-partum haemorrhage – loss of blood after giving birth.

It was agreed that the delay in getting her to the Hospital, caused by the prior engagement of the air ambulance, probably led directly to her death, as the medics would probably have saved her if they had been able to act earlier.

For the second time in less than a year, Hassan was faced with a family tragedy, but this time tempered by elation at the birth of a grandson.

Again he was called upon to act quickly – this time to decide who would foster the orphan Karim – away from the prying eyes of Press and public, both substantially unconcerned about the effect of their attentions on a young child unprotected by his natural parents.

Fortunately, Hassan's daughter, Mari (aka Marijah), and her husband, Tom Sutherland, stepped into the breach and volunteered to adopt Karim informally, much to Hassan's relief.

Mari and Tom had 2 daughters aged 12 and 8. The Sutherland family were resident in Dubai where Tom, who was British by birth, worked as a partner in an international law firm.

Hassan assured the Sutherlands that he would make available to them substantial financial assistance to take care of Karim's maintenance, education and security – he was sure it was the least he could do.

It was decided that Mari and Tom would tell their daughters and friends they had decided to adopt a baby boy whose parents had died. They would say they had always wanted a son but that Mari had not been able to have any additional children of her own, so adoption was the only way forward.

Over the next few weeks and months, they looked after Karim and bonded with him in the same way as his natural parents would have done, had they survived.

Mari and Tom resolved to treat Karim with as much love and care as they had treated their daughters, and Karim responded by being happy and healthy.

Rod had been devastated by Caroline's untimely death and it wasn't until 10 days afterwards that he managed to recover his composure enough to socialise and start living again.

Financially he knew he would be secure as Hassan had arranged some time ago for Rod to be on his payroll, following HMG stopping his salary after the verdict of accidental death by the Italian Coroner's Court.

With regard to his employment by Hassan, there was an unspoken condition that Rod would keep a low profile and not publicise at all his role in protecting Caroline during her pregnancy.

Two weeks after Caroline's death, Rod sent a text to Smiffy, whose number had been given to him by Caroline.

The text read:

Dear Marigold Smith. I very much regret to inform you that Caroline died 2 weeks ago giving birth. Unfortunately the baby – a boy – also died. Please give my condolences to Prince Richard – I will try and get in touch again if or when I get back to London.

Kind regards, Roderick (Caroline's minder)

Underneath the tough exterior, Rod was a kind hearted man and the reason he lied about the baby was to protect him from unwanted attention. He had no way of knowing how Smiffy or Richard might react to the knowledge that Richard had an infant half brother. Rod therefore decided to play safe.

Rod never did return to London – he decided to cut loose – changed his surname, grew a beard and worked in security at various locations in the Middle East over the following couple of years.

Sadly he was killed in a shoot out with Islamist kidnappers who had targeted a wealthy businessman who Rod was contracted to protect.

Hassan arranged for the recovery of his body to Morocco, where he was cremated, in the presence only of Hassan plus Zaid, his wife and daughters.

Hassan paid for the Sutherlands and Karim to have a minder, Mike, who was not told about Karim's real parentage.

Mike's main responsibility was security but he was also expected to help out with such mundane tasks as shopping and chauffeuring.

The Sutherlands decided early on that they would, one day, tell Karim who his natural parents were, but had not decided when. For the time being his name was Karim Ali Stuart Sutherland and that was the way it was going to stay until the Sutherlands might decide otherwise.

3

"My father didn't deny his celebrity. He treated the Press the way you would do a dog – if you run away, it will chase you and bite you, but if you play with it, it may lick your hand."

Paloma Picasso.[*]

March 1995, London Docklands

When they discovered Andy Sheikh's office block had an exclusive gym, squash court and swimming pool in the basement for use by him and his fellow Directors only, Sheikh's friends knew he'd arrived – big time.

Andy had come a long way since he'd started as an office junior at The Sun in the late 70s and he was very proud of his achievements.

He had quickly got himself noticed as a bright spark and been taken on to write sports reports – that was his day job.

In the evenings he managed to build up a very

---

[*] *Quoted in "Picasso's Animals" by Boris Friedewald, page 41.*

healthy magazine and newspaper distribution business, employing various family members and working out of a warehouse in Bethnal Green.

In late 1987, just before the crash, Andy floated his business on the Stock Exchange which netted him personally a 7-figure sum – around the same time he got promoted to joint Editor news and current affairs at The Sun and then found himself sitting on a pile of cash when the 1988 property slump hit. At that point he invested in a large portfolio of cut price commercial and residential property and a substantial shareholding in The Sun and its holding company, which the original proprietor was happy to offload.

From there he'd not looked back, to the extent that now, in 1995, he and his family had a controlling interest in The Sun and he was able to dictate editorial policy.

By this time Sheikh had developed a keen interest in politics. Additionally he had not forgotten about his Muslim roots – after all, he was the son of an Imam, hailing originally from Pakistan. His commercial acumen he had inherited from his mother's side of the family. Her father had been a prominent and successful businessman back in Pakistan, complete with 3 wives, as was commensurate with his financial and social status.

The days of 6.00 am starts to his working day were now over and today he had started work at a more leisurely 8.00 am in readiness for an editorial conference at 9.00 am.

But it wasn't that meeting that was of particular interest to him – it was a later meeting scheduled for 11.00 am with Hassan Khaled that was exercising his mind right now.

He had met Khaled on several occasions before – they were both prominent members of the Muslim community involved in charity functions and events.

But why was Khaled insistent on bringing a lawyer with him and why did he ask for The Sun's chief lawyer to be also present at the meeting?

The meeting had been set up by Khaled's lawyer, a Mr Ben Fitzsimmons, a partner with a pukka firm near Lincoln's Inn. All he would say was that the matter was confidential and they wanted it kept that way – for the time being.

The 11.00 am meeting convened on time.

Sheikh was accompanied by his lawyer, David Gibbs, who was a specialist in libel and commercial contracts and a partner in a "top 10" city firm. Hassan Khaled had with him the said Ben Fitzsimmons, an expert in commercial litigation.

Hassan opened the bidding by saying:

"I have come here to offer you the scoop of the century. It's information relating to my son's partner, Caroline, the former Princess of Wales."

"Is she alive?" asked Sheikh.

"I need a confidentiality agreement from you before I can answer that question. You won't be disappointed. Are you both okay with that, in principle? What I'm saying is that I want to buy time – then in return I can give you the whole story which you can go public with, when I choose."

"How long will we have to wait?" asked Sheikh.

"Several years maybe."

"We could all be dead in several years."

"That's true, but our companies will still be around hopefully as will our lawyers or their successors who have a professional duty of confidentiality."

"So what exactly are you offering?"

"Initially I'm offering your company £50,000 to sign a confidentiality agreement plus £25,000 to you personally as a sweetener – that should be enough to fill the fuel tank of your yacht or executive jet," joked Hassan.

"I haven't got a yacht or executive jet."

"Maybe not, but by the time you've done this deal you should be well on the way to having more than enough cash for both" – Hassan continued – "what I'm suggesting is that our lawyers here thrash out the finer points of a confidentiality agreement which we both sign and hand over the money – we have brought Bank drafts with us – and then meet again, in say a week's time, when I will disclose items and material to you which are likely to be of interest.

We can then conclude a more detailed contract with a payment to me when you actually use the material, which will not be before a date in the future specified by me."

"What happens if we ignore the confidentiality agreement and publish the story regardless?" asked Sheikh.

"Over to you on that please Ben," said Hassan.

"There will be a substantial penalty clause in the confidentiality agreement which would be more than enough to discourage you from cheating or leaking," said Fitzsimmons.

"Also, there's the point that the sweetener I will be paying you personally reinforces the point that it's also a question of honour between fellow Muslims. A manly embrace between us when the deal is done should have the same effect honour-wise as a handshake would have between our British friends."

"Yes, I see what you are saying – any views David?"

"Is there a down side if we sign the confidentiality agreement but then don't sign the contract?" asked Gibbs.

"Yes, there will be a provision to claw back 80% of the £50K payment if the contract is not signed within 4 weeks," responded Fitzsimmons.

"What about payments in the contract?" asked Gibbs.

"Yes, there will be payments required under the contract but I think Hassan will agree that it's pointless to discuss the amounts until your side has seen the material."

"Yes, I agree," said Hassan.

"Okay, we'll agree to go ahead – in principle," said Sheikh " – apart from anything else I'm curious to see the evidence – sounds like it could be box office stuff.

Hassan, how about us having a tour of the newsroom and so on while the lawyers sit down and thrash out the confidentiality agreement?"

"Sounds fine by me," replied Hassan.

"I prepared a draft agreement earlier so we shouldn't be more than an hour," Fitzsimmons commented.

"Okay, let's adjourn till 1.00 pm then we can re-convene for a working lunch," responded Sheikh.

Sheikh phoned his secretary to say they wanted lunch for four at 1.00 pm in the boardroom.

By the time the meeting re-convened, the lawyers had earned themselves another £500 plus VAT each, not that their wealthy clients were likely to complain – they would regard such as money well spent – as well as being tax deductible.

"Do we have a deal?" asked Hassan.

"We have a confidentiality agreement – aka non-disclosure agreement – for you both to look through prior to signing," responded Fitzsimmons.

"Fine, we'll read it – I hope it's in plain English!" joked Sheikh.

The agreement was produced in duplicate and Sheikh and Hassan took a few minutes to absorb the main points which had already been carefully sifted and refined by their lawyers.

"Are you okay with this now Andy?" enquired Hassan.

"Yes, it looks reasonable enough – are there any drawbacks David?"

"It's fair so far as I'm concerned," replied Gibbs.

"I have the Bank drafts here, one for £50,000 made out to Star Media Plc, owners of The Sun, and the other for £25,000 made out to Mr Sheikh personally," volunteered Fitzsimmons.

"Fine, let's rock and roll then" said Sheikh, sitting down with pen poised – "where do I sign?"

With the signing done, the agreements and money changed hands and the parties said their goodbyes which included Hassan's version of a manly embrace of Sheikh, to seal the deal.

A week later the same four men met again in the same location.

This time Fitzsimmons extracted a file from his briefcase.

"Here is the material Hassan has asked me to disclose to you – I've brought hard copies of it."

"Isn't it on your laptop?" asked Sheikh.

"No – to cut down on the risk of hackers getting hold of it – so far as we are concerned it's the Holy Grail in this story and we have to protect such, as best we can."

"It's a long story," said Hassan, "but essentially Caroline was not killed in the car crash in Italy – she went to ground after that tragedy – she was pregnant and she stayed with a friend of mine in Morocco, but sadly died in childbirth – the baby, a boy, was born healthy – he is my grandson, Karim.

Here is a copy of Caroline's Death Certificate in her unmarried name of Gibson-West. Here is Karim's Birth Certificate with my son, Ali, named as the father."

There was a 15-second pause while Sheikh and Gibbs examined the certificates. "I see what you mean about scoop of the century, but how can we be certain these certificates are genuine – in the nicest possible way, of course?" asked Sheikh.

"Because they are solicitor certified true copies – ie personally signed by me, having seen the originals," responded Fitzsimmons.

"Also there is the photo of Caroline pregnant in Morocco holding a copy of Paris Match," commented Hassan.

Fitzsimmons produced the photo of Caroline in

bikini, obviously pregnant, holding the magazine with a well known French actor on the cover.

"To enable you to check the date," Fitzsimmons continued "I have here the front cover of the magazine – it's the April 21st 1994 edition – nearly 4 months after the crash in Italy."

"So who is bringing up young Karim and where?" enquired Sheikh.

"You don't need to know that right now," replied Hassan. "In the fullness of time you can have the complete story exclusively. I want to protect Karim's privacy while he's a child, so he can have as normal an upbringing as possible."

"So why are you telling us about his existence, even?" asked Sheikh.

"I calculate that the truth will out at some stage and I am trying to manage how and when the story emerges and also make money for my family and Karim, in particular, out of the story," Hassan continued. "Also the contract will provide for you to protect Karim and his privacy until he is 21, at which point you can publish the story. Meanwhile, what you have should be kept under lock and key – apart from anything else, Karim may be regarded as a threat by the Royal Family and the Establishment generally and there are plenty of 'rogue elements' in MI6 etc who would be keen to neutralise Karim, particularly as he is being brought up as a Muslim. By the time he's 21, I am expecting him to be able to look after himself."

"So please let us have the financial details," responded Sheikh. "We need to know firstly how much you expect us to spend on protecting Karim's privacy and secondly how much we need to find to enable us to publish the story when Karim is 21, or earlier if someone bumps him off before then."

"Don't say that," said Hassan "I hope and pray it never happens."

"To be a tad mercenary, we will want to protect our investment," said Sheikh.

"To answer your question, I would not expect you to pay out anything before he's 21 unless there is some kind of emergency, like my running out of money due to a major business crisis. Hopefully I may just need your advice from time to time plus maybe legal help and support if it looks like another paper may be about to get hold of the story from another source." Hassan continued, " – regarding the story itself, I reckon £5 million on publication would be fair – index linked to take into account inflation – and to include disclosure of background information about my family in general and Karim in particular."

"In principle, I'll agree 4 million provided the contract looks okay," replied Sheikh "and provided we have some access to Karim personally once he's 18 –

Karim would have to agree this and if he doesn't I can only agree 1 million. We would also want book and film rights included in the contract – that almost goes without saying."

"You're driving a harder bargain that I expected," replied Hassan "but I'm not going elsewhere with this as things stand, so the answer's yes – provided we can have half the net profit on any book or film."

"Yes, agreed," said Sheikh. "Okay, let's all re-convene at, say, 2.00 pm for a late lunch, which should be enough time for the lawyers to thrash out the finer points?"

"Yesterday I spent 2 hours working on a draft agreement in anticipation so I reckon a further 2 hours should be long enough to amend and agree it – are you okay with that David?" asked Fitzsimmons.

"Sounds fine to me," responded Gibbs.

"Okay, Hassan, I'll show you my embryonic art collection while the lawyers put their heads together – no old Masters yet – I'm trying to encourage living artists – it's cheaper that way!" said Sheikh.

By the time the meeting re-convened at 2.00 pm, the lawyers had each racked up an additional £1,000 plus VAT in costs. As far as they were concerned it was well deserved, as they both felt exhausted after 2 hours of unremitting mental concentration, under pressure, to agree the final wording.

"Okay guys, are we ready to roll?" asked Sheikh.

"Yes, I reckon it's doable and reasonable – I don't have a problem with it," replied Gibbs.

"The agreement's now 17 pages – you'd better read it – we've prepared 2 copies so here you are," said Fitzsimmons, handing them each a document.

"Why do you lawyers always have to be so verbose?" said Sheikh.

"One reason is that we try and avoid punctuation, which leads to clerical errors, so there's loads of ands, ifs and buts," said Fitzsimmons.

"Steady on with the buts, I may be the owner of The Sun but I'm also a practising Muslim," joked Sheikh.

Gibbs just managed to suppress a snigger.

Hassan was mildly shocked at this contribution but let it pass.

"Okay, we'll read it while we have lunch," Sheikh continued.

He then rang his secretary to say they were ready to eat, and 5 minutes later the food appeared.

Sheikh had a sharp eye, having proof read in the newspaper business off and on for years, and quickly spotted 3 or 4 typos which were corrected by Fitzsimmons on his laptop and the final versions of the document were then printed, signed and exchanged, much to Hassan's relief and satisfaction. It might not be ideal but, in the circumstances, it was the best he could do for his family in general and Karim in particular.

4

Dubai 1995 – 2012

Tom Sutherland had 3 main objectives in his life – in approximate order of importance as follows:

Firstly to earn enough as a lawyer to put food on the table and educate his children, which in Dubai meant at least £175K p.a. (or the equivalent), as fee paying education was the only option.

Secondly to make sure his wife, Mari's, nagging tendencies were directed towards external rather than family targets, which these days usually meant Mike, the minder. Tom loved Mari very much, but if the nagging was directed internally, ie towards him, he found it destructive in respect of their otherwise healthy relationship.

Mike was a tough ex-Para, took the nagging on the chin and with good humour, earning Tom's eternal gratitude. Mike once jokingly asked Tom what the Arabic word for nagging was so he could ask Mari to stop doing it. Tom said there wasn't one, though they do it all the time!

Tom's third priority was to find enough time in his busy schedule to indulge his passion for jazz in general and playing the trumpet in particular, emulating his hero, Miles Davis.

Tom had a shed load of jazz CDs which included most, if not all, of what Davis had ever recorded.

While a student at Oxford, Tom had spent some of his vacations in Morocco which was where he'd originally met Mari, and some working in the U.S., particularly in New York and New Orleans feeding his jazz habit.

After passing his law finals, he did his training with a London firm which had offices in the Middle East, which was how he'd eventually ended up in Dubai. The location was Arab enough for Mari to feel at home and yet partially westernised, particularly in the business world, so Tom was also content with it.

Tom had no problem at all with fitting Karim into his life – he looked forward to teaching him to play football on the beach, only a 5-minute walk from the family home in the Jumeirah district.

Additionally, Hassan's promise of generous financial help to bring up Karim meant there was no need for Tom to worry about the expense of having another mouth to feed.

Little Karim fitted in well over the next 3 years or so, to the routines of the Sutherlands' family life. He grew to love his adopted sisters, Alina and Safaa, and they in turn were affectionate and protective towards him.

Then one day, shortly after his third birthday, came the inevitable bombshell.

"Mummy – are you and daddy my real mummy and daddy, or just pretending?"

Mari and Tom had rehearsed many times how they would respond to this question and were thinking of broaching the subject without being asked, but Karim had beaten them to it. Maybe Safaa or Alina had said something. The important point was to be truthful.

"Your daddy and I love you very much but we are not your real mummy and daddy. They died."

"So where are they now?"

"They are both together in Paradise."

"Where is Paradise?"

"It's a wonderful place you go when you have died if you have been a good Muslim in the eyes of Allah. Some people call it Heaven or Xanadu. There are palm trees and white sand."

"Like where we live now?" said Karim.

Mari laughed, "yes, a bit like where we live now, but everyone is happy all the time and never ill."

"My real mummy and daddy, were they nice?"

"Your mummy was very beautiful and charming and your daddy very clever and kind – like you," said Mari. "One day when you are older I will tell you all about them, but for now just be happy that everyone in this family loves you very much."

At that moment Tom came into the living room from his study and Mari said, "Karim wants to know about his real parents, so I've told him one day when he's older I'll tell him all about them."

"Okay Karim, how about some more football? Come on let's go," said Tom, ruffling Karim's hair.

Karim, who had been pensive, sprung to life at the mention of football and for the time being his chat with Mari was put to one side.

Apart from the question mark in his own mind about his real parents, Karim's childhood was as normal as many of the other kids in Dubai. He went to the English speaking School in Jumeirah district until he was eleven.

He enjoyed being taken sailing by Tom and driving and racing 4 x 4s across dune and desert, known as Wadi bashing.

Mari brought him up as a Muslim, teaching him the essentials of that religion as her parents had taught her. A useful side effect of this process was that Karim acquired the ability to read and speak enough Arabic to be able to read the Koran in the original and make himself understood in that language.

Tom always spoke to him only in English, so Karim became genuinely bi-lingual.

At age eleven, Karim started at Dubai College, the leading secondary school in the area, and cultivated his interest in sport, in particular football, and also music, which Tom had encouraged. Karim had started on the recorder, then graduated to guitar and trumpet, much to Tom's satisfaction.

Shortly after his thirteenth birthday, Tom and Mari raised the subject of his parents' ID with Karim when Safaa and Alina were away.

"We just want a quick word, darling, about your real mum and dad," said Mari.

"Fine, who were they?"

"Your dad was my brother, Ali, so I am your aunt officially. So Grandad Hassan is your real Grandad, not pretend."

"That makes sense, the girls keep saying I look like you – I thought they were just being annoying! That's great news about Grandad as well."

"Your mum was English – she was Caroline, formerly married to James, Prince of Wales."

"You're kidding!" said Karim. "Why the secrecy?" he continued.

"For the time being we think it should remain secret as we don't want to attract the world's media to this neck of the woods, potentially being a nuisance," said Tom.

"Would they regard me as important?"

Tom replied "Probably yes – mainly because of who you're related to – Prince Richard in England is your half-brother."

"So how and why did they die?"

"Your mum was in Morocco when she gave birth to you – there were complications and she died, sadly, shortly after giving birth to you."

"And my dad?"

Tom continued. "This is the problem, it's all a bit of a mystery – we think he may have been killed possibly by the Mafia, but it was made to look like an accident."

"Why would someone want to kill him?"

"This is a difficult question – possibly someone who didn't want Richard to have a Muslim half-brother or sister. Please keep the content of this chat secret for the time being, darling, it's simpler that way," said Mari. "When you are a bit older we'll talk some more, okay?"

"Will I ever get to meet Prince Richard?"

"Hopefully yes, but not until you have passed all your exams with A grades, preferably," joked Tom.

"Come on, let's have a jam session while your mum puts the supper on – okay?"

"Yeah okay – whatever."

Over the next few weeks and months, Karim's curiosity got the better of him and using the internet, he researched Princess Caroline, Prince James and their son, Prince Richard. He found Press reports on the romance between his father and mother. He then widened the scope of his research to take in some historical background, including scandals and rumours involving the Royal Family and British politicians. What troubled him more than anything was the apparent hostility to Islam and what seemed to him the aggression of the West in general, and England in particular, against the Islamic world, starting with the Crusades.

At one point he brought up the subject over supper with Mari and Tom, when the girls were out.

"Don't you think it's racist the way the West has attacked the Islamic world over the centuries?"

"Up to a point, yes," said Tom, "but they all thought God was on their side – it's like the Dylan song we used to sing in the Sixties."

"But there was so much violence."

"Most religions are violent from time to time – Islam is no exception, look at the Jihadis."

"Yes, I suppose so, but to me it looks like the West started it—"

"I think you'll find it's not as simple as that," said Tom.

"I like History – I reckon I'll do it for A Level, so I can find out about these things," said Karim.

"Just one word of advice," said Tom. "Be careful about using the word racist when you talk about religion, they aren't the same thing. There are Arab Christians in Egypt, for example."

"Okay," said Karim, "so where are there European Muslims?"

"Well there's plenty in Bosnia" said Tom. "The West defended them up to a point against the Serbs."

"I don't think I even know where Bosnia is," said Karim.

"Well you better do Geography as well as History hadn't you – it's unwise to get strident about these things until you know the facts."

"I don't like these arguments," said Mari, "it feels like my family's tearing itself apart."

"Darling – we are debating rather than arguing," said Tom, "it's part of Karim's education – it's good he's interested."

After passing most of his GCSEs with flying colours, Karim started in the sixth Form and chose History, Politics and Arabic as his A Level subjects.

He was clever academically but also prepared to get stuck in to some serious socialising – he was quite happy doing what his pals did most of the time: things like getting false ID to go clubbing in Trilogy and go to listen to live music at Jambase – what didn't suit him, however, was alcohol, much to Tom's amusement.

After two bingeing sessions following which he'd been violently sick on both occasions, he became teetotal. Mari was over the moon about this – "It's all that alcohol aversion therapy you keep throwing at him," joked Tom.

"He's following the example of his ancestors who were all good Muslims," suggested Mari.

"Tell you what, Karim, you can get dressed up in Dish Dash when you go out and you won't be allowed in the bars," Tom helpfully suggested. "Just don't get stuck into weed or pills instead."

"Okay dad, don't rub it in – my mates are already taking the mickey big time," said Karim.

"Cheer up – it's not the end of the world, there's still women and song to think about, just no wine."

During his first year in the sixth Form, Tom arranged for Karim to have a week's work experience at his law firm on the fifth floor of the Al Fahidi Tower in downtown Dubai.

Tom promised Karim he would get a taste of what it's really like to work in a law firm, ie that only a tiny percentage is spent in courtroom dramas, contrary to what many US and UK media people would have you believe. The result was that Karim spent day one photocopying and day two learning about the post room and accounts departments.

It wasn't until day three he was permitted to look at some real law and that was a small research project on the gripping topic of the law relating to oil rigs and pipelines. Karim still managed to show up on day four and his reward was to spend the day in the civil courts with one of the firm's litigation Partners, followed on the morning of day five by a session in the criminal courts. There then followed a slap-up lunch at a fancy restaurant courtesy of Tom.

"Well, have you learnt anything?" asked Tom during the lunch.

"I suppose the main thing I've learnt is I don't reckon I want to be a lawyer."

"Probably wise, though I reckon a lot of it's an acquired taste – and the money can be good if you stick at it."

"Maybe, but loads of it is so boring."

"Yes, at the start 80% is boring, 20% interesting if you're lucky. If you continue to be lucky, you should find the work gets a tad more interesting as you progress. Also the more senior you are, the more able you are to farm out the chores to more junior people. The downside to being senior is that you have to carry the can if and when things go wrong. Even though we're insured, we still have to pay the excess, and that can be a four or five figure sum."

"Seems like it's all about money and none of it's about justice," said Karim.

"Well, some large firms sponsor and help in law centres and clinics and they wouldn't be able to afford to do that if they didn't make profits in other areas."

"I reckon I'm more interested in politics than law – you can make more of a difference in politics."

"Fine – personally I think the best politicians are or have been lawyers – Lincoln, Lloyd George, Lenin! The list is endless – why don't you do Law and Politics at Uni?"

"I think law may be very hard work – I'm thinking of doing a Politics and Arabic degree – I'm already doing A Levels in those subjects – mum's taught me Arabic so I'm halfway there already."

"Okay which Uni?"

"How about London? You are always saying it's a great city."

"Okay, why don't you try for SOAS? That's the School of Oriental and African Studies – I've heard it's very cosmopolitan and it's quite small, so everyone knows everyone else, which makes it seem friendlier than these massive Uni's like Manchester or Leeds."

After toying with the idea of trying for Oxford, Karim eventually took Tom's advice and applied to SOAS as his first choice. He had received good reports from his teachers, who had predicted he would get at least three Bs at A Level. SOAS offered him a place conditional on achieving three Bs to read Arabic and Politics. He achieved two As and a B, the latter in History. He did not mind dropping a grade in that subject, he had concentrated more on the other two.

After a summer spent sailing and absorbing some more work experience in Tom's office, Karim arrived in London in October 2012 for his first year at SOAS.

Tom had kindly offered to help Karim settle in to his Hall of Residence and showed Karim around some of the sights, the highlight of which was a trip to Ronnie Scott's Jazz Club in Soho.

Karim quickly decided that London had much to offer and he was going to enjoy his three years in town as a student – he had been told about the 'secret Trust Fund' created for him by his grandfather, Hassan, so money wasn't going to be a problem, so long as he didn't overdo it.

At the Freshers week, held in the University of London Union jointly with King's College, Karim mingled and was pleased to join the Jazz Society, the Islamic Society and the Rock Music Society – the latter contained several embryonic bands who were looking for kindred spirits to join them, so Karim agreed to turn up to a couple of jamming sessions to see if he was keen enough and if they wanted him as a band member.

The first session did not go well – at least one of the group was on a major ego trip and the band did not seem to be going anywhere collectively.

The second session with a band called Rainbow Warrior went extremely well. The band was mainly green politically, but musically they were quite sophisticated and eclectic.

Karim liked them and liked their style. He particularly liked their lead singer, Kirsty, who was Scottish with big red hair, and a strong personality to match.

Early on they got chatting and it turned out that Kirsty was doing Music at King's College.

"What was the attraction of London – why didn't you go to Uni in Scotland?" Karim asked her.

"Oh I've got contacts here and although there's drawbacks to London, it's still the centre of the universe musically," she replied. "So what brought you here from Dubai?"

"My dad was always on about how great London is so I thought I'd see for myself," said Karim.

"How did your dad know London, is he British?"

"Yes he's British and did most of his legal training in London. My mum is Moroccan so I'm a mixture – how about you?"

"Oh my dad's an SNP Councillor and businessman and my mum's a music teacher – both Scots through and through."

"Does that make them both anti-English?"

"I suppose so – up to a point – they both voted for independence in the referendum and so did I."

"I think I'm anti-English," volunteered Karim.

"I reckon the English establishment has shafted Muslims and Arabs for centuries and the West is now paying the price."

"Isn't that disloyal to your dad?"

"No, because he's not establishment, he's cool, he likes jazz – anyway I think he's at least half Scots!"

Karim didn't just play hard, he worked hard as well – he was ambitious and driven. He was especially interested in the lectures and tutorials on Middle Eastern politics and rapidly reached the conclusion that the Palestinians had been unjustly treated, mainly at the hands of western-backed Zionists. He was not a fundamentalist by conviction or temperament, so he did not turn into a Jihadi, though he understood the sense of grievance that such had in relation to the West.

Neither was he a Holocaust denier, though it seemed Europe had shifted the burden of compensating wronged Jews onto Arabs and Palestine, who were innocent of the crimes perpetrated against Jews in concentration camps.

Interestingly, David Rosenthal, one of his Jewish classmates, agreed with him and mentioned the name of a well-known Jewish Labour politician who regularly criticised Israeli government policy towards Palestinians in the House of Commons.

Karim was pleased to discover that Kirsty was happy to discuss politics as well as music. Her agenda was markedly different to his, but they were both indignant about what they regarded as injustices.

In Kirsty's case, her emphasis was on Scottish Nationalism and green issues – with a mainly socialistic slant on most matters.

Karim decided that he needed to ask her out.

After breaking the ice on two dates, the couple wound up at Kirsty's flat in Kilburn. One thing led to another and they found themselves in bed together. Despite their relative inexperience, they made it happen – sap rose – the swelling wave broke at the right moment – the earth moved – momentarily, in Karim's eyes, Kirsty became an additional super-hot star in the firmament. Post coitus tristis did not set in, so Karim found himself in love.

He went to sleep and woke up a happy man.

5

Sheikh's Media Empire and the Scoop of the Century: 1995 – 2014

In the years following his acquiring a controlling interest in the Sun and doing a deal with Hassan on the scoop of the century, Sheikh built up his media empire to include several TV channels and magazine titles.

At an editorial and management conference in early 2002, the subject of 9/11 arose.

"One of the problems is that the West doesn't understand Islam," ventured Sheikh, "I'd like to promote some aspects of Islam that people in the West can tolerate and even find attractive."

"Such as?" asked Nick, one of his sub-editors.

"There's some elements of Sharia law in relation to family and criminal matters that could acquire support in the West – I'll give you a couple of examples – take paedophiles – they could be chemically castrated with repeat offenders being physically castrated."

"Are you serious?" said Gibbs, the lawyer. "What about their human rights?"

"The average Sun reader doesn't reckon paedophiles have any human rights. This doesn't have to be a campaign to change the law, just a softening up process whereby people's mindsets are gradually changed."

"I see, what other campaigns do you have in mind?" asked Gibbs.

"Right – look at the state of divorce in Britain and the numbers of children left fatherless. The Islamic world has for centuries permitted polygamy, and as a result, in my view, there is nothing like such a widespread crisis in the family."

"I'm not convinced it's cause and effect," said Gibbs. "Part of the deal is the oppression and subjugation of women that most people in the West won't buy into."

"I'm not advocating the oppression of women." Sheikh wasn't going to be put off that easily. "If you know anything about polygamy, you can see that the wives in many ways have a better deal than their monogamous sisters."

"In what way?"

"Take childminding – they can divide up that task between them – trusting each other with their children. There is also chat – women and men often prefer to discuss different things so the women are often better off chatting with other women than with men. Their monogamous sisters have a frustrating time trying to discuss girly issues with their husbands then accuse them of not paying them enough attention. It then turns into a vicious circle. In case you think defending polygamy is groundbreaking stuff, it's worth noting the greatest polygamist was Abraham, the Biblical patriarch who is revered by Muslims as well as Christians and Jews, in the latter case for thousands of years."

Sheikh had managed to reduce the meeting to silence – after a pause lasting several seconds, Gibbs said "Okay, give it a go – I dare say it will increase circulation initially even if it doesn't change anyone's mind – just don't ask me to support stoning," continued Gibbs.

"Stoning's a good example of where the modern Islamist radicals have distorted and brutalised what went before – someone's recently carried out a study of Ottoman legal history over five centuries and there's only one stoning to death recorded. Okay, we'll try our readership with polygamy for a couple of days then consider other proposals like opposition to gay marriage and the public flogging of football hooligans."

"Yes – one thing at a time I reckon," chortled Gibbs.

Over the next three weeks the Sun's current affairs editor, Harry Bennett, and Laura Bradford, the women's issues editor, combined forces to get the lowdown on the current state of polygamy in Britain and internationally.

At the end of the two-week period, they had a meeting with Sheikh and Gibbs to discuss progress.

"Well we seem to have established that informal polygamy is more popular and widespread in Britain today than you might imagine," said Harry.

"Let me explain," said Laura. "For a start, many of the baby boomers, now in their 60s, were hippies and/or influenced by 1960s libertarian ideas, so many of them have been informal polygamists for over 40 years."

"Yes, but it goes back much further than that," suggested Harry. "Henry the Eighth was probably the most famous English polygamist."

"True," said Laura. "We must not forget the Bloomsbury group in the 20s who lived in squares and loved in triangles."

"Yes, that's all very interesting," said Sheikh, "but what about formal polygamy with a man and his wives living under the same roof?"

"As you probably know," continued Harry "the Koran permits a man to marry up to four wives."

"But a woman may only take one husband," commented Laura.

"We reckon that's related to the importance of determining who the biological parents are of any given child," suggested Harry. "Obviously if a woman is having sex with more than one man, she's never going to know who the father is in relation to any given child – like in the film Mamma Mia. This problem doesn't arise when a man is having sex with several wives – barring infidelity, you are always going to know who every child's biological parents are.

Apparently, in Britain there is a reluctance on the part of Muslims to admit to being in a formal polygamous relationship as bigamy is a crime under British law." Harry continued "However, what many of them don't realise is that the traditional Muslim wedding, the Nikah, on its own, is not recognised as a legal marriage under UK law. So the would be polygamists who don't know this are worrying about nothing!"

"We commissioned Cyclops, the opinion pollsters, to carry out a survey on the issue of acceptance of polygamy," Laura continued. "The two main questions were what are the drawbacks to polygamy? And if polygamous marriages can be shown to be more stable (ie less likely to end in divorce), would you support its legalisation? On the drawbacks issue, the main problem was the welfare of women – polygamy was thought to be too man centred – a charter for randy and chauvinistic males, if you like—"

"And responses on the second question – about legalisation?" asked Sheikh.

"Ninety per cent of Asians said yes, as did sixty five per cent of the rest of the population," responded Laura.

"Interesting," said Sheikh – "the drawbacks points are debatable – my mother always said my grandfather's wives were all very happy."

"Well there is a paradox that people in the West don't generally know about," said Harry.

"What's that?" asked Sheikh.

"In a 2005 joint study by the Social Sciences department of Karachi University and the Health Sciences department of the University of Lahore," Laura continued, "it was found that where a husband had two wives, each wife had more sex than their monogamous sisters. Where a husband had three wives, they each had about the same amount of sex as their monogamous sisters. The psychologists put this down to the happier state of mind of the husband, increasing his libido. It was only when a fourth wife arrived that the husband's performance started flagging."

"Okay, let's run with it," said Sheikh, "call the article Pros and Cons of Polygamy – can Everybody be Happier? – something like that, we'll see what our readers make of it."

Over the next few months other issues were raised in the paper, gay marriage, paedophiles, public flogging of football hooligans – each article carefully recorded the Muslim viewpoint which, with the assistance of the Cyclops pollsters, was shown to coincide with majority opinion in the non-Muslim population.

The articles also included at least one on Islamic finance and banking. The point was made that Islamic Banks followed a policy of investing on a partnership basis with customers rather than lending or charging interest – and that such a policy was fairer and less likely to lead to financial meltdowns requiring bailouts as had occurred all too often in the West.

Towards the end of Karim's first year at SOAS, Hassan set up a lunch meeting with Karim at Hassan's flat in Cadogan Square, Belgravia.

On arrival, Karim was embraced heartily by his grandfather who was still spritely, despite now being in his 80s.

"How are you? Do you like London? Have you got a girlfriend yet?"

"Steady on Granddad – too many questions at once – one at a time please."

"Well they say you don't drink – that's good. How about food – I assume you eat?"

Karim nodded.

"Fine – I've got some proper Moroccan food from

the restaurant round the corner, it's tajine and couscous followed by peaches and apricots."

"Great – Mum often cooks tajine back home – I'm feeling hungry just thinking about it."

"Good, let's get started. It's all laid out in the dining room – let's go through. My staff have the rest of the day off, so we've got the place to ourselves."

The two settled down at the large dining room table and started to eat – in Karim's case as though he'd not eaten for a week.

"Fine – you seem hungry," said Hassan. "Doesn't anyone feed you?"

"Yes, Kirsty my girlfriend is a very good cook – she does some traditional Scottish dishes like haggis and neeps."

"This Kirsty, where did you meet her?"

"One of the fresher dos – she's doing music at King's and we're in a band."

"What a brass band?"

Karim knew when he was being teased but let it go.

"No, a soft rock band, if you like, we do all sorts of music, blues, rock, folk – protest."

"Protest eh – what are you protesting about?"

"Injustices mainly."

"What injustices?"

"Poverty, pollution, the Palestinian issue…"

"Sounds like you've inherited some of Caroline's

indignation – so what are your answers to these problems?"

"Persuasion and politics hopefully – I'm not a Jihadi."

"I'm glad to hear it – what's Kirsty's view on these matters?"

"We both tend to agree on political matters, though we have slightly different priorities – she's more interested in green and Scottish issues rather than the Middle East, for example."

There was then a pause while Hassan contemplated what had been said.

"I think I can help you, but probably not until you graduate when you're 21," said Hassan.

"In what way?"

"I know Andy Sheikh quite well and I know he would be interested in your views, particularly when he knows you're my grandson."

"Andy Sheikh – he's the proprietor of The Sun isn't he?"

"Yes that's right – he would I am sure like to meet you and get hold of some background information to get the interest of his readers. Eventually he could also introduce you to some useful contacts, I'm sure – politicians, media people and so on."

"That sounds good – what do I have to do?"

"Well, to really get his attention you'd have to admit

to being Ali and Caroline's son – I can tell him I'm your grandfather and he can put two and two together – I'm sure he'd like to hear it from you as well though, about your upbringing etc. However, I would keep this under wraps until you're 21 in the year you graduate, otherwise it is likely to disrupt your life as a student and attract the wrong kind of attention. For the time being concentrate on your studies and having a good time while you can – that's my advice.

I can introduce you socially here on the understanding he will just chat and leave you alone until you've graduated – would that suit you?"

"I'll need to chat it through with Kirsty, but it sounds a good idea to me."

"Fine. Additionally there's a letter from Caroline to Richard that I need to show you to give you an idea of her wishes and plans, if you like, for the two of you."

"A letter? Written when?"

"Written about 6 months before you were born when she was in hiding in Morocco, staying with a friend of mine."

"Why was she in hiding?"

"Because the Press were constantly harassing her and because we thought the car crash quite probably a deliberate attempt to kill both Caroline and my son – your father, and that it was made to look like an accident."

"Does that mean I will be in danger when I admit to being their son?"

"Possibly – you can have a bodyguard if you like but Sheikh is a powerful media mogul and once you are under his wing, then your would-be enemies are likely to back off – up to a point."

"I don't want a bodyguard. I'll take my chances. So what's in this letter – can I read it?"

"Yes, I've got a copy, I'll get it."

"When was it sent?"

Hassan didn't answer.

He returned a couple of minutes later with a photocopy of Caroline's letter.

"Have a read of this."

Darling R

I have been advised my life is in danger, which is why I have gone to ground, ably protected by Rod, who has been very attentive and understanding – a hero, in fact.

I am now 3 months pregnant and have a strong feeling the baby will be a boy, in which case my greatest wish is that you and he should be friends, particularly if anything happens to me.

I intend to call him Karim, which is Ali's grandfather's name – they were very close.

I realise your father will probably try and prevent this, particularly as Karim will have been brought up a Muslim.

I hope and pray you do not end up enemies – blood is thicker than water, as they say.

I will try and write again soon –
God bless
Fondest love
Mummy"

"That's fine" said Karim. "I wish she'd written me a letter, even if it only said the weather's fine today…"

"She created a Trust with you as main beneficiary and me as Trustee, so she provided for you," said Hassan.

"By the way, when did you send the letter to Richard?"

"I've not yet sent it."

"What?!"

"Timing is everything and I thought I would send it after consulting with you and Sheikh – if it's sent to coincide maybe with an article by or about you in Sheikh's paper, then it's going to have more relevance. If I send it too early it may just create a problem for you."

"I see – so it's going to take around 20 years for this letter to be delivered to Richard…"

"Maybe, but I've already turned this over a thousand times in my mind, and there's no easy answer to this type of question. I promised Caroline I would get the letter to Richard, I didn't say how or when. I'll speak to Sheikh about it – I'll also arrange a lunch with Sheikh so I can introduce you."

"Okay, but I would want to bring Kirsty. There are no secrets between us."

"Fine. I don't think Sheikh or I will have a problem with that."

Three weeks later Hassan, Sheikh, Karim and Kirsty meet at Hassan's flat.

After the initial meeting and greeting, Sheikh opened the conversation:

"I was a great admirer of your late mother. We would like to go public with a story about you after you have graduated. Please be aware this will be a scoop, a world exclusive, and we need to all agree now that all the details, including this discussion, must remain private and confidential between the four of us for the time being – is that agreed?"

Everyone present nodded in agreement.

"I don't want to appear tactless, but what about payment?" asked Kirsty.

"No, you're absolutely right to ask, remuneration will be substantial," said Sheikh.

"I'm suggesting it goes into the family trust fund with, say, twenty per cent into a charity," remarked Hassan.

"Yes, Grandad can handle that side for us – he's the businessman," said Karim.

"On the political side, I can introduce you to many people from a wide spectrum who will be fascinated to meet you," continued Sheikh.

"First things first, we need to agree on when to send Caroline's letter," said Hassan.

"Yes you told me about the letter – perhaps I could have a look at it before I contribute to this discussion further."

Hassan produced the copy letter and handed it over – Sheikh had seen the letter many years previously as part of the process of verifying Hassan's story about Karim's birth, but Sheikh and Hassan, for now, had agreed not to disclose anything about their deal to Karim for fear of him getting the wrong idea. It was better for everyone if Karim took decisions about his own future with Hassan and Sheikh's advice – if his decisions happened to coincide with what Hassan had had in mind all along, then fine.

Sheikh refreshed his memory by reading Caroline's letter again.

"I've still not sent it – I was thinking I'd send it to coincide with the first article about Karim in The Sun."

"How do you make sure he gets it?" asked Karim.

"Send the original 'Special Delivery' post and also send a copy first class in case he refuses to sign for the original – that's how my lawyers deal with this kind of problem," suggested Sheikh.

"My own lawyer can arrange to send the original, he's totally discreet and trustworthy," said Hassan.

"I'm desperate to meet Richard face-to-face," said Karim. "I just hope this is the best way of achieving that ambition."

"The wishes of your mother are clearly expressed – it will be difficult for Richard to ignore that," said Hassan. "I think we are agreed, are we not, that we send the letter to arrive just after the first article in The Sun?"

"That's fine by me," replied Karim.

"Can you please tell me about your upbringing? Our readers will be fascinated."

"Let's discuss this over lunch – there's a smoked salmon salad in the dining room," suggested Hassan.

Over lunch Karim spoke about his adoptive parents with great affection and gratitude, and about his life in Dubai as a child and teenager.

"Did they talk much about your natural parents?" asked Sheikh.

"Occasionally – when I was about three they told me I was adopted but that they loved me very much." When Karim said this, he could feel the tears welling up – Kirsty noticed and put her hand on his arm, reassuringly. Karim passed on as quickly as possible to the occasion when Mari had told him his parents were famous and who they were. He must have been about thirteen at the time he recalled.

He said he remembered spending a couple of hours on the internet looking up the details. Partly as a result, he later developed a keen interest in history and current affairs.

"Fascinating," said Sheikh, "truly fascinating."

Karim continued by describing his life as a sixth former, his work experience in Tom's office and why he had chosen SOAS in which to continue his studies. When he had finished, Sheikh gently clapped his hands a few times and said:

"Well done, Karim, I think you have shown great resilience and courage to get this far – I hope I can help you go further. May I say I have many of your views about politics, particularly regarding Islam and the Middle East – also you have your mother's charisma, I can see that, and that makes your view of the world all the more compelling."

As the months went by, Karim concentrated on working hard on his academic studies and playing hard, mainly in his band – he realised he may never again have the opportunities that his lifestyle gave him as an anonymous student in London.

On several occasions he met with Sheikh again in Hassan's flat.

They discussed the content of the article that Sheikh planned to publish following Karim's graduation.

At their second meeting, Sheikh produced a draft of the proposed article headlined:

SON OF A PRINCESS – WORLD EXCLUSIVE
My life so far by Karim Khaled

The article contained a summary of Karim's upbringing in Dubai followed by his life as a student in London. It printed a photo of a letter from Hassan's Solicitors confirming that they held documentary proof as to Karim's parentage.

Karim asked for some amendments, all of which Sheikh agreed to, and he also agreed not to mention the Sutherlands by name, although Karim conceded this would probably emerge, via the internet.

The following summer Karim took his finals at SOAS and was awarded first class honours in his chosen subjects – Politics and Arabic.

Three weeks later Sheikh's lawyer posted the original of Caroline's letter to:

HRH Prince Richard
St James's Palace
London SW1

by Special Delivery post, and also posted a copy by first class post to the same address.

The following day, a Wednesday, the completed article was published in the main edition of The Sun, complete with fanfare on Sheikh's TV news channel.

There was the promise of a Press Conference on the Friday morning, to be held at the Hotel Russell, Russell Square, London WC1.

Meanwhile, at St James's Palace, on the Wednesday the story broke, Prince Richard, his wife, Sophia, and Smiffy were conferring in the sitting room of Smiffy's apartment.

"Mummy's bodyguard sent you a text saying the baby died at the same time as Mummy didn't he?" asked Richard.

"Yes that's right, but he may have just been protecting the baby – this Karim person has a Birth

Certificate and is stating that your mother, Caroline Gibson West, to use her maiden name, is his mother. Also his grandfather and Sheikh seem entirely to believe in him," said Smiffy.

"You could ask him to submit to a DNA test," suggested Sophia.

"Maybe, but first we need to get someone to go to the Press Conference on Friday."

"I should send your secretary, Vanessa, she's very sensible and a good judge of character," suggested Smiffy.

"Okay, we'll do that, I'll tell Pa."

At a meeting in Sheikh's office on the Thursday evening before the Press Conference, Hassan, Sheikh, Karim, Kirsty and Gibbs met for supper and to discuss tactics.

"Is everyone pleased with our choice of the Hotel Russell as the venue for the Press Conference?" asked Sheikh.

"I must say the Hotel Russell, which I know well, is a really good choice of venue for this Press Conference in my view, it's just the right mix of traditional and stylish," ventured Hassan.

"Good, I'm glad you like it, it was David's choice.

He prides himself on being an expert on London landmarks and Hotels in particular – I think you wanted to entertain us with a couple of anecdotes about the Hotel Russell, didn't you David?"

"Yes, thanks Andy – the Hotel was designed by the celebrated Victorian architect, Charles Fitzroy-Doll, in about 1898 – he paid particular attention to the design of the interior and the Hotel was very lavishly fitted out. It was said the dining room was identical to that on the Titanic, which was also designed by Fitzroy-Doll."

"I hope it's not a bad omen," said Sheikh.

Gibbs ignored that comment and continued:

"I've got an extract from the current website which talks about guests being able to "marvel at the beautifully crafted statues of all the Prime Ministers to have 'serviced a Monarch' since the first modern Prime Minister, that would have been Walpole in the eighteenth century. The only problem is that I think they've chosen the wrong word – it should be served, not serviced. The latter, I think, is too awful to contemplate!"

Kirsty was the first to get the joke and managed to stifle a giggle. Hassan and Karim made no comment and Sheikh would only say: "That is a typical lawyer's joke – based entirely on a slight discrepancy – talk about pedantic!"

Despite this mild reprimand from his client, Gibbs was satisfied that he'd managed to amuse at least one member of the party.

The following morning at the Hotel Russell, the Press Conference started at 10.30 am.

Admission was by ticket only and no TV cameras were allowed apart from those owned and operated by Sheikh's company.

Sheikh, Karim, Gibbs and Hassan sat at the top table hosting the Conference.

Most of the questions were addressed to Karim – Sheikh had anticipated this and, although he had a lot of confidence in Karim and believed him to be very bright and personable, they had agreed that if any question was too sensitive, then, on a pre-arranged signal, Gibbs would answer it.

Oscar Byron of The Mail on Sunday was the first to input a question.

"This question is addressed to Karim – can he please explain why he does not prefer to remain anonymous?"

"I wish to continue with my mother's projects, I am also very interested in finding political solutions to international problems. I would like to do things that my parents would have been proud of, even though they're no longer around to witness such."

Someone else asked:

"We understand you were brought up a Muslim from an early age. To what extent do you have an Islamic agenda?"

"I think that mainstream Islam is misunderstood in the West and probably there are various Islamic people who misunderstand the West. I would like to provide a bridge between the two. Some would say, having regard to my parentage, that I am the ideal person to do such."

The next question was:

"Would Karim be prepared to submit to blood/DNA testing to prove his parentage?"

The pre-arranged signal went up at this point and Gibbs replied by saying:

"That will not be necessary as we have verified Karim's Birth Certificate. It would be demeaning and unnecessary for Karim to submit himself to medical tests in these circumstances."

Before anyone else could comment or stop him, Karim said:

"Wait a moment – I would only submit to blood/DNA testing if Prince Richard asked me to, personally."

Somewhat to Karim's annoyance, there was

the usual journalistic pre-occupation with money/ funding.

"What is happening to any payments you are receiving personally from Mr Sheikh's companies, Karim?"

"We are splitting such payments 50 per cent to go into a family Trust Fund and 50 per cent to charity," (Karim had succeeded in overruling Hassan's suggestion of an 80:20 split).

Various other questions were put, mainly concerned with verifying Karim's identity, and these were fielded diplomatically by Sheikh and Hassan, to whom they were addressed.

After the Conference, Sheikh, Karim and Hassan had a brief meeting in one of the Hotel's Board Rooms, by way of post mortem.

"I reckon that went well," said Sheikh, "they seem to like you – and why wouldn't they?!"

"Fine, but why did you make it a ticket only function?" asked Karim. "And why so expensive, and why exclude other people's TV cameras?"

"We had to exclude timewasters and hangers on. Five hundred pounds a ticket is neither here nor there to serious media people. Besides, I have to recover some of my expenses and that's also why I needed to only have my own company's cameras present."

"I think he's right," said Hassan. "Leave the money side to Andy and me."

Sheikh was encouraging – "Don't worry, Karim, with your charisma and my common sense, we should go far…!"

6

"So the voters don't know about this Rainbow Crescent Alliance then?"

Dinner taken and cleared away early, Karim was sitting with his arm around Kirsty's shoulder as they watched the election TV debate on her sofa. As political theatre, they were enjoying it but the outcome was predictable. Each party set out its agenda for a better Britain as if they had a chance of winning power on their own but everybody knew no party was going to gain an absolute majority.

"No," was Karim's reply. "Andy Sheikh will only promote it if Labour need such an alliance to stop another Tory Government."

Kirsty still looked puzzled. "And why would an alliance of a more left-wing Labour party and the Muslim Party appeal to the voters, let alone work in Government?"

"Because the model already exists, in Bradford. Jeff Jefferson, former Labour MP, won there against the odds in 2012, remember? In secret talks, he's now pledged his considerable following to join the alliance."

Three weeks later, the predictability of the election result was borne out. No party had won an overall majority so after swift negotiations, Rainbow Crescent was announced to the nation with Labour's Dave Berriman as prospective Prime Minister, being leader of the largest party. Together again on the same sofa, Karim and Kirsty watched the news with growing unease as events unfolded. Based on intelligence provided by MI5, even though not open to scrutiny because of anti-terrorism legislation, the Muslim Party had yesterday been proscribed as a legitimate democratic force because it was deemed a front for a banned terrorist group and its leadership arrested. Without all its MPs, the Rainbow Crescent alliance could not govern, despite winning more seats than the Tories.

"You know what, Karim?" frowned Kirsty, shaking her red locks. "This country looks like it is becoming ungovernable, like Italy in the 80's."

From the kitchen, Karim's phone was ringing. Kirsty listened as he went out to take the call. "When?", "Where?" and "Fine" was all she heard him say. As he reappeared, her blue eyes widened as she looked at him for an explanation.

"That was Andy, Kirsty. I've got to see him

tomorrow. There's only one person who can help us get out of this and Andy wants me to combine what influence I have with his."

"So who's that?"

"Ibrahim Irani."

The broadcasters were right about the security alert except Karim hadn't thought it would extend to an armed police presence outside Andy Sheikh's dockland offices. Surprised at being asked what his business was, it took a phone call to the proprietor to verify he was attending a meeting with him. "I'm assured it's for our protection," Andy told him as he met him coming out of the lift on 25th floor. He took him along the corridor to his boardroom where Karim stopped to take in the stunning view of the tranquil-looking Thames before settling his focus on the man he was being introduced to. Sporting a well cut grey suit and an open collar mauve shirt, Ibrahim Irani smiled benevolently as he greeted the well born young man.

"You so remind me of your mother," he said. "Her desire to do the right thing in the world beyond the call of duty, made such an impression on me. I only met her once in person, but I will never forget her."

"It's our hope that Karim here will follow in her

footsteps," said Andy. "He already seems to have captured people's hearts."

Karim let his momentary embarrassment subside before replying. "And I'm delighted to meet you too, Mr Irani. You did so much to lift the nation when you led us to win the World Cup a second time."

A youth international footballer who played for his native Iran, Ibrahim had become a naturalised Briton when he was brought to England as a teenager. Within a year, Aston Villa had recruited him and he was soon back on the international stage as the first player of Muslim extraction to captain the national team. Hugely popular as a TV pundit following his playing career, he was liked also for his progressive views on religion and society which he put into effect in his role with the Football Association channelling TV revenue into the grass roots of the game in England. He was almost alone as a political operator who people trusted as honourable and Andy Sheikh's best hope to unify the anti-Tory vote as well a personal hero of Karim's.

"Now he has come out of retirement to help us face an even greater challenge," beamed Andy Sheikh. "This time, Ibrahim is going to be slipping tackles and striking goals against the Government which is cooking up allegations against the Muslim Party. We are going to court to demand evidence. If it's not forthcoming we will take legal action against an unconstitutional Government."

Karim looked at Andy Sheikh across the big table. "So why am I here?" he asked.

"People need someone to revere who sits above politics, as Queen Elizabeth did in happier times," said the media tycoon. "When the going gets rough with the political and legal processes, you will be the figurehead to keep the public on side. People see your mother's compassion in you."

Karim felt some discomfort and looked from one to the other.

"But Prince Richard is perceived similarly, isn't he?"

"Yes indeed. But he has the handicap of being the figurehead of institutions that are past their sell by date."

"Like the House of Lords you mean?"

"And the Church of England," said Andy Sheikh, "riven by internal conflict about gays and women, and whose numbers of worshippers is in terminal decline."

Karim raised his dark eyebrows. "The Windsors have always adapted to changes in society."

"Not so as to embrace the demographic ones happening now. The Muslim population will be looking for a new politics to reflect their cultural influence;

which is why we must act at once, to give confidence to the population as a whole that a Government with strong Muslim representation can be democratic in principle and practice."

"We need to arrange a meeting with the Quilmod Foundation," said Ibrahim.

"I've heard of them, but what do they do?" asked Karim.

"They're an association of academics, clerics and activists who see the salvation of Islam being in a reinterpretation of scriptural authority."

"What's that got to do with Rainbow Crescent?"

Andy Sheikh reached for the telephone on the mahogany table as Ibrahim explained further.

"It's our meal-ticket to Government, Karim. If the Koran can no longer be used to excuse the actions of terrorists or those in sympathy with their methods, then we have a much better prospect of securing power in this country."

Karim sat fascinated as he digested this information and watched Andy Sheikh on the telephone as he began to discuss arrangements with the only agency that was apparently capable of acting as midwife to assist the creation of his new alliance. The political life of the country of his mother's birth had frozen. Only Quilmod could thaw it, break the logjam and restore its onward flow.

Before joining Ibrahim at the Royal Kensington Hotel for his meeting with the Quilmod Foundation, Karim needed air and space so he could digest what was happening. He had often spent an hour or two in Kensington Gardens where he liked to go when he needed to ponder his fate and purpose in life. The palace had been where his mother lived her royal life and the home of his half-brother Richard, already blessed with popular appeal that seemed also to be accruing to him. If he envied Richard at all, it wasn't for his wealth or status; it was that he never knew the Princess of Wales, a devoted, imaginative and demonstrative mother as even her harshest critics agreed. But he would not be complaining as he had been raised by loving adoptive parents in Dubai in what was surely a more relaxed household than the royal House of Windsor.

After the publicity had subsided, he was now part of the celebrity circuit, subject to nods and greetings in the street regardless of the slant on his political views pushed by the right wing press. Despite the political tension arising from the election result, he had never thought his life would be in danger. The same car that had parked in Bayswater Road the week before was again outside Kensington Gardens at the High Street end. Today it was a different minder who walked around the orangery while he read the newspaper on the bench in front of the big golden gates. Flattering to think the British state thinks the bastard offspring of a maverick Princess is worth 'looking after' too.

He got up from the bench and headed across the park in the direction of the V&A. Keeping to the side streets behind the Albert Hall, he was crossing over the road when a car suddenly accelerated as it approached from the left of him. He paused momentarily to catch the eye of the driver before throwing himself forward onto the pavement; had he not lunged, history might have recorded him in a footnote rather than as a rival contender for the throne. As the car carried on at speed, he recognised the number plate.

Unhurt but frightened of staying so exposed in a public place, he hailed a taxi. Before he arrived at Kirsty's flat, his phone rang. It was Andy Sheikh. Ibrahim Irani had been arrested outside the Royal Kensington Hotel.

"Don't even think of going to the police," he warned Karim when he heard of the attempt on his life. "And don't use this phone again as it is most likely bugged. I will reach you on email."

By the time he arrived at Kirsty's, the news about Ibrahim had already broken across the media. To calm their fears, they took refuge in her bedroom for the afternoon before getting up several hours later when hunger got in the way of their efforts at intimacy and consolation. As Kirsty clattered around the kitchen, Karim switched on his laptop to see if he had any messages from Andy. He didn't get so far as opening his mailbox before the horror of the latest news bulletin made him shout in anguish.

Kirsty was straightaway at the door from the kitchen to enquire. "What is it?" she whispered.

Karim said nothing as they watched the chaotic scenes playing out on the screen in front of them. Smoke still not cleared, what had been recognisable as the imposing facade of the Bank of England was now charred and deformed, with ambulances crews and police performing their grim tasks of securing the building and carrying out the bodies of the bombers' victims. Karim finally opened his mailbox. The message from Andy Sheikh was short. Don't move or open the door, it read.

Recent election results had been shock enough to the UK body politic. Now it was unravelling further with ugly looking consequences. London was now on the highest level of security alert. On account of Star Media's support for the Muslim Party, calling for reinstatement of its MPs and the release of Ibrahim Irani, several of its journalists had been arrested for treasonable offences. Next day, the tension level ratcheted up further with the news that caretaker Prime Minister Smithson had employed new draconian emergency powers to shut Star Media down in London. Then in retaliation, local authorities in constituencies won by the Muslim Party at the election would sanction moves to starve the Treasury of taxes. Leeds City Council in particular invited Andy Sheikh to base his operation there, making office space available for Star Media, and charging no business rate.

Karim waited for further instructions from Andy Sheikh before he moved. With the United Kingdom now so obviously dividing against itself, Karim would have left London anyway, had he not been summoned to Leeds by his minder. Knowing his British history, this Young Pretender took the trouble of disguising himself, though not as a woman like Bonnie Prince Charlie before he set about rallying troops to his cause.

On a grey March morning he set off from Kirsty's flat in her Ford Fiesta, dressed in a boiler-suit and a woollen hat. On arriving at the TV studios in Leeds, the Star Media mogul was waiting for him. As he got out of his car, Andy Sheikh threw his arms around Karim.

"Allah be praised you're safe. If you had been killed, my dreams really would be in tatters. Politics would be over."

"What is to be gained by killing me?" Karim asked with a look of boyish innocence.

"Look, it's clear the Establishment are intent on crushing any threats to their interests," said Andy. "That means all of us. Ibrahim because he's the most popular Muslim, you because you're a possible pretender to the throne, and me because I'm a nouveau-riche upstart who has wrecked the cosy monopoly in the media."

Pointing him toward the reception area of his studios, he took Karim's arm. "Come on, let's go inside. We don't know if we're under surveillance out here."

Inside Andy's office, Karim was keen to air his anxieties.

"So who bombed the Bank of England, Andy?"

"Our informants in MI6 have informed us it was Israeli intelligence."

Karim laughed. "That's ridiculous. Like the al-Qaeda propaganda that Israel was behind the 9/11 attack on New York."

"So why would jihadists destroy the chance of getting the Muslim Party into Government?" Andy shook his bald head. "No, if they were the bombers, they would be playing into the hands of Smithson's Government which has arrested Ibrahim, the man trying to negotiate getting that party into Government."

Karim groaned, "we've somehow got to find a way forward from here."

"Non-Muslims must be given confidence that there are no extremists in government but compromise will be necessary. For one thing, the Muslim Party I expect will not play ball unless we accept the adoption of Sharia Law in predominantly Muslim areas."

Now Karim shook his head. "No, I don't agree. Stoning and amputation as punishments in the 21st century? I'm not happy to be the figurehead of an alliance that aims to implement that."

Andy got up from his desk and opened a filing cabinet.

"Well," he said, "my newspaper sales boomed when our editorial line supported flogging football hooligans," throwing a copy of the Sun across his desk toward Karim. "And the forcible chemical castration of paedophiles."

Karim stared grim-faced at the headline **'TIME TO GET TOUGH ON CRIME'**, with pictures of a birch and a syringe.

"Look," continued Andy, "you support a socialist agenda, right? The Left on its own will never get into power in Westminster now that Labour cannot win any Scottish seats. An alliance of Muslims and Socialists is the only way we can get rid of the Tories and their wealthy clients. And also the Greens – they will never have influence unless they join our Rainbow Crescent."

"Green as she is, I'm not sure Kirsty is comfortable with Muslim attitudes to the status of women either."

"That's for our Muslim brothers in the Quilmod Foundation to sort out with the clerics. Leave the alliance politics to me, Karim. It will work out in our favour, I guarantee that."

WINDSOR CASTLE, FEBRUARY 2016

The door opened to the butler carrying a silver tray with the Prince's morning coffee and a set of newspapers for his perusal. On top of the pile was the Sunday Star with a picture of his half-brother beaming confidently. '**King for a new Britain?**' ran the caption.

"Has my father seen this?" Richard asked.

"Not yet, sir. He's not yet returned from walking the dogs."

"They're getting cocky, putting a picture of Karim with Balmoral in the background."

The Scots were doing all they could to help the Rainbow Crescent it seemed. Richard turned to Sophia. "One advantage he doesn't have as a rival to the Crown though. A queen like you."

Sophia stroked her husband's hair as she poured them both a coffee.

"I don't think we have anything to fear. Your father will be King a good while yet."

"There is concern that he hasn't been doing enough to bring the sides together. If he is seen to support Smithson in refusing to honour the election result, he may have to abdicate."

"But we can't have a Government which includes terrorists."

"You're right. I would have to refuse accession to the throne if father abdicated. Unless something can be negotiated with this Ibrahim fellow."

They turned as the door opened and King James III entered the breakfast room.

"I see you've got the papers. I expect the paedophile scandal in the Church has pushed the run on sterling and our collapsing economy off the front pages."

"Good morning Papa – we haven't got further than this one," said Richard, pointing at the Sunday Star's picture of Karim. "My half-brother is Rainbow Crescent's candidate to succeed you as King."

The King laughed. "Well after waiting for so long, I'm in no hurry to go, my boy. Anyway, are people going to accept any young upstart claiming to be the son of your mother by another man?"

"Well, the Sunday Star is challenging us to a DNA test. If we don't supply the material, we are the ones who lose credibility."

"Goodness, Rich, you are heir to the throne and that is the end of it." Sophia sounded determined.

"But people identify me with a privileged Britain, while support for Karim is growing as he becomes the heir of the 'Queen of people's hearts'. The Windsors may not survive this, Papa."

Smithson picked up his office phone but paused before dialling. What troubled him, as he ran his hand through his tousled red hair, was keeping him sweating. Normally he would have showered by this time in the morning but there was no point. He would continue to sweat until the urgency of the situation with Ibrahim Irani had eased.

The problem was that the police could not detain him any longer without charging him. He had been arrested several times before on the grounds of being a member of a proscribed jihadist organisation – then tried and acquitted. His current arrest was so that the UK could prevent a renaissance of the Rainbow Crescent intended to incorporate moderate Muslim political activists rather than Islamist extremists. Smithson's Tories needed their opponents to be terrorists to have any chance of legitimately excluding Muslim representatives from Parliament.

The downside to this of course was the continuing threat of violence, the most recent instance of which was the Bank of England bomb. The latest scandal to hit the stock markets had noticeably driven the rhetoric against bankers up to a higher pitch than even that of ten years before; and despite the Muslims not claiming responsibility for the atrocity, the suicide bombing had all the marks of their involvement. While Muslim fanatics were still active in the UK, their activities MI5 assured him were run from Bradford, now under martial law imposed by the Rainbow Crescent administration in Leeds. Any attempt by his Government therefore to eliminate the threat at source was confounded unless he sent overwhelming force against that nest of vipers. Such would inevitably become a full scale civil war with unacceptably high civilian casualties.

And then there was the funding of the opposition. With HM Treasury reserves depleted by a weakening currency and falling tax revenue, it really grated that Saudi Arabian money was rumoured to be keeping the Rainbow Crescent alliance buoyant. Only as long as the Muslim Party was part of it though.

He dialled the number of the Met's anti-terrorist Tsar.

The rear door of the taxi parked outside Wormwood Scrubs opened and Andy Sheikh stepped out to greet the man exiting the prison gates.

"Welcome back to freedom, brother." When visiting London in such a tense political climate, Sheikh had abandoned his sleek limo and his bald head was covered by a baseball cap.

Ibrahim's response was serious. "This time it had better be for good," he said.

"It will, Ibrahim, never fear. You've been acquitted of any terrorist-related activity and they have just shown us their hand – they have nothing to charge you with." Andy Sheikh gestured to Ibrahim to get into the cab.

"But still we have no time to waste. The Quilmod Foundation are impatient to meet you. Only through their good offices can we hope to see a change to the articles, tenets and behaviour of our Islamic faith."

"Like Christianity 500 years ago, it needs reformation or this country is doomed to a second civil war."

"Karim shares your opinion. And I am tending to agree with it now. If we are to unify this country again, it will be because of the healing influence you and Karim bring."

Ibrahim touched Andy's sleeve in a gesture of caution. "If Karim is to become King, he would do well to keep his opinions to himself."

"Not like James, eh? He always did want to meddle in politics."

Ibrahim had some sympathy for James. If he himself was King, he would find it difficult to stand back while his Government supported Israel in the conflict with the Palestinians, for example.

"Let's go, Andy. We've got work to do."

Andy Sheikh knocked on the cabbie's glass screen and the taxi moved off.

7

THE EU REFERENDUM CAMPAIGN –
FEBRUARY-MARCH 2016

At the Rainbow Crescent meeting and debate held in Leeds City Hall, Karim spoke passionately in favour of voting Remain in the EU Referendum.

"We are supposed to be internationalist in our approach to politics – London is the most cosmopolitan city on this planet – I am cosmopolitan, therefore we should not seek to sever ties with the EU. Immigration and the free movement of labour is desirable economically, culturally and socially, particularly for those of my generation – the under 30 age group – and our leadership must campaign for a Remain vote otherwise it looks like the UK is turning its back on Europe and the rest of the world."

Kirsty also made a contribution to the debate.

"My politics are green through and through. The EU has promoted policies on climate change, for example, which would be threatened if we vote Leave. Global problems can only be addressed by an international approach so I urge everyone to vote Remain – our children's future may depend on it. Also there has been peace in Europe for over 50 years and that's mainly down to the EU – give credit where credit's due."

From the platform Ibrahim acknowledged the sincerity of the speakers on both sides of the debate.

"This question is complex – there are powerful arguments on each side and for that reason we should not officially recommend either a Remain or Leave vote.

Personally, I support the Leave side. The free for all on immigration isn't fair on people already here or on the immigrants. It leads to unacceptable pressure on infrastructure and public services.

My view is that we should look at re-discovering EFTA – the European Free Trade Association – as it was before the UK joined the EEC back in 1972. People are happy with a free trading block and that way we could invite countries like Turkey to be full members without worrying about having to accommodate millions of Turks in our labour force. The more we mess Turkey around, as at present, the more likely it is they will lose patience and allow the jihadis to gain more traction..."

Karim interrupted at this point.

"Leaving the EU, I still say is going to look like UK is turning its back on Europe and the rest of the world – it's isolationist when we need to be global in our approach to politics."

Ibrahim responded:

"I agree we need to be global, the problem is the way the EU is set up is holding us back. For a start, there is the compulsory delegation to the European Commission of the power to negotiate international trade deals. That means we are literally unable to negotiate deals with our natural allies in the Commonwealth, like Australia, India and Pakistan. The UK has turned its back on the Commonwealth for more than 40 years.

Churchill said back in the 20s the British Empire is the world's greatest Muslim power.

The UK needs to stop feeling ashamed of its imperial past and start capitalising economically and politically on the residual loyalty that still exists in the Commonwealth.

The UK still has political and diplomatic influence – soft power, if you like, in dozens of countries around the world – it's just we are not yet taking full advantage of the opportunities that such soft power confers."

Karim again spoke – "I never thought I'd hear you defend Churchill and British imperialism…"

"Well, I used to be a bit of a radical firebrand when I was your age, but I'm now older and wiser," responded Ibrahim.

The meeting then voted against adopting a party line on the issue, which meant that supporters were to be free to vote according to their individual beliefs.

The polls were showing a pro-Remain lead, possibly as a result of the Prime Minister being pro-Leave – the British never like their leaders to get too complacent. The BBC also exhibited a pro-Remain mindset, in its choice of speakers, in particular, though it was always quick to deny any bias.

Scotland was generally pro-Remain by a comfortable margin and at one point Ibrahim said to Kirsty:

"Why don't you vote Leave as a tactical move? Scotland's more likely to get its independence if the rest of the UK votes Leave!"

Ibrahim was half joking, but Kirsty wasn't amused.

Koco Dine was an economic migrant from Albania. He was also an illegal – he'd unsuccessfully applied for asylum on the grounds of religious persecution – he was Catholic in a predominantly Muslim country. His asylum application had been turned down on the basis that the "evidence" he'd produced consisted of some bruising on his back which was actually self inflicted by intentionally falling down some stairs.

He was now surviving on free handouts from charities and what little he could earn as a part-time cleaner. He had wanted to be a taxi driver but there was no way he could get a loan to get started in that occupation. He was starting to get clinically depressed – some nights he could not sleep.

He was also harbouring a grudge against the British. His father had told him how one of his uncles had been in a group of anti-Communist exiles who had been betrayed by the British spy, Kim Philby.

They had been promised full support by the British and had been parachuted in 1946 into Albania to start a counter-revolution against the Communists. Philby had betrayed them and they had all been surrounded by Communist Partisans and shot on landing.

His father had always said the betrayal meant that Albania had to endure Communism for several decades, presided over by Enver Hoxha, an admirer of Mao Tse Tung and enthusiastic promoter of his own personality cult.

The point that Philby was a double agent working for the Russians made no difference to Koco Dine, aka KD to his few friends – Philby was British and employed by the British, so the betrayal of the Albanian exiles was the fault of the British, who now owed him a living.

KD was now being let down again by the British

and he was convincing himself that Britain and the British were the cause of all his problems, rather than the answer to his prayers as he had hoped.

That morning KD stopped at the mobile cafe in a lay-by within half a mile of the Brent Cross Shopping Centre where he'd been doing some unofficial cleaning work.

Eleni, the Greek girl he half knew, served him a black coffee.

"Don't look so miserable KD – cheer up!" Eleni remarked.

"I fed up of this shit Referendum," replied KD.

"I know all the anti-immigrant right wingers have come out of the woodwork to persecute the likes of you and me," offered Eleni – she continued "that Marcus Love on the Leave side is one of the worst – he's on about repatriating people who can't pass an English language test. Spoken and written."

"You pass tests like that if you want but me no – I no read English – I no write English."

"So why don't you make an effort and learn how to?"

"I no have cash to pay for lessons and no ID to get loans, that's why I depressed."

An idea was slowly taking shape in KD's mind – why not end it all and take down some shit politician like Marcus Love, so people like Eleni would think him a hero.

But – how to do it – where, and when?

He knew the date of the Referendum was 23 March, so he had about 5 weeks to get organised – that was the when – up to a point.

What about the how?

He could probably get a gun by joining some jihadi group or criminal gang, but neither idea attracted him as he might easily get busted before he had a chance to achieve his aims – problem was he would never be able to get close enough to use a knife on Love, who was a prominent politician usually surrounded by minders.

"So how about a bow and arrow?" he said out loud to himself when on one of his solitary cleaning assignments. He said it just to keep his spirits up – then he hit upon a solution – how about a crossbow?

He knew enough about computers to use one in a public library and, the next day, went to the only public library in Brent, and managed to google the word crossbow on one of the public computers. With the use of a dictionary and after some time-consuming research, he established that he could buy a lethal crossbow for the princely sum of £26.95 and a pack of 12 6.5-inch alloy bolts for £4.75. The next problem was how to pay and take delivery – he had no credit card and no fixed abode – he often took refuge from the rain in the Brent Cross Shopping Centre public toilets open 24/7, but he didn't reckon that was an acceptable address for delivery purposes.

He then googled archery products for sale in Hertfordshire and Essex and came up with 2 stores, one in Barnet and one in Epping. After phoning each he was able to establish that the Barnet store had more choice and at cheaper prices.

The next day he took a trip on the Tube out to Barnet armed with £52.47 which he had saved from the previous week's cleaning.

"Good morning sir, how can I help you?" was the encouraging greeting from Bill, the shop's proprietor.

"I look for crossbow pliz."

"Certainly sir – looking to do a spot of poaching are we?" was the jocular response.

"Poaching – what is this?"

"You know, someone's rabbits, pheasant."

"Yes I get hungry."

"Don't we all – there are several here from about £25.00 upwards."

"On target at 40 metres pliz?"

"Well, that's a bit far – 30 metres, perhaps, with practice."

"Pliz show me how to work it then I buy."

"Okay, we'll go into the yard – follow me." Bill gestured to the door at the back of the shop.

Bill carried the crossbow with some loose alloy bolts into the yard and KD followed.

The yard was about 20 metres long with targets at the far end.

Unaware he was instructing a potential political assassin, Bill patiently explained the basics of the crossbow theory and practice to KD.

"Practice makes perfect – find yourself a quiet spot, say on Hampstead Heath or Epping Forest, and you'll get more and more accurate – the beauty of these bolts is you can use them time and time again."

After about 15 minutes of instruction, KD said

"Okay, I buy now – thank you."

"Fine. I suggest you take 2 packs of bolts and you can have some targets 12 for £2.50 – they're on at half price."

A few minutes later KD was walking back to the Tube having completed his purchase – on the way back to Brent Cross he was thinking about the where question – up to a point he'd already sorted the when and how aspects of his project.

Marcus Love was the target and KD needed to focus on when and where he would be speaking in the London area, probably within the last 10 days or so of the Referendum campaign.

The following day he visited the library again and, with the help of Google and a dictionary, was able to establish that Love was due to visit Finchley on 21 March, 2 days before the vote. There would probably be a walk-about in the car park of the Asda supermarket in Ballards Lane, according to the What's On section of the Leave campaign HQ.

Later, in the afternoon, KD, with the crossbow, target and bolts in his rucksack, visited Hampstead Heath for some target practice. He managed to find a sequoia tree with a wide trunk. He nailed a target to the tree and then, from an initial distance of 7 or 8 metres, took aim and fired. To start with he lost a couple of bolts in the undergrowth, but gradually improved his technique and accuracy, working his way further back from the tree.

After several hours of practice over a 5-day period, he found he could hit the target from 20 metres, 80 per cent of the time.

He reckoned he might get a second chance so he also practised re-loading, which he perfected in about 6 seconds.

The crossbow was virtually silent when he fired, so it would take time for a minder to work out from where the weapon was being fired.

The following Sunday, after Asda had closed, KD carried out a reconnaissance to the supermarket car park and found a good place on the day to wait for his target to appear – it was the first floor level of the multi-storey car park – there was a pillar providing cover but there was also a clear view over most of the car park over the top of a brick parapet.

That was definitely the "where?" side of the problem sorted.

Over the next few days he followed a set routine of working in the early mornings and evenings at his cleaning job. During the afternoons he would practice with the crossbow, usually on Hampstead Heath. He was now able to hit the target from 30 metres 80 per cent of the time.

"Pliz, I need more bolts for crossbow."

KD had decided to re-visit Bill's Sports Shop in Barnet as he was needing to replace bolts he'd lost in the practice sessions.

"Fine, bud – how many?"

"Twenty, maybe."

"Okay, I can do 24 at £8.50."

"Okay, I buy."

"Fine – tell me, have you hit anything yet?"

"Two pigeons and tree, but I practice like you said."

When he got back to Brent, KD decided to have a chat to Eleni in the trailer cafe.

"Hi – will you have drink with me when you finish tonight?"

"No, KD, I have boyfriend and he won't be keen on the idea – thanks for asking though."

KD knew his prospects were minimal but he fancied Eleni big time and decided to try again.

"How about when you boyfriend at work?"

Eleni laughed. "Sorry KD – I like you but I also like my boyfriend and I don't want to lose him."

"I save up and take you West End one day."

"Dream on KD – here, have another coffee – this one's on the house."

"What means 'on the house?'"

"Free – it's a gift from me."

"Thanks, I know you nice girl."

KD's state of mind was such that his rejection by Eleni confirmed what he thought he already knew – that he had no status, no prospects and very little money.

His desperate circumstances made him even more determined to carry out his plan.

There were now only 10 days to go til 21 March and his unofficial rendezvous with Marcus Love.

His routine did not change – by now he had acquired a tent which, for now, he pitched amongst some bushes on Hampstead Heath to be near his practice range. This enabled him to practice firing at least 3 hours per day and it was easier and more comfortable to sleep in the tent than some of the other locations he had had to put up with previously – bus stations, shop doorways, garden sheds, you name it he had tried it.

He also found time to access a Leave HQ website in order to check that Marcus Love had not changed his plans about visiting Finchley on 21 March. Sure enough, Love was still scheduled to speak – the likely topic being immigration and the need to repatriate those whose English language skills were not sufficient to pass the tests he was proposing.

During the afternoon of the 20th, KD went to see Eleni, knowing it was probably going to be the last time he spoke to her.

"I go away, probably for long time, so I say goodbye."

"Sorry to hear that, KD, where are you going?"

"Not decided yet… maybe Birmingham or Manchester."

KD was finding it hard to resist the temptation to confess everything to Eleni about his wish to get even with the likes of Marcus Love, about the crossbow, the endless practising – his desperation and his plan to "end it all."

He eventually decided telling her would worry her and she might be tempted to shop him, which would be even worse.

When they eventually parted company, they shook hands and KD grasped Eleni's hand firmly but gently, using both his hands. He was welling up, but just managed to suppress the urge to weep openly.

"I Catholic, Eleni, please pray for me."

"For sure, KD – I'm not religious, but if you think it will help I will pray for you."

"Thank you."

At that point he released her hand, turned and left her – 20 metres away he turned and smiled. Eleni waved, and that was the last time she saw him.

The next day KD got up early – 5.00 am – packed the tent away and hid it in some undergrowth. He packed the crossbow and bolts into his rucksack and started his short journey to Finchley on foot. He got the Tube for part of the journey and arrived at the Asda store Ballards Lane at 7.30 am. He went into the cafe for coffee and breakfast and contemplated his plan. He was still depressed, but able to focus on what he felt he needed to do. He reckoned he would be doing the other illegals a favour, and would be applauded by the likes of Eleni – he was on a mission and was sure God would forgive him.

Marcus Love was due to speak from his trademark soapbox at 10.30 am in the open air area to the side of the multi-storey section of the car park. The police had already erected barriers in anticipation of a crowd, and by 9.30 am various people had gathered at the venue, including protesters, mainly from the Socialist Workers' Party (SWP), with placards reading "Immigrants welcome – Tories out."

KD loitered for about 10-15 minutes in the open air section of the car park biding his time.

Then he made his way up to the first floor level of the car park and re-discovered the pillar he had found on his last visit. He extracted from his rucksack a hi-vis yellow gilet which he put on to look, at first glance, like a Council workman or car park attendant. He was able to stand to the side of the pillar and only be seen by anyone in 3 or 4 cars parked to the side of it, and also by the crowd in the open air section of the car park below, if he leaned forward. He looked over the parapet and surveyed the scene for a few minutes, then carefully extracted the small crossbow, which was wrapped in a cloth, and placed it out of sight on a shadowy area of the parapet. He took two alloy bolts from his pocket in readiness.

It was now 10.15 am and Marcus Love and his entourage of 3 or 4 minders had arrived. Love was limbering up by pressing the flesh of various supporters, many of whom were brandishing Vote Leave and Pro UKIP placards.

At 10.29 precisely, Love stood on his soapbox and proceeded with his speech.

"Good morning ladies and gentlemen – I am very pleased to be here again in Finchley – the constituency of the late great Margaret Thatcher..." There were then cheers from many in the crowd and boos from the SWP.

"Some of our opponents routinely call us racist, but your race is not defined by the language you speak..." KD took the cloth off the crossbow and loaded.

"… there are white folk who can't speak English and there are coloured folk who speak English very well…"

KD took aim at Love's chest about 25 metres away.

"… the point is that English is the language of UK business and people working in this country…"

KD pulled the trigger – he scored a direct hit – on Love's left eye – KD quickly re-loaded.

People in the crowd were screaming – the minders had rushed forward – Love had slumped forward and rapidly lost consciousness.

KD fired again, but this time he missed and the bolt skidded away after hitting the ground close to Love's motionless body.

A policeman with an interest in shooting and archery saw the bolt and yelled "it's a fucking crossbow bolt" – the crowd gasped.

KD calmly surveyed the chaotic scene below him, took a 6-inch kitchen knife from his rucksack and, with it, he slit his own throat 15 seconds before 2 policemen got to him – one of whom had noticed a glint of metal – the barrel of the crossbow – shortly before the second shot was fired.

In the distance the siren of an ambulance could be heard.

Love never re-gained consciousness and died in the ambulance 20 minutes later from loss of blood and shock.

KD died a few minutes after the police got to him – the cause of death was asphyxiation and loss of blood – he had managed to sever the main artery in his own neck.

KD had wanted at least Eleni to know he was the perpetrator and the police found a letter addressed to Mr Koco Dine c/o Brent Law Centre. The letter was from the Refugee and Asylum section of HM Immigration Service, Croydon. It read:

Dear Sir

We regret to inform you that your application for asylum on the grounds of persecution in Albania has been rejected.

The medical practitioner who examined the injuries you have sustained believes such injuries were probably self inflicted and were so recent as not to have been inflicted before 15 November 2015, your stated date of arrival in the UK.

You may appeal against this finding, but we have to tell you that we will strongly resist any attempt to alter the decision we have taken.

Yours faithfully

During the 36 hours left approximately until the Referendum started, the Press and media had a field day. The assassination of Love seemed to the pro-Leave papers a vindication – not that they ever believed they needed vindicating.

As just about every 10-year old English schoolkid knows, King Harold, the Anglo-Saxon king, was killed by an arrow through the eye by the invading Norman French Army at the Battle of Hastings in 1066 – hence the headlines:

"950 YEARS LATER – IT'S GROUNDHOG DAY"
was The Sun's offering.

The Express went with:
"1066 RE-VISITED – ENGLISH STATESMAN FELLED BY FOREIGN ARCHER – AGAIN."

The Mail decided to try and capitalise on Love's death:
"DON'T LET MARCUS'S DEATH BE IN VAIN – VOTE LEAVE TOMORROW"

The King called for calm.

It eventually looked as though 3 per cent of the Electorate listened to The Mail, as Vote Leave won the vote with 52.5% of the vote, having had 49.5% in the poll of polls the night before Love was assassinated.

Naturally, Ibrahim was content with the result but saddened by Marcus Love's "martyrdom". He made sure all the journalists who spoke to him knew this and that he was not in any mood to be triumphalist, although he thought the right result had been achieved.

In any event, his own prestige as a politician and statesman were enhanced by being on the winning side.

"Now that Leave has won, I feel like I must be a member of the Establishment," he joked with Karim next time they met.

"Kirsty and I are very upset – if it wasn't for Love's death we reckon Remain would have won. In the end it was an old fashioned sympathy vote that clinched it," observed Karim.

"Let's just thank our lucky stars the perpetrator was not a Muslim…"

At least Ibrahim was right about this… and Karim knew it.

8

The King entered the morning room and greeted Sophia and Richard.

"A Happy Easter to you both. I was expecting to see my grandchildren out hunting for their eggs. Don't tell me they are still in bed?"

"No James," Sophia replied. "They've been out and back and are getting ready for Church."

"Ah, splendid."

A knock at the door announced the children's nanny.

"We're ready, sir," she announced to the King.

"Very well, Harriet. Let's go down. We've been advised to drive to church in three cars, for security reasons. Clarissa and I will go in the second car and you can go in the third. We'll see you in church."

The King's car moved slowly along the lane that led from Sandringham House to the village church.

Each car was identical with blackened windows so that any attacker wouldn't know which was carrying royalty. Out of the woods from both sides of the road some forty masked gunmen emerged to open fire on the first car, prompting the convoy to stop and the King's armed guard in the attending vehicles to open doors and retaliate. But they were hopelessly outgunned.

Once the armed escorts were all dead, the gunmen shot the driver of the second car and opened the door. The bodyguard in the passenger seat succeeded in shooting three of the attackers until he was killed. The terrified King and Queen were pulled out and bundled into a van, that had parked up alongside, and driven at furious speed through the village toward the main road to Kings Lynn.

There being no surviving police or intelligence officers, by the time the authorities were informed of the attack, the getaway car had despatched its precious cargo into another vehicle which was now heading up the motorway to Yorkshire. Within an hour, the BBC was broadcasting the kidnappers' terms: the immediate recall of Parliament including members who had won seats at the election and to enact the establishment of Sharia Law in any borough that had a preponderance of Muslims living there. If these terms were not met within 48 hours, the King would be executed. Within

30 minutes of the announcement, GCHQ confirmed the source of the terrorists' command and control. It was Bradford City Hall.

9

At the Inland Revenue offices in Bradford, the Assistant Chief Finance Officer took a call from a senior official in Whitehall.

"So now you've got rid of your bad apples, Malone, when can we expect our dues at the Treasury?"

Malone took the phone across to the window overlooking St. Blaise Way and groaned. The picket line preventing any of his tax collectors entering the building was being reinforced by an army of Government opponents showing muscle and voice enough to deter any but the bravest of his loyal HMRC staff from pushing through. There would be insufficient numbers anyway to reverse the procedure their colleagues had implemented before they were sacked, whereby any tax due from postcodes with constituencies won by Muslim Party MPs would not be collected.

"I haven't the staff to restore normal tax collection, Mr Gunridge."

The tone of his superior's reply was condescendingly

sharp. "Then we will have to put the matter into the hands of tax offices elsewhere," he said. "That won't help your application for promotion of course."

Malone was favourite in the running for the Chief Finance Officer vacancy in Bradford. He paused as he resolved not to let this threat rattle his composure.

"The unions won't let that happen," he retorted, conscious of the satisfaction in his voice. "They have instructed their members not to revise the procedure." He waited for a reaction but none came. "Until the Government reinstates Muslim Party MPs," he went on, "we will have to accept that no tax due on income or services will go to HM Treasury from areas where Muslim Party MPs have been elected."

The debate in the council chamber was getting heated.

"You can't expect those earning below the tax threshold to pay more council tax. It unfairly penalises them. It's a case of double standards when Labour objected so strongly to the supposed poison of the Poll Tax…" The Conservative speaker's interruption was drowned out in a cacophony of jeers from the crowd of Labour Party supporters that had packed the room.

"Order," called the Chair. "Let the proposer make

his final point so we can at last take a vote on this motion."

The Labour councillor for Queensbury stood.

"In summary, Ms Chair, if the Government is withholding our block grant, we've got to get our revenue from somewhere.."

As the Bradford City Council prepared to vote on the motion to raise council tax by nearly 200%, members of the public were still pushing through the doors of the chamber. Security staff tried to hold them back, and persuade them to leave the building but managed only to block the stairway as more people were entering the town hall from the street. What relieved the bottleneck was entirely unpredicted, both by the victims of the stampede and its perpetrators.

The loud bang that was heard from two floors above the council chamber was a stun grenade being detonated. This was followed by cries and shouting as a door was flung open and several men in Muslim garb came tearing down the stairs. Seeing them pursued by masked gunmen, the crowds two floors down outside the council chamber panicked. The gunmen did not need to fire. Thanks to the blocked staircase, they were able to apprehend their prey within moments, but not before a crush on a corner of the staircase had rendered unconscious several of those seeking to attend the council vote.

By the time the emergency services arrived – police first to take over from the SAS – then ambulances 20 minutes later, six people had passed the point of recovery and expired before paramedics could revive them. Public resentment about the suspension of parliamentary democracy was now fuelled by outrage that the Government was responsible for the deaths of innocent people in a blundered attempt to secure the release of the monarch from a terrorist group covertly run from Bradford City Hall.

Jim McCosh took a slug of whisky from the bottle sitting provocatively on the First Minister's desk. He paused to reflect before standing up and hurling the bottle at the wall opposite, narrowly missing the framed photograph of his beaming face as a young man with his arm around the shoulder of his mentor and founding father of the SNP, Sandy Wallace. He was furious, not least for letting himself slip back into his old habit of indulging in a tipple during working hours.

He tried to persuade himself he had an excuse this time. Ivan Smithson's suspension of the Westminster Parliament had closed the only avenue open to his party to influence British economic policy and its relations with the rest of the world. After the SNP had been defeated in the independence referendum, the annihilation of the Labour Party in Scotland had provided Westminster with an anti-austerity block of SNP MPs that punched above its weight. Labour in England would have to adopt the same platform if it was to win its vote back and challenge for Government in the UK in future. This scenario had vanished in a puff of smoke now that Ivan Smithson had suspended Parliament.

McCosh pressed the buzzer on his phone. He didn't need to. The door of the office was already opening and his PA Lorraine frowning her concern as she surveyed the whisky-stained wall and fragments of glass on the floor opposite his desk. The First Minister didn't offer her an explanation, preferring to impress on his PA the urgency of the task he wanted her to perform.

"Would you take down a letter, please Lorraine? I want it sent to Smithson right away."

He began dictating.

'*Dear Prime Minister,*
The news that the Monarch has been kidnapped and held to ransom is shocking, and we in Scotland share the wish of the majority of the British people that he and the Queen come to no harm at the hands of this despicable so-called caliphate.

I cannot accept however that such an act justifies the suspension of Parliament. I have decided to declare Scotland an independent country. This will be de facto with immediate effect. The overwhelming support in Scotland for continued membership of the EU in the recent UK referendum is cause enough for us to reject England so that a second referendum on Scottish independence is not necessary.

I await your acknowledgement pending implementation of my Government's intention to recover our assets from the British state.

With sincere wishes for cordial relations between our countries

James McCosh First Minister'

Kirsty was torn. Her politics were too green for her to feel comfortable with playing a gig on an oil platform, yet she was Scottish enough to support her Government's UDI. What swayed her was the fervour of the band's drummer, Nick. He was passionate that McCosh's Government should not allow itself to be bullied out of securing the oil off the Scottish coast for the Scottish economy alone, by diverting all tankers to the Grangemouth refinery in the Firth of Forth . Hence the Rainbow Warriors had accepted an invitation to play for the oil workers to keep up their morale as Smithson's Government threatened to send the Royal Navy to restore the transportation of crude oil to the Humber refinery in Lincolnshire.

The gig was being televised and thus guaranteed exposure to an audience outside their London base. But Kirsty had misgivings about this. Instead of a matey slot on BBC's Later with Jools, their manager Martin had arranged a lucrative deal with a television company based in Riyadh. Saudi Arabia was keen to present an image of British imperialism to the world as it put more pressure on Smithson to reinstate Muslim MPs to Parliament. The news channel Al Ekhbariya would like nothing more than to film the gig against the background of the Royal Navy confronting the Scottish oil tankers in the North Sea. Kirsty the flame-haired political activist with a heart for radical political change was now feeling that the waters she was wading into were becoming rather too deep and turbulent for her taste and comfort.

The weather was also turbulent as the road crew set up the stage on the oil rig platform, there being no room elsewhere on the rig for an audience of more than about 50. Wind mixed shriekingly with electronic feedback as it howled around the PA system but the squally rain eased enough to allow the Rainbow Warriors to mount the stage and launch into "Everybody's Bully", now their most recognisable number.

"War is his game and he's playing for kicks
He has them all fooled with his cheap little tricks",

belted out Kirsty after introducing it as a reference to the Smithson's RUK, the Government derived from the rump of a UK Parliament that still tried to boss the Scots.

Hardly had they got into the song when they were startled by a loud explosion some distance from the rig. They stopped playing as their audience leapt to its feet and crowded to the rail. Two warships, bristling with high tech antenna and weaponry, were facing off in an otherwise grey featureless sea. The Royal Navy destroyer had fired a warning salvo across the bows of a frigate commandeered by mutinous nautical supporters of the Scottish Government to protect the tankers that were being primed with crude oil from the rig.

The bully had arrived.

On the screen Andy Sheikh was transfixed by the sight of his protégé Karim contorting himself as he solo'd lead guitar while Kirsty bopped and jived to the rhythm of the song. He heard the Royal Navy cannon. The camera then went quickly off the Rainbow Warriors to catch the incident taking place across the water. Sheikh was on the phone at once.

"I want you to get the rights to these pictures, Bernie. For tomorrow's front page, with the headline:

'PRINCE KARIM, SON OF PRINCESS CAROLINE, ROCKS FOR SCOTLAND.'"

Resisting the temptation to open the new bottle of Lagavulin on the desk in front of him, Jim McCosh took a sip of tea in an effort to maintain calmness in mood and tone. Smithson had just called him.

"The Scottish economy can't function since the Bank of England froze our assets," he reiterated to Smithson. "Until we negotiate our membership of the EU, our offshore oil is our only lifeline now."

"I'll use force if I have to," Smithson barked back down the phone. "Blasting out those terrorists in Bradford should have proved that to you, McCosh."

The Scottish First Minister laughed. "But look where it got you." He didn't bother to hide his derision. "Mass protests on the streets of ungovernable cities against your regime, and still no sign of the King and Queen because your intelligence didn't tell you the caliphate had relocated their hostages. If you don't restore Parliament you won't just have lost Scotland but large parts of England, Wales too probably. I..."

Smithson was still listening but could hear only muffled but frantic chatter in the background.

"McCosh, look, all you have to do is let those tankers pass so they can get to the Humber refinery and I will order the Royal Navy to withdraw. Otherwise, the frigates you have commandeered will become the first victims of conflict between our countries since the Jacobite Rebellion and your mutineers will be charged with treason."

"Sorry, Smithson... I'm not able to respond to that just now. Something more urgent has come up..."

"What – more urgent than a stand-off between those two warships?

"Yes. I've had a call from Admiral McKinley in Faslane. Some mavericks calling themselves the Culloden Brigade have threatened to take matters into their own hands if your forces attack ours. Whether intentional or not, a cruise missile launch has been triggered from a Trident submarine. It's primed and heading for GCHQ."

"Christ, how did that happen?"

"Never mind, I just have to tell you we can't stop

it… but we can re-target it onto a large town north of Cheltenham, according to my computer nerd friends up here."

"How about Burnley? I know a couple of total arseholes from there. We'll have to retaliate you know, like for like – what Scots town do you particularly dislike? Dundee's a bit of a shocker isn't it?"

"No I like Dundee, I went to Uni there – I'll agree Paisley – Graham Blackson's old constituency – he's always trying to scupper us as well as being allegedly the worst British Prime Minister since Lord North."

"Okay it's a deal."

The live coverage of the North Sea faceoff kept running. Kirsty could see the cameras were still rolling and ran back to her microphone.

"If proof were still needed, the Smithson Government's contempt toward our nation is there for all to see, how it is prepared to use brute force to get its way. Well, I for one won't be a subject of your King, Smithson, even if you find him…"

Shouts from the rail interrupted her. "Come here, Kirsty," came Karim's voice. "They are withdrawing."

Sure enough Karim's words were borne out as Kirsty rushed back to the crowd of riggers at the rail.

Four destroyers had turned from the frigates defending the tankers and were sailing away southwards. Had McCosh caved in to Smithson when he had demonstrated his intention to use force?

"So what the fuck are you going to do?"

"I've asked the admiral to abort the attack," said McCosh. "They are trying to down the missile on open land but it's not guaranteed. Just now it is crossing the Lake District."

"One gem of British landscape ruined for hundreds of years then," grimaced Smithson, "though minimal human casualties at least. I will get onto the BBC at once."

"Will you call off your warships too?"

"That will depend on where the missile lands and the number of casualties."

Assuming the incident had passed, Al Ekhbariya's cameras were now back filming the Rainbow Warriors who had resumed their set. Still watching from his office in Leeds, Andy Sheikh was in the middle of another call about declaring Karim as the rallying point for opposition to the Smithson Government when the broadcast was interrupted by a news announcement in Arabic showing a picture of the Prime Minister. He flicked onto the BBC News Channel on another screen.

"... a grave state of emergency," Smithson was saying. "Fringe nationalist elements have launched a nuclear missile from a Trident submarine. All attempts to abort it have failed. Government control of the local situation for people close to GCHQ is now being directed from nuclear bunkers in Gloucestershire. If you are in the vicinity, your Government strongly advises you to find whatever shelter from the fallout is available to you within the next 25 minutes. 'Duck and cover' was the slogan Mr Macmillan would have used in the 1950s. I am sorry I cannot offer any better advice now."

Andy Sheikh looked back at the Al Ekhbariya broadcast from the oil rig. Its cameras were now showing the retreat of Smithson's destroyers had halted. They were now turning to face the rig again.

Next morning's papers had sold out before Ibrahim had reached Andy Sheikh's office. He had hoped for a more complete picture of events before he met his political backer. He got more information from his taxi-driver than the scrambled conversation he had with Sheikh at 6 a.m. All Sheikh would say was that he was not going to say anymore over the phone and that Ibrahim should come in person to his office. With grim irony, Ibrahim reflected that there would have been no need for such caution, had GCHQ been devastated.

After the brinkmanship and tension of the past 24 hours, and while back in Sheikh's office once more, Ibrahim experienced a sensation he had never felt before. He trembled with relief as he kissed the hand of the woman proffering it to him. Dressed in ill-fitting khaki trousers and a red sweatshirt, Queen Clarissa of England smiled wanly on being introduced to him.

"Ibrahim is the man who will lead this country forward as it comes to terms with a new multicultural constitutional arrangement, your Majesty," said Andy Sheikh.

"I'm afraid I don't know where this is all leading, Mr Sheikh. Are we to believe that the Muslim population of this country are not breeding violent extremists?"

"It won't if I have anything to do with it, Ma'am," said Ibrahim. "Contrary to what you may have heard, not all Muslims hold extremist views. The whole purpose of the Muslim Party is to represent those strands of Muslim belief that are consistent with the democratic and pluralistic traditions of this country."

"And that includes advocating equal rights for minorities and women," said Andy Sheikh.

"As well as the rule of law", added Ibrahim. "So how did you get here, Ma'am?" he asked.

"I was driven here blindfolded. I don't know where they were holding us. It was about an hour's drive away."

"Why is the King not with you?"

"Because whoever paid those scumbags their ransom didn't pay enough. That's what I gathered from my captors' conversation during the car journey. They seem to think Mr Sheikh is sympathetic to their cause and my appearance in his media will put pressure for acceptance of their demands – more money and Sharia Law for Muslim areas."

"And has there been a response from Smithson?" asked Ibrahim.

"Yes, my reporters are with him now." Andy Sheikh unmuted the TV that dominated the wall of his office so they could hear what the Prime Minister was saying. Smithson was addressing the massed ranks of constabulary preventing anyone gaining access to Bradford City Hall. Many had been bussed in from other police forces to tackle the crowds protesting against the closure of the council on the orders of the Government since the events of the previous week when the SAS had stormed the building. Their banners read 'Police brutality – Orgreave again', and 'Time for another Civil War'.

"… nothing changes my resolve to restore law and order here," the PM intoned, "and to defeat the forces of terror, whether they be Islamist or nationalist…"

As the Prime Minister was being guided into a Daimler by his bodyguards so as to be promptly driven away, pictures of a Tesco superstore appeared on the TV. The smoking remains of a missile clearly marked by the symbol of a trident was lying next to the Tesco sign that had fallen from the front of the flattened building. Bomb disposal experts had not yet started work to establish why the warhead had not detonated. The TV picture switched back to Smithson.

"What can you tell us about the Trident missile that was fired at a Tesco superstore in Burnley, Prime Minister?" asked a Daily Mail reporter.

"Only that the people of Paisley will be relieved we shan't be retaliating," he replied with a grin. "They will be wiser too in the knowledge that their country's nuclear arsenal is hardly safe and effective in the hands of those they elected to be in charge."

The broadcast again reverted to Burnley where local residents were crying and shouting their outrage to the camera as Sheikh's reporter was interviewing them. By some miracle the superstore was closed for a refit and the only casualties were 3 shopfitters enjoying a tea break and 3 trespassing teenagers intent on a looting spree.

There was now something else on Ibrahim's mind.

"Forgive my ignorance, Andy," asked Ibrahim, "but what was meant by that banner outside Bradford City Hall – about another civil war?"

"My colleague Harry can help with that I expect."

"In 1641 King Charles I shut down Parliament and they went to war," Harry said.

"How did it turn out?"

"The king lost," Harry continued. "Not just the war but his head too."

Ibrahim saw Queen Clarissa wince.

"I fear for my husband if this conflict turns out like that one," she shuddered, "even if he survives his capture now."

Seeing the Queen of England looking scruffy and strained on the evening news had an effect on Kirsty she didn't expect. Although highly critical of British royalty she was surprised at her feelings of pity for the woman. James might be a self-opinionated prat but he was still Clarissa's husband who she had waited years to claim as her own. Now he was still absent. When asked by the Star Media reporter why she thought she had been released but not him, Clarissa just expressed her dismay, offering no explanation.

"She must have been given a job by the caliphate people," was Karim's sceptical observation. "They released her to persuade the Government to do something for them before they are prepared to release the King."

The next news bulletin gave some foundation to Karim's suspicions. In talks between the Government and Bradford City Council, the Home Secretary had agreed a compromise whereby the police would allow council business to resume, provided due tax was passed to the Treasury. This was in return for the Government preparing a bill so that all courts within the jurisdiction of Bradford City Council would be administered according to Sharia Law.

"Do I really want to be King?" said Karim. "I'm happy as I am, with you, and rocking the world for a good cause. So they love me in Scotland. Well, big deal. The Scots aren't part of the UK now. I'd be more than happy being a journalist or charity worker."

"But you've got a huge following down here too. English areas opposing Smithson's emergency rule are holding you up as a poster boy." Kirsty paused to ponder then smiled. "If we ever have an election again, the Greens are going to have a field day."

Kirsty and Karim were on their way back to Leeds after playing a gig in Manchester, followed by a midnight meal to celebrate Kirsty's birthday. It was now 2 a.m, raining, and they were tired. Karim was glad there was very little traffic, though a white van seemed to be keeping them close company after leaving the restaurant. As they drove up the slip road onto the M62, they were startled by the van pulling past them at speed, to disappear quickly into the gloom ahead. "Was there a need for that?" grumbled Kirsty. "Oh well," replied Karim, "keep talking will you, I need to stay awake."

It wasn't Karim who first noticed the figure through the rain, some 200 yards ahead of them. "Slow down, Karim," Kirsty yelled. "Look," she pointed. "He's obviously drunk, with no idea where he is.."

Karim saw the man staggering hazardously across the motorway and immediately pulled onto the hard shoulder. There was no other traffic going in the same direction so he leapt out and pulled the man into their car. He was wearing no coat, just a tracksuit and a blindfold. His hands were tied behind his back.

Tearing off the blindfold, the two of them stared at their charge in disbelief. The King of England, unmistakable despite his long bedraggled hair and a beard, looked from one to the other before addressing Karim.

"You… I recognise you… not one of my captors … no."

"My name is Karim. Are you his Royal Highness the King?"

"I am." King James paused. "If you are the Karim I think you are from the pictures I have seen in the newspapers, how extraordinary that I should be in the car of my first wife's second son."

Karim thought quickly. "I suspect it was intended that we would be the first to see you. You're not wet through so I assume you were not on the motorway for long."

"No, just a matter of minutes."

"Pushed out of a white van bound and blindfolded so you would be found by the first car that was behind. I get it."

"Does that mean you are part of my captors' plan to carry out their designs or can I assume I am safe with you?"

"You are safe. We have no connection with jihadis and don't support their agenda. Where would you like us to take you?"

"To the Queen, if you would," said King James. "I trust she is safe?"

"Yes," answered Kirsty. "She is at St James's Palace."

"Then please, take me there."

"It is nearly 3 a.m, sir," said Karim as he started the engine, "and we are in Yorkshire."

"Then please, if you have a phone, would you let me call her?"

"Of course," replied Kirsty, handing him her iphone. Realising he couldn't use his hands since she had nothing to cut his ties, she asked him for the number which she typed in. The number connected but there was no answer.

"She'll be asleep, sir. I suggest you come with us. We are staying at the Hilton in Leeds. I'm sure there won't be any problem."

"That's kind of you, er.."

"Kirsty is my name, sir. We are staying there courtesy of Andy Sheikh who has been protecting Karim since he made public his identity. We were advised to leave London as it is not safe for him there."

"I see. Well, I cannot very well walk into a hotel with my hands bound. Haven't you got something to cut the ties?"

"No, sorry."

"Then I'd be grateful if you could take me to the nearest police station."

Kirsty logged on to her phone's search engine. "So you are happy to sleep in a cell?" asked Karim.

The king laughed. "I shall ask them to take me to York. I will stay at Bishopthorpe Palace where the Archbishop will hopefully restore my determination to do what is right for the country. Then I will be fit to brief the Prime Minister."

"What will you tell him?"

"My captors told me he is passing legislation to establish Sharia Law as an option in cities such as Bradford. How appalling. I don't recall seeing that in his party's manifesto."

"I believe it was the condition of your release, sir, " said Karim.

"Well we can't have that. The terrorists will have won."

"We already don't have democracy under the Conservatives."

"You mean because he banned the Muslim Party? But they are the people who kidnapped me."

"No, sir. They are your best bet as a firewall against the extremists who want a caliphate regardless of the will of the people."

"Take this exit, Karim," said Kirsty. "There is a police station half a mile from the first roundabout."

In no more than a couple of minutes, they were pulling up outside.

"Do you mind if we don't come in?" said Karim. "It would be too much if I was recognised too. The press would no doubt think I kidnapped you. There would be a feeding frenzy."

King James smiled as he got out of the car. "Thank you for rescuing me. I hope I can return the favour and we can spend time together in less troubled times. Your mother would have wanted that I am sure."

10

It was late next morning when Karim's phone serenaded him out of a deep slumber.

"Hot news just going out on Star Media." Andy Sheikh's voice was supercharged with excitement. "King James has been released by his jihadi captors. Can you get to my office by 4pm?"

Karim yawned deeply. "I know. It was Kirsty and I who found him wandering on the motorway last night."

"What?" Sheikh sounded wounded. "And you didn't think to phone me?"

"We were too tired, I'm sorry, Andy."

"For crying out loud, there is a story here. I could run the headline '**KING BROUGHT TO SAFETY BY HIS ILLEGITIMATE "STEPSON."**' It will give you all the credibility you will need with our opponents."

"Nobody is going to believe that of all the motorists on the motorway it was me who stopped for him," replied Karim testily. Still tired, he didn't bother to hide his impatience. "Anyway, why do you want me to come to your office?"

"I've got someone coming to see me who wants you to be here too."

"Who?"

"Your law tutor, Lena Khan."

Karim did not reply immediately. Andy Sheikh was unsure if this meant disapproval or that he was just computing the possible reasons for Lena's request.

"Why should I come?"

"Because she wants the Labour Party to join forces again with Ibrahim's party and by implication back your claim to the throne."

Karim was not in the mood for being groomed to be Head of State but was curious as to the political players he might have to work with.

"What influence can she bring to bear on Labour's policy?"

"Dave Berriman is going to resign due to ill-health," replied the media mogul. "There's going to be a leadership contest in the Labour Party and she wants to go for it."

The daughter of a wealthy Pakistani landowner, Lena Khan had come to Britain as an Oxford law student.

During the 1980s, she had risen to prominence as a barrister successfully defending left wing activists against deportation to Chile and other Latin American dictatorships. She had become a protégé of Tariq Ali, leading light of the International Marxist Group (IMG). When the IMG infiltrated the Labour Party, she was smart enough to rise above the factionalisation the IMG fell victim to as a result of the miners' strike. Nor was she too closely identified with New Labour when that brand of left wing politics had turned stale. It was as though her political career was following the example of the leader of the Chinese Communist Party who was careful to offend no-one, because her rise to a place on Labour's NEC was uncontroversial and apparently preordained.

It was realising Labour wouldn't be fit for government again for several years after New Labour was defeated in 2010 that Ms Khan took a sabbatical academic post at SOAS. Here she made a strong impression on a young student with a keen social and political conscience. A course in the law of international relations was part of Karim's degree. After Sheikh rang off, Karim started to wonder what her approach to him might be.

While a student at SOAS, Karim had been incensed about Israeli treatment of its Palestinian neighbours to the point that he became a fellow traveller of Hezbollah;

as had Dave Berriman it seemed, a friend of Hamas too as the Tories didn't cease to remind him. Did Lena Khan take the same view? He thought it unlikely she would excuse the shelling of Israeli civilians from across the Lebanese border. He remembered an essay he wrote challenging the purpose of the UN which had allowed the massacre of the Muslim population of Srebrenica under its watch, failed to implement its resolutions against Israeli occupation of the West Bank and also failed to stop the US and UK going to war against Saddam without a UN mandate. Ms Khan gave him a good mark for his logic and use of supporting material but left a comment in red on his paper:- *What alternative would you offer the world if there's no international guarantor of collective security like the United Nations?* He had not offered a reply. Would she remember?

He arrived in Sheikh's office to find Lena Khan already there, wearing a business suit; no salwar-kameez on this occasion, the loose-fitting trouser suit that she wore the last time he had seen her in the SOAS lecture theatre a year or two before, with a draped scarf over her head. Lena Khan wasted no time in getting to the point.

"Andy tells me Ibrahim is keen to have you on a Rainbow Alliance ticket as the royal figurehead. The symbol of British unity across faith and racial lines that divide our society."

"I'm flattered, Ms Khan. Ibrahim is a good man. I'm not clear though why you are setting me against my half-brother as a potential heir to the throne."

"From our contacts at the BBC," Sheikh explained, "we gather there is evidence that the King and Queen are very hostile to Muslim political influence. Without a coalition of anti-Tory opinion, this country is going to see social breakdown. The King and Queen appear to be reactionary and partisan which is a toxic mix. Some people already want them to abdicate."

"I have a question for you Karim," Lena said, "are you prepared to stand above the political fray as is expected of the royal family?"

"In principle, yes." Karim paused to take a sip of coffee from the mug in front of him, emblazoned with the caption 'GOTCHA – only in The Sun'. "But you are assuming I want to be King. I don't want to be considered as a candidate for monarch unless possibly the King and Prince of Wales abdicate. I'm happy just now supporting my partner, as she gigs around the country in support of good causes."

"Which makes you very popular in Scotland, I hear. You could be the catalyst for a repaired United Kingdom."

"Well I would support that."

"And Ibrahim too, a pluralist who advocates liberal values?"

"I'm no jihadi if that is what you are implying."

"Being aware of your links in the past with groups supporting suicide bombing, I have long since wondered."

Karim went on the defensive. "You're referring obviously to Hezbollah whom I went to meetings with during my student days but I have never promoted such behaviour. It is against the teaching of the Prophet."

"I'm asking because you will need to be prepared for the press opening cupboards where you may have left some skeletons."

"I will think about it. Let me speak to Ibrahim and I will let you know my decision."

"Don't be long. To have any chance of winning the party leadership, I need to have a convincing strategy Labour will accept. And the Tories may call a general election now Scotland no longer have MPs to challenge them."

Still tired from the exertions of travelling back home the night before, Karim left the meeting. Lena confided her fears to Sheikh of joining forces with the Muslim Party to defeat Smithson.

"Wasn't Ibrahim a follower of Mawdudi?" she asked.

"Yes. He inspired hundreds of young men when he started up the first Muslim political movement and advocated the establishment of Sharia Law."

"Mawdudi opposed women's emancipation, didn't he?"

"True. Mawdudi may have drawn him into politics but Ibrahim's always been a secularist. There are women in Ibrahim's party. Ibrahim's got a problem though. Saudi Arabia doesn't just export oil. His party organisation is being infiltrated by Saudi-backed hardliners who want to limit women's rights."

"Are these people jihadists too?"

"Islamic State draws on Wahhabi doctrine so most likely yes."

"Then the Labour Party will want to hear Ibrahim is tackling this head-on."

"What makes it harder for Ibrahim is his party is facing a funding crisis. A large donation occasionally goes into their coffers indirectly from the Saudi government. They will withhold funds unless the party supports Sharia law, for example." Andy Sheikh paused. "A bit like the trade unions withholding funds if Labour doesn't hold to their agenda."

"OK, point taken," Lena winced. "But we really cannot have Saudi Arabia dictating terms if it serves to encourage jihadism."

"If Labour is to have any chance of returning to government, you will have to ally with Ibrahim."

"I agree but it's a dilemma – a headache."

After pouring tea, the royal butler walked backwards to the door of the King's drawing room and quietly closed it behind him. Smithson looked at the teapot he had left on the tray. How archaic the royal insignia looked now that the lion and the unicorn had parted company.

"I've asked you to come because I fear for the direction this country has taken since I was kidnapped," said the King. "It's hard enough to stomach the loss of Scotland but what I won't countenance is the establishment of Sharia Law in this country, Smithson."

The Prime Minister's cup rattled in its saucer, as if in sympathy with his jangling nerves.

"It is only as an option in certain towns in Yorkshire and Lancashire, your Majesty. With respect, you would not be here if I had refused the demand."

"It's the thin end of the wedge, Smithson."

"But we have to repair relations with the Saudi government or we run the risk of falling out with OPEC, which they dominate. The economy won't survive for long based on what we can extract from the North Sea."

"Repairing relations means giving in to their demand to reinstate Muslim Party MPs, I take it?"

"We cannot afford to upset our Arab friends, sir. They are threatening already to give the Scottish government special status at our expense."

"Well then I can't see why you don't call a general election. It is one you should win now Scotland no longer has MPs to challenge you."

"And I have your Majesty's blessing if I allow the Muslim Party to participate?"

"My blessing? Good God no, but I take your point about the economy. I don't wish to see my Kingdom freezing to death as well as shrinking into oblivion." The King stood up. "Besides, there is no legitimacy for an unelected government of the RUK."

Taking his royal cue,Smithson also got to his feet.

"Thank you, your Majesty. I will set the wheels in motion."

Back in Downing Street, Smithson was straightaway on the phone to his party chairman Sean Markinson at Conservative Central Office.

"I am going to go to the country at the earliest opportunity, Sean. I have the King's blessing for this. Give me a date in about two month's time, would you?"

Markinson made a quick scan of his diary.

"June 30th, Ivan," he said. "Labour may not appoint their new leader till the party conference in October so we should have a clear run."

Markinson was later to be proved wrong as no-one

stood against Lena Khan, so she emerged as Labour leader in early May.

Markinson could hear the sound of uncorking; then something being poured and a gulp.

"What are the chances of another Rainbow Alliance to spoil our chances?" was the eventual response.

"Few I think," said Markinson. "There is a lot of unease in Labour about their joining forces with the Muslim Party while it seems to be infiltrated by jihadi sympathisers. I can't see Ibrahim sorting it out in time or even still being leader."

"Is Lena Khan your preferred candidate for Labour Party leader?" Karim was in Hyde Park with Ibrahim. Where Obama or Trump would have been talking political tactics during a round of golf, they were kicking a ball around. "The Sun is supporting her bid and talking of a potential electoral pact with your party as a marriage made in Paradise. As if it is a done deal."

"I've met her and am impressed," Ibrahim replied. "She has concerns though about joining forces with my party. I don't blame her, as I do too."

"How do you mean?"

"The Muslim Party has problems, Karim. Our organisation is riddled with factionalism. Entryists from fundamentalist groups are controlling the selection of candidates for Parliament. If pluralists like me try and counter them, we find our finances from Saudi backers are withheld. What is worrying me is that the Saudi Government wants to approve our candidates."

"Why should they do that?"

"The Saudi Royals are in an alliance with a brand of Islam that is not like yours or mine. It is intolerant, strict and puritanical. They certainly would not approve of your lifestyle."

"So what is your plan?"

"I've arranged to meet a backer who has Saudi connections but is independent of the regime. I'm going to ask him to fund my party for the election. As you will be on the ticket for another Rainbow Alliance, I would like you to accompany me. His wife is charming I am told. Kirsty would surely like her so she must come too."

"Like Lena Khan, you are assuming I want to be King to preside over a Rainbow Alliance government. You will both need to get your act together before I agree that."

"I understand, Karim. No-one is going to pressurise you."

The appointment Ibrahim had arranged was for lunch at an Indian restaurant in Westminster. Sultan was a Saudi banker in his early thirties who was financial adviser to four government ministers. Ibrahim pointed through the window to where they were already seated when his taxi pulled up outside the restaurant. Despite Ibrahim briefing Karim and Kirsty that Sultan was much more liberal and cosmopolitan than most Saudis, his wife, Shaya, was wearing a veil.

On seeing Ibrahim enter the restaurant, Sultan called over a waiter. A makeshift partition was arranged so that the party could have some privacy, whereupon Shaya, to Karim's surprise, removed her veil. She smiled at Kirsty and started to chat fondly of London where she had met her husband who in turn spoke warmly of his time there, particularly his placement at Coutts as a trainee banker in 2005.

Without thinking, Karim ventured a question that was to change the atmosphere noticeably.

"You were there on 7/7 then?"

"Oh yes," replied Sultan with a shrug. "And predictably that was blamed on Bin Laden too."

Kirsty looked uncertainly from Sultan to his wife. Both seemed nonchalant about the matter. She looked at Karim.

"Well the bombers were home-grown British jihadis, it's true," said Karim. "That doesn't mean Bin

Laden was any less responsible for their preparation than when he provided resources and training for the 15 Saudi men who blew up the twin towers on 9/11."

"No," replied Sultan without hesitation. "No, because Saudis were not behind 9/11. The plane hijackers were not Saudi men. One thousand two hundred and forty-six Jews were absent from work on that day and there is the proof that they, the Jews, were behind the killings. Not Saudis."

Karim looked at Ibrahim who had decided to study the menu as if he suddenly wanted to order a chapatti to go with his tandoori chicken. Shaya interjected.

"The number was higher than that, Habibi. And what was that film that predicted 9/11?"

"Yes," Sultan said. "The Americans produced a film depicting the destruction of the twin towers by Jews before 9/11. They knew it was going to happen so they released a film. And now they blame us."

Ibrahim looked up from his menu.

"And what was the name of that film?" he asked.

Sultan put down his knife and fork to take his phone from his pocket and call a friend. Not just one but several. None of them could remember the name of the film. He promised Ibrahim he would email him when he got the answer as he returned to the subject of bin Laden.

"We all like Osama; we just don't like the bother he

created for us," he said. Then pointing to his wife, said her best friend was Osama's niece.

"Really?" said Ibrahim.

"We know the bin Laden family," said Shaya. "They are very humble and don't show off like the newly rich Saudi families and people respect them for that. One of the wealthiest men in the world, Osama gave up everything."

Shaya now addressed her attention to Kirsty in particular.

"Osama wanted Arabs to be great again, as we were in the past. He wanted us to do this through jihad." Perhaps noticing Kirsty looking very uncomfortable now, she paused for a brief moment.

"The Americans are forcing our government to remove references to jihad in our school textbooks and most people are very angry about this", she continued. "I will teach my children jihad and the true Islam that is taught in our Saudi schools. You won't find me wearing a coloured headscarf like they do in Egypt or Yemen where they teach a deviant form of Islam."

There was silence.

"Now what is it you intend for your Muslim Party, Ibrahim? To promote Muslim teaching obviously. I will be very happy to back that. What sort of money are you thinking of?" Sultan enquired.

"Oh, enough to pay our election expenses – £10 million should do. With enough MPs to ensure Islam is respected and understood throughout Parliament and beyond. You may need to channel it through English based companies."

There was a pause in the discussion while the table was cleared. Karim and Kirsty took their cue from Ibrahim who declined Sultan's offer of a dessert and coffee.

"More important than the sum is what precisely you stand for," said Sultan. "I don't represent the Saudi government but I would like a say as to what goes into your manifesto."

"We need to move fast, Sultan. If you can advance half of what we need today, we can get the party organised for the election we expect to be called in June. The manifesto will be written as soon as our constituency parties are ready to launch our campaign."

Ibrahim's authoritative tone was sufficient for his donor to acquiesce. In their taxi on the way back to Kirsty's flat, Karim was effusive in his praise for Ibrahim's masterful diplomacy. He had got the funds he wanted but not committed to any details for an agenda that his donor was clearly pursuing.

"So what Islamic agenda can we expect to see in the party manifesto funded by our friend Sultan?" asked Karim.

"Oh, that as the Koran repeatedly reminds us, the vast majority of the world's population will not become believers, to quote the Prophet 'as to you your religion and to me mine.'"

But as Karim and Kirsty murmured their approval, Ibrahim counselled caution.

"It's going to be a difficult period for us now if we are to find our way to gaining a significant presence in Parliament. The money we have we will use to purge the party of Jihadi influence, otherwise we cannot appeal to a wider electorate. As a condition of membership, there will be no longer be a written undertaking to promote and defend Islam. But Muslims will make an oath of allegiance to the British Monarch when elected to the House of Commons like anyone else."

Kirsty and Karim both applauded in spontaneous approval.

"And when this is done," Ibrahim carried on, "we will rename the party. So that there is no ambiguity in case people continue to think ours is a sham commitment to the democratic process, our party will go forward into the election campaign as the Muslim Democratic Party."

11

After their ordeal at the hands of the Jihadi kidnappers, James and Clarissa retreated to Highgrove for a time to lick their wounds. At the suggestion of Smithson, anticipating a political dividend at the expense of Ibrahim's supporters, James and Clarissa agreed to be interviewed by Piers Wheatley, the BBC's Chief Royal Correspondent.

The interview took place in the garden at Highgrove in June.

Wheatley's opening question was probing and calculated.

"Did you seriously think that your jihadi kidnappers might kill you?"

"We had no idea what their plans were," responded James. "Sometimes I felt they didn't know either – many of them seemed just to be teenagers."

"With Yorkshire accents," contributed Clarissa.

"It was really a case of ACHAB – anything can happen at backgammon," continued James. "The leader, we nicknamed him Don, after Don Quixote, seemed volatile and unpredictable."

"Does this experience colour your opinion of British Muslims?"

"To be frank, a lot of them would ruin our lives at the drop of a hat," remarked Clarissa. "Khaki coloured scumbags if you ask me."

"You'd better delete that last bit," said James.

"Don't worry, we'll doctor it," Wheatley promised, having no intention of doing any such thing.

"Talking of Muslim youngsters, do you have a view on Karim Khaled?"

"Yes, I've got a view," said Clarissa. "He's clearly an upstart and an imposter along the lines of Perkin Warbeck – the monarchy has seen this kind of thing before and we're still here!"

A few days later the interview was broadcast with Clarissa's remark about scumbags left in.

The Palace complained but it was too late. Wheatley wrote a letter of apology to James and Clarissa, blaming his Editor, but the damage was done.

Sheikh watched the programme with Harry Bennett and some other colleagues in his office.

He seemed less concerned about the scumbag comment than the reference to Karim.

"Who on earth was Perkin Warbeck?"

"Yes, I can help you on that," said Harry, drawing on

his knowledge as an Oxford History graduate. "He was a claimant to the English throne in the 15th Century. It was alleged he was one of the Princes in the Tower supposedly murdered by their uncle, Richard III, but his claim fizzled out amid reports that he was actually the son of a Flanders boatman."

The following day, The Sun ran an editorial stating that Clarissa's comparison of Karim with Perkin Warbeck was unfair and unjustified. Reporting of Clarissa's racist remark was limited to a brief mention on page 4. Sheikh sensibly decided that the racist allegation would be better left for the likes of The Guardian to consider.

Various papers, and other sections of the media, took up the cudgels against Clarissa on the grounds of her reactionary and racist views.

James additionally courted unpopularity by writing to the Home Secretary suggesting a substantially beefed up citizenship test for all immigrants, and to the Education Ministry suggesting that the National Anthem should be sung in all schools every day in morning assembly.

Both letters were quickly leaked – the beefing up of the citizenship test was described as potentially discriminatory and the National Anthem idea was widely ridiculed as being old fashioned and inappropriate.

On Sheikh's instructions, The Sun adopted a fairly low key approach on the leaked letters, as Sheikh was happy to let others stick the knife into James. After all, The Sun was a monarchist paper with monarchist readers and Sheikh did not wish to be seen to overegg criticism of the Royals.

Macmillan, British Prime Minister during the 50s, was once asked what he thought dictated politicians' policy and actions, to which he responded by saying "Events, dear boy, events."

Smithson re-discovered the truth of this statement when three crises hit the government in quick succession.

The first related to the Spanish naval manoeuvres and infringements of territorial waters around Gibraltar – Smithson was obliged to despatch three destroyers and two companies of Marines to beef up Gibraltar's military capabilities, just when he needed these Forces to deal with the Scots and Jihadis at home.

Some of the Press predictably got worked up about the Spanish government's opportunism. Additionally, Smithson appeared to delay and dither before the Forces were despatched and he was unfavourably compared to Mrs Thatcher and her handling of the Falklands crisis.

The second crisis related to revelations about paedophiles among the senior echelons of the Anglican Church. In some of the cases the allegations went back 35 years or so.

As with the earlier Catholic Church scandal, the Church establishment had seen fit not to sack the culprits. Instead, many were simply moved to new Parishes and in a few cases promoted to Bishops.

As the Monarch and government were involved in the appointment of Bishops, neither could escape responsibility, so James and Smithson, the current incumbents, suffered serious criticism, particularly from the tabloids, not least The Sun, which called for the resignation of the Archbishop of Canterbury.

Partly as a result of misplaced loyalty, the King and Smithson stoutly defended the Archbishop and his Bishops, which enraged the tabloids, and no doubt many of their readers still more.

The third crisis could not have arisen at a worse time for Smithson and the Tories – just five weeks before the Election.

Alan Croft, the Tories' Chief Whip, was the first to alert Smithson.

"Prime Minister, we've got a major problem brewing at the Treasury," Croft said at their weekly meeting in Number 10. "The Guardian has today printed the first of what promise to be several articles by a whistleblower alleging that various Treasury staff used taxpayer funds to bet on currency and futures."

"What's wrong with that? I thought hedge funds in the City did that all the time," said Smithson.

"Well it might be okay with the investors' consent, but in this case the taxpayer hasn't consented – it's no joke."

"Maybe not, but if they've not gained personally, then it's not criminal – interview the culprits with Keith present and we'll see what gives."

Keith was Keith Dyson – Chancellor of the Exchequer.

Gavin MacDonald, the Number 10 Press spokesman, aka chief spin doctor, briefed a couple of journalists off the record leading to a headline the following day in The Telegraph:

"SOURCES CLOSE TO THE PM SAY THERE IS NO EVIDENCE OF CRIMINALITY."

This approach duly led to a headline the day after that in The Mirror as follows:

"CONSERVATIVES CONSENT TO CASINO CAPITALISM – USING YOUR MONEY."

Three days later Smithson spoke to Dyson in private in Number 10 after a meeting with the Cabinet.

"What was the outcome of the interviews of your boys at the Treasury using hedge funds without authority?"

"Trust me, Ivan, it's a storm in a teacup," Dyson responded. "We don't leave taxpayers' funds in a Building Society Account earning 0.1% interest. As well as gilts, there are a mix of investment vehicles we use to maximise returns for the taxpayer, less than 5% of which are hedge funds. The whistleblower was some kind of Marxist who didn't fit in – we had to get rid of him."

Smithson nodded in agreement, but Dyson would live to regret his complacency.

The whistleblower, an LSE graduate with first class honours by the name of Jeremy Gilmour, had further cards to play, if only someone would allow him to play them. At long last, he'd managed to arrange a meeting with Pete Shelley, the current editor of the satirical magazine, Private Eye.

The pair met at a run-of-the-mill pizzeria in Islington so as not to attract attention. The meeting took place one week after the story first broke in The Guardian.

"So how can I help you?" enquired Shelley.

"I can't persuade The Guardian to go out on a limb and use the really hardcore evidence I've accumulated," replied Gilmour. "They seem to be terrified of the potential legal consequences."

"Is it just defamation they're worried about?" asked Shelley.

"Primarily defamation, but also information accessed from government computers could be criminal in some circumstances, and hacking into computers to see people's bank accounts."

"So you did that?"

"Not personally – I got a friend to do it, and I've collated the information which is quite damning."

"What does it show?"

"It shows about four members of the Treasury team siphoning off profits into their personal bank accounts in places like Panama in relation to profits derived from hedge funds, while losses were posted to travel disbursements and sundry miscellaneous expenses."

"Okay, can I see the evidence?

"Sure – most of it's copied onto a couple of discs I've brought with me. I'll show you a couple of examples on my laptop."

After about 20 minutes of looking at various bank accounts, ledger entries and e-mails, Shelley declared himself to be satisfied.

"Yes, I reckon we can run with this – I'll get something put in the next issue – it's a pity Paul Foot isn't still with us, he would have loved to get stuck into this."

"Would you get your lawyers to check this out?" enquired Gilmour.

"Yes we'll probably run it past them, but whether we take any notice of what they say is another matter!"

"Fine, that's what I like to hear – publish and be damned, as they say," said Gilmour. "By the way, I've got some more material in the pipeline from a mate of mine who's been working in the banking sector – watch this space!"

True to his word, Shelley put a half page article in the next issue in the "Business News" section – the headline was:

HEADS WE WIN, TAILS YOU LOSE – H M Treasury.

The article mentioned the names of four Treasury officials apparently caught up in the scam, including dates and amounts involved.

There would be no hiding place for the culprits – they would be questioned by the Public Accounts Committee of the House of Commons and then by the Police – the former might turn out to be more brutal than the latter.

At the next Cabinet meeting in Number 10, Smithson remarked:

"The fallout from this could be serious, Keith."

"I'm sorry, Ivan, I was only told part of the story by my civil servants."

"Well it's up to you to find out the rest of the story, preferably not by reading it in the papers. This makes us, or more particularly you, look complacent and cynical, and additionally calls into question your competence."

"Well if this was China and I was President, we'd close down Private Eye," remarked Dyson.

"Well it isn't, and you're not," Smithson said helpfully – "I'll stand by you for now as you've shown me loyalty in the past, but if this gets too hot to handle you may have to fall on your sword. It looks like Labour and Ibrahim's lot are limbering up to hit us hard with this."

The rest of the Cabinet looked sombre and most managed to nod silently in agreement.

Sure enough, Ibrahim and Labour's Shadow Chancellor, Ben Keyes, were dissecting the Private Eye article and scandal generally that night on BBC2's Newsnight, with the programme's presenter, Dan Nicholson.

"It's the contempt shown for the taxpayer that's truly shocking and scandalous," opined Keyes.

Ibrahim nodded in agreement – Keyes continued "We undertake to clean up government departments so the spivs are rooted out."

"There's no doubt this is criminal behaviour and we are calling for the Police to investigate and arrest the culprits," said Ibrahim.

"Don't you accept that this was perpetrated by corrupt civil servants and their political masters are not to blame?" asked Nicholson.

"Not for one moment," said Keyes.

"The politicians must take responsibility for their teams," said Ibrahim – "they are supposed to create a culture of integrity and honesty in relation to public money – the first time questions were asked about this, the government spokesman said there was no criminality and left it at that – that's just not good enough."

"Various leading politicians don't seem to get it," remarked Keyes, "and it's likely the Electorate will punish them – and rightly so…"

12

In the words of the respected British economist, John Kay, modern banking in the West has represented a union between a utility and a casino.

The utility side of the business comprised the low risk retail banking sector holding deposits, dealing with money transfers and vanilla lending.

The sexy casino side of the business comprised investment banking, higher risk lending, trading in futures and other activities involving high risks in return for high returns... or heavy losses.

The important point is that the old fashioned retail banks could expect to be bailed out by the Government if they failed, whereas the higher risk investment banks could not.

The legal separation between retail and investment banking had been imposed in the United States by the Glass-Steagall Act of 1933, passed as a consequence of the stock market crash of 1929.

However, the rot set in again with the repeal in

1999 of the Glass-Steagall Act when President Clinton's administration caved in to the powerful banking sector and repealed the 1933 Act, thus allowing the banks to carry out retail and investment activities under the same roof.

To retain an active international banking sector and remain competitive, the UK banking authorities followed suit with the abolition of certain key regulations.

Ed Ruskin, an Australian working at the Bank of England, knew in broad brush terms most of the above historical and economic facts as a result of his degree course at the LSE.

However, the narrative he was more personally concerned about related to two dates in Australian history when the British Establishment had, in his view, shafted two relatives of his by killing one and destroying the political career of a second.

The first date was 1915 when the Gallipoli landings saw his great-grandfather, a Captain in an Australian Infantry Regiment, cut down by Turkish machine guns within five minutes of landing on Turkish soil.

Gallipoli had been Churchill's idea while a Minister in the British Government. Churchill was made the scapegoat for the disaster, resigned and duly took his place in the trenches on the Western Front.

No amount of contrition on the part of Churchill,

or any other British politician, could heal the fatal wounds sustained by Captain Ruskin and the thousands of other ANZAC troops who perished in the same campaign, leaving heartbroken family members at home, including the agonised surviving members of the Ruskin family.

Ed Ruskin's view was that his great-grandfather and the other dead ANZACs had been murdered thousands of miles away from home by Churchill and the British State to further the dubious objectives of the British war machine and British imperialism.

The other date etched on the collective memory of the Ruskin family was 1975, when Gough Whitlam's Labour government was controversially dismissed by the Governor General, the Queen's representative, after the Liberal dominated Senate blocked the Government's money bills.

The subsequent general election saw Labour thrown out and Ed's father, Chris, then a promising Labour politician, lost his seat.

Chris never got over this. It seemed like the British Monarch's rep had behaved in a biased manner, which resulted in a radical Labour government being replaced with a Conservative/Liberal administration.

Further evidence of British hostility and callousness towards Australians, if more was needed, was Ed's 2.1 Degree in Economics and Philosophy from the LSE. He reckoned he should have got a First – he saw himself as bright enough to get a First and he'd certainly worked hard.

In his opinion, he'd been penalised for being radical and having anti-British views.

He denied he was anti-British – he was just anti-British Establishment.

However, Ed's Degree was good enough for him to be taken on as a Graduate trainee at the Bank of England. He showed promise, and after two years was seconded to the Financial Conduct Authority (FCA), still under the umbrella of the Bank.

Ed's immediate boss at the FCA was Trevor Morris – they did not get on.

Ed saw Morris as stuffy, self serving and bureaucratic. Morris had got on by being polite to the right people and filling in forms on time.

They co-existed for five months and then Ed faced a career threatening crisis of conscience.

He had jointly, with Morris, conducted an audit of Broad Bridge Bank (BBB), chaired by Sir George Petersham, a leading City luminary and substantial Tory Party donor.

In Ed's view, certain aspects of the Bank's management of financial risk were not kosher and he fully intended to broach the subject with Morris, who would be responsible for signing off the FCA Report.

Ed was certain there'd been substantial mixing of deposits and investment funds amounting to a clear breach of the guidelines fully re-imposed following the 2008 banking crisis.

After a day spent rehearsing what he was going to say, when Ed eventually spoke to Morris about the problem, the conversation was as follows:-

"Trevor, I need to speak to you about BBB."

"Okay, fine, fire away."

"I think there's been a clear breach of the guidelines – deposits and investment funds have been mixed – we can't sign it off as having a clean bill of health."

There was a slight pause.

"Well, for a start, it's me that does the signing off – you're just my assistant," responded Morris. "Secondly, I know what you are alleging and I've mentioned the potential problem to George Petersham, who has undertaken to put things right asap. We were at school together and I've every reason to trust him, and I'm not prepared to blow the whistle on him."

"But you must know it's not as simple as that – we've – you've got a responsibility to flag up breaches like this – you don't have a choice."

"I decide if I have a choice or not – not you – and if you rock the boat on this I'll make sure you get fired, and I've got enough clout in this town to ensure you never work in the City again."

For 4 seconds Ed stared at Morris open-mouthed – it was then as much as he could do to restrain himself from calling Morris a typical Pommie bastard and decking him then and there.

"Okay, message received – I'll let you know later if it's understood or not…" Ed replied, and left the room.

That evening, Ed worked late and with the office empty, he decided to see what, if anything, he could discover by snooping discreetly in Morris's office.

Morris's desk was locked, but Ed easily found the key in a receptacle for pens and paper clips between the drawers and the rim of the desk.

The desk was full of various forms and the usual paraphernalia of an office desk. After about 5 minutes Ed had found nothing of interest and was about to give up, when he noticed a small leather credit card case at the back of the lowest drawer. The case contained, not a credit card, but a UFB Bank debit card complete with international sort code and account number in the name of Trevor D Morris.

Though UFB's HQ was in London, it was very much an international bank with a reputation for having active branches in several tax havens including the Cayman Islands and Isle of Man.

Ed knew he was now on to something as a Bank of England official having a bank account, probably in a tax haven, though not illegal in itself, would be regarded as "irregular" if the Bank of England's authorities got to hear of it.

Ed used his phone to take a snapshot of the card and then replaced it where he'd found it.

For the following few days, Ed was out of the office dealing with another audit.

He was in for a surprise a week later – he knew something was wrong when the receptionist studiously ignored him when he got in, instead of being her usual friendly self. He soon discovered the reason – his desk had been cleared of all papers and clutter. Such had been deposited in a bin liner and left at the side of the desk, apart from the computer screen and a letter addressed to him which read as follows:-

Dear Mr Ruskin

Your contract of employment has been terminated with immediate effect, due to gross and dishonest conduct, being the use of your office telephone to make two long distance phone calls to Australia at a total cost of £45.73 which you have not paid for.

In any event, this is contrary to the Bank of England's staff Code of Conduct paragraph 3 sub-section 2.

We know these calls were made by you as it's the Bank's policy to record all calls, as you know.

The calls were discovered during a routine

audit – a copy of the Invoice showing the numbers called is attached to this letter.

Please do not attempt to access e-mails on your computer any more. The password has been changed and further access will be denied.

A completed P45 form is enclosed.

Yours sincerely

Tracey Trimdale, Head of Human Resources

Ed realised it was true and that he was snookered. He had intended to pay for the calls but had then forgotten about them. One call was to his parents and the other to a girlfriend.

The thought of some ferret at the Bank listening to his personal calls upset him more than getting fired.

He picked up the bin liner and made for the exit without acknowledging anyone or saying any goodbyes.

As soon as he got out on the street, he phoned his mate, Jeremy Gilmour.

"Jezza – it's me, Ed. I've got some good news and some bad news – the good news is I've got a story for you as I half promised a couple of days ago, the bad news is that I've had the boot from the Bank – no doubt they sensed I was onto something. Are you still in touch with that hacker friend of yours? We're going to need him."

The following evening Jeremy Gilmour and Ed Ruskin travelled to Walthamstow on the tube to see the hacker known only as Ahmed.

"How much do we have to pay this guy?" enquired Ed.

"It's £75 a shot – cash – that's however long it takes. Usually with a Bank Account it's one or two hours."

"What if he can't get access in two hours?"

"He will ask for an additional fifty quid and try for another hour. If there's still no joy he will give up or refer you to his more expensive friend who owns more powerful equipment."

Twenty minutes later, Jeremy was introducing Ed to Ahmed, at the latter's flat, a loft conversion in a Victorian warehouse.

Jeremy handed Ahmed the £75 cash.

"Okay, guys, what do we know about the target punter?" asked Ahmed.

"His name's Trevor Morris, he's a Bank of England employee and he's about fifty."

"And his e-mail address?"

"It's here." Ed handed over one of Trevor's business cards.

"Fine – any ideas about date of birth?"

Ed shook his head.

"Okay, we'll try the Magistrates Court website. You can often get it if there's been a speeding fine imposed, failing that we'll try for a copy Birth Certificate online from Somerset House. I think you've got a photo of the debit card?"

"I'll e-mail it to you now from my phone."

"No, best get a hard copy off your phone – even hackers' e-mails get hacked sometimes!"

About 3 minutes later they had a hard copy.

"Yes, you're right, this is a Cayman Islands Bank Account – we're lucky it's not Swiss – they are next to impossible to hack into as there are no names, just numbers and the data is encrypted," commented Ahmed.

"So why didn't he choose a Swiss Bank Account?" queried Jeremy.

"The Swiss Banks are gradually opening up under pressure from various European and other Governments hunting tax evaders," explained Ed.

"The Caymans are still relatively private unless, of course, you get hacked – and you don't get hacked if people don't know you have an account there."

After about an hour Ahmed had produced copies of the last 4 months' bank statements. There were only 2 or 3 entries per month, but Ed found what he needed – for each of the last 3 months there was an entry of £20,000 shown as being received from GP Enterprises, Isle of Man – described as consultancy fees.

At home that evening Ed searched the Isle of Man

company on line that had made the payments and established that George Petersham was sole Director and 100% shareholder – so it didn't take a genius to work out that, at the very least, there was a conflict of interest involved in Morris's receipt of the payments and that, in itself, should be enough for Morris to consider his position at the Bank.

"Consider his position terminated before it gets any worse," said Ed, thinking aloud.

He phoned Jeremy.

"Jezza – I've got what I need – time to organise a meet with that Private Eye dude – what was his name – Shelley?"

"Correct – I'll get on the phone to him tomorrow. We have to act quickly as the Election's fast approaching, or how about cutting a corner and going straight to Sheikh at The Sun? He'd lap it up I expect – there's no love lost between him and Smithson's Government."

"Okay, fine by me – do what you can."

By 6.00 pm the following evening, Jeremy and Ed were conferring with Harry, one of the editorial team at The Sun.

"Our readers are only interested in this kind of thing if public money is being put at risk, which it is, by the look of it," remarked Harry. "It's definitely political, as the Bank and FCA are the Chancellor's responsibility.

By the way, you asked about money and, as you stuck your necks out, we can pay you five grand for this story.

Okay, so you've got bank Statements and company records re the Isle of Man company – anything else?"

"I can give you a transcript of my last conversation with Morris at the Bank – I can remember it word for word."

"Okay good – if I give you an office to sit in, could you write that up straight away – I can get someone to fix you up with tea, coffee or whatever?"

"Yes, that's fine," responded Ed.

"Meanwhile I can run the whole thing past Andy Sheikh with a view to getting a scoop in the paper's first edition tomorrow – let's re-convene in an hour."

An hour and fifteen minutes later, Harry, Jeremy and Ed were back in the same board room.

"Andy's fine with it – if sued, one of our lawyers said we can use the public interest defence," said Harry. "How about this for a headline" – Harry handed over a facsimile.

"DODGY *ANKERS AT IT AGAIN"

It was in 2-inch high lettering.

"That looks fine to me – sock it to them!" commented Ed.

The fallout from The Sun's front page article the following day was at first inconclusive.

Trevor Morris at first denied any wrongdoing, but under pressure admitted a potential conflict of interest.

With a week to go to the general Election, the following day even the quality Press went on the rampage.

The Telegraph, usually highly supportive of the Tories, went with:

TAXPAYERS' MONEY AT RISK AGAIN – THIS TIME IT'S CORRUPTION AT THE BANK OF ENGLAND

Again, the Chancellor seemed complacent, provoking yet more Press hysteria, and prompting Smithson to promise a full investigation – after the Election.

Would the Chancellor resign – no, not immediately, that would be an admission of guilt "sources close to the Prime Minister" divulged.

Smithson dithered.

Five days later the electorate of Leeds West made a decision for him. The Chancellor lost his seat, having previously been elected with a majority of 14,000.

As before, Smithson's Government's complacency, arrogance and dithering presented Labour and the MDP with a gold plated opportunity to make political capital which both parties seized on with enthusiasm, offering, if elected, to make sure the culprits were sacked, prosecuted and a rigorous clean-up operation effected in relation to banking and it's "so-called regulators."

Labour even promised to hire Ari Stavros, the investment guru, to act as a banking and financial services trouble-shooter on an 7-figure annual salary if necessary. The latter proposal was the brainchild of Jeremy Gilmour and Ed Ruskin, who had been taken on by the Labour Party machine as consultants to advise on economics, finance and banking.

13

After a meeting held to discuss progress and tactics in the election campaign, Ibrahim and Karim were left alone.

"There's been something I've wanted to ask you," said Karim.

"Go ahead."

"What's your real view on Israel and the Palestinians and how can that problem be resolved?"

Ibrahim pondered the question even though he'd spent what seemed like a lifetime thinking about it.

"The problem with the two-State solution is that if they started fighting and trying to destroy each other, where would it end? Armageddon?"

"Some say this problem could be overcome by the Palestinian State being de-militarised in return for its borders being guaranteed by the UN Security Council. Surely the Palestinians deserve a homeland, and they have been unjustly treated?" responded Karim.

"Yes, it's true, many had title deeds to property

issued by the Ottoman Empire from which they were evicted by force, but I wouldn't have much confidence in the UN guaranteeing anyone's freedom and security – look what happened at Srebrenica – 5,000 Muslims got massacred by Serbs, despite the town being declared a UN protected safe haven complete with a so-called peace keeping troop contingent. Personally I think we need to consider financial compensation in return for acknowledging Israel's right to exist. For a start there's plenty of oil money around to pay compensation to the dispossessed. The problem is that there are extremists on both sides who don't want peace."

"What Israelis don't want peace?"

"People like Rabin's assassin – the ultra orthodox types – scratch the surface of them and you will find racists and fascists, yet they are the first to complain about others with those mindsets."

"Is that why Jews have been unpopular throughout history – their religion?"

"It's far more complicated and has to do with their tending to be clever and rich, neither attribute will make you popular. What it does is to make people jealous. Still, no-one can accuse me of being anti-Jewish – my ex-wife was Jewish and we had two kids."

"That sounds like the film, 'Sleeping with the Enemy.'"

Both laughed.

"I had a friend at University who used to say the Jews were certainly right about one thing," said Ibrahim.

"What was that?"

"The second Messiah – his name's Bob Dylan!"

While he did not aspire to being a Messiah, Ibrahim was respected and charismatic enough for Lena Khan, the new leader of the Labour Party, to have no problem with his proposal that the MDP and Labour enter into a non-aggression pact in several key constituencies.

When they met to discuss the mechanics of the pact at Labour's HQ in Millbank, London SW1, Khan was in a playful mood.

"Some people are comparing you to Mandela, Ibrahim – that's a statesman, not merely a common or garden politician like me!" Khan was only half joking.

"Don't go public with that statement – frankly I find it highly embarrassing," countered Ibrahim.

"That's misplaced modesty, if you ask me – you should be flattered and be prepared to lap up all the compliments you get, even those provided by political rivals such as myself!

By the way, how's your friend, Karim, my former

student? You're very lucky to know him, he's extremely bright and charming."

"Yes, I'm keeping him busy at our campaign HQ – he mentions you from time to time as someone whose views he respects."

"Well, we do our best don't we? I might poach him off you one day, if I manage to play my cards right."

"Unlikely I would say – he's not so keen on some of your fellow travellers – Communists and atheists among them," explained Ibrahim.

"Well, like every political party, we're a broad church, we have to be, that's democracy. Anyway, I used to be a Marxist when I was his age, it's a phase loads of my colleagues have been through. There was a time, say, 30 or 40 years ago, when it seemed like a reasonable response to the world's problems – you had the Vietnam War, fascist dictators running Spain and Greece, to say nothing of Pakistan, and Apartheid in South Africa, in case you've forgotten," continued Khan.

"Well, he was brought up in the UAE where they don't assume democracy is that desirable and regard Communism as the work of Satan, as you know. Anyway, while we're on the subject of Marx, I also see my function is to make history, not just write about it."

"I couldn't agree more," said Khan.

"Okay, then, can we deal with this beneficial carve-up of constituencies," Ibrahim continued, "I think you've already agreed in principle that a pact is the way to go with this first past the post system?"

"Okay, fine, I've got a full list here", said Khan. "It comprises the voting details from the last 2 General Elections and some comments relating to ethnic and religious composition in various key constituencies, which could be relevant."

Ibrahim spent several minutes looking over the papers supplied by Khan and said:

"This all looks fine, can we look in particular at the Tory held marginals where Labour came second last time – we could probably split those between us, say, two-thirds to you and one third for us?"

"We'd be looking for at least eighty per cent of those – how about if we give you twenty per cent of those plus all the seats where the Lib Dems came first or second, apart from those where Labour came first, of course?"

The haggling continued along similar lines for another three hours, by which time they'd agreed on a carve-up of around 275 seats. At that point they decided to call it a day.

By then, there were 170 where MDP had agreed to give Labour a clear run, and 105 where Labour had agreed to do likewise for the MDP.

Meanwhile, in the Sun's offices, Sheikh was busy contemplating a plot that could land the MDP with enough seats to hold the balance of power.

The original proposal was that the Saudis would discount the price of their oil heading to the UK by fifty per cent, provided at least 50 MDP candidates were elected to the House of Commons. This proposal was quickly dropped as being a likely breach of electoral law.

The crowning glory of the revised proposal was that the Saudis would pay across a large sum, say three hundred and fifty million dollars, to various charitable and educational projects, including at least half of such sum to be divided between the top ten charities in RUK.

Sheikh understood perfectly that, whereas there are loads of Brits who will do just about anything for money, there are possibly more, who will do just about anything for charity.

The whole scheme was later to be dismissed by the Telegraph as "the Tesco clubcard approach to politics", to which Sheikh responded by saying "What's good enough for Tesco is good enough for me!"

The idea had originally been floated three weeks previously at a dinner at the Pakistani Embassy at which the Saudi Ambassador had been guest of honour. The Ambassador had been complaining about the Americans always wanting to call the shots on all international issues, from the failed invasion of Cuba through to the Middle East crisis via the Vietnam War and numerous overt and covert interventions in Iran, Chile, central America and so on.

Sheikh, half jokingly, had said why don't you get your own back by using your cash to influence some Elections in the West, starting with the current RUK General Election.

The other dinner party guests fell silent at what seemed like a challenge, leading Sheikh to think he may have spoken out of turn.

Perhaps surprisingly, the Saudi rose to the challenge.

"What do you suggest?"

"Well, the West needs oil to survive, so why not agree to discount the price in return for people voting for Ibrahim and the MDP?"

"That's a bit too obvious, I don't think the MDP would agree that and it might be illegal."

"Okay, then, have regard to public relations – how about a massive donation to charity of, say, $350 million, whichever way people vote – but let it be known that you would welcome more MDP MPs?"

After a thirty-second pause, the Saudi eventually smiled and said "Okay, I'll put it to my government if Ibrahim Irani will agree it in principle…"

Later, on meeting Ibrahim, Sheikh broached the subject of the proposed Saudi deal.

"Why would they want this?" said Ibrahim.

"It's a combination of public relations and influence and to teach the Yanks a lesson. It was my idea in the first place, not theirs," said Sheikh. "Your justification for agreeing it, if you need one, can be the charitable donation – the British will forgive virtually any activity if there's a charitable side effect or spin off."

"Okay, that might do as a moral justification, but what about political justification – the Americans will call it bribery and corruption," said Ibrahim.

"Don't be scared of the Yanks – put the boot in if necessary – they're probably much less popular here than they realise. Say they are hypocrites if they criticise you – they purport to support democracy, but since 1945 they've engineered the overthrow of democratically elected governments in Iran in 1952 and Chile in 1971 – Gaza is currently a work in progress – there are countless other examples of interference. By veiled threats, they even attempted to influence the EU Referendum here. Besides, you know what they say, don't look a gift horse in the mouth – or maybe in this case, that should read camel instead of horse!"

Ibrahim laughed. "Okay", said Ibrahim, "I'll go along with it on two conditions – in your coverage in The Sun, first you say it's your idea and not theirs or mine, and secondly that we're not giving them any favours in return – it's a goodwill gesture on their part and that's all."

"Fine, I'll run that past Rashid, the Saudi Ambassador."

That evening, Sheikh met the Saudi again at the Pakistani Embassy – neutral ground, you might say.

Sheikh recited the deal on offer –

"This is the basis on which Ibrahim will approve our arrangement – it's got to be like this as anything he might agree formally in return, would compromise his integrity and potentially sink him."

At first, the Saudi was reluctant, but Sheikh sold it to him on the basis of the need to counter the often negative image the Saudis had in the UK and that the deal would be good public relations.

Rashid was a mid-ranking Saudi Royal, and was able to clear the proposal quickly with his uncle and cousin, the ruler and Minister of Finance respectively in Saudi Arabia.

At first, the English Press, apart from The Sun, was hostile, as were the Americans. With regard to the former, Sheikh went on a charm offensive using The Sun's paper and online versions, and with regard to the latter, Ibrahim, on Sheikh's advice, accused the Americans of being hypocrites and told them to stop lecturing the British people on how they should vote.

The polls started to swing round to show Ibrahim's MDP was gaining ground.

Several leading charities spelt out in detail what they would do with the twenty million pounds or so, they were each expecting to receive.

On the day of the Election, Karim remained at the MDP's HQ coordinating the Party's organisation, together with various other Party workers, in a bid to get all potential MDP voters to cast their vote, however elderly or infirm.

That night, Karim and Kirsty stayed up all night watching the Election results on a BBC TV Newsnight Election Special programme chaired by Dan Nicholson.

Much to Karim and Kirsty's delight, Ibrahim secured a landslide victory in his Birmingham constituency – the result being declared at around 5.00 am.

By 7.00 am, the results in around half the seats had been declared and the MDP had secured 70 seats so far.

Karim, naturally, was over the moon and, while hugging Kirsty, said, "No-one's ever seen anything like this before – we're going to easily hold the balance of power – we can really make a difference now."

"Don't overdo it, darling, not all seats have been declared yet," – Kirsty counselled caution, but Karim was having none of it.

"I'll always remember this day, it's just fantastic!"

"Yes, Darling, I know you've done amazingly well, congratulations – just remember don't speak too soon to the media, I'm going to bed."

Even if Karim had then tried to sleep, he wouldn't have been able to, he was high on a mixture of adrenaline, excitement and caffeine.

By 11.00 pm the following night, all the results had been declared and Karim still had not slept.

With no seats now allocated to the Scots anymore, the number of seats being declared was down to 591.

The result looked like this:

Conservative Party	184
Labour Party	213
Muslim Democratic Party (MDP)	142
Green Party	32
Others	20
	591

14

Following the election result, it quickly became apparent that Labour was the only Party able to form a government – even if substantially dependent on the co-operation of the MDP.

Lena Khan, Labour's leader, was duly summoned to Buckingham Palace for an audience with the King, who invited her to form a government, an invitation she was very pleased to accept.

That same day she had a meeting with Ibrahim, who was ebullient following the MDP's election successes.

Ibrahim showed up at No. 10 with his close political ally, Majid Sharif.

"Congratulations Lena, on Labour's successes and your appointment as PM – what's it feel like now to have the keys of the kingdom?"

"Congratulations to yourselves as well, Ibrahim. It's not rocket science what we agreed but the results are truly satisfactory, if not spectacular. Obviously I now need to ask you for another deal – how about Deputy

PM and Foreign Secretary for you as the price of the MDP's co-operation?"

"That sounds fine if you can also give Majid here education – he's dead keen to try his hand in that area. He's got Degrees in PPE from Oxford and Economics from Harvard, so he's well qualified, surely?"

"That sounds okay to me so long as the approach is pluralistic rather than exclusively Islamic...?"

"Yes, I reckon we can agree that, subject to some re-visiting of the issue of faith Schools – our manifesto promised as much."

"I will introduce you to the permanent Secretary in the Department and together you can produce some written proposals for me to place before the Cabinet."

"I am very happy to accept what you say about pluralism. In particular I'd like to see Oxbridge Colleges adopt a more pluralistic approach in regard to their names – having regard to their funding from the State. How about less emphasis on Christianity and more on some of the other beliefs, and that would mean not just Islam but also Hinduism, Buddhism and Marxism, for example?" contributed Sharif.

"Yes, certainly, the more isms the better, I expect," joked Khan, perhaps not realising how serious Sharif was on this point.

"Well, at the last count only 44% of the British public were prepared to call themselves Christians, with 48% other religions or none, and 8% don't know," commented Sharif.

"Yes, I expect 48% included a substantial number of Jedi Knights so I hope you're not proposing to impose on Trinity College a new name with a Star Wars theme, like Interstellar College or Darkside College, perhaps!" countered Khan.

"In fact we are very serious about this. The two best Universities in this country are dominated by Christian and Imperialistic symbolism and people wonder why it is that they only manage to attract and accept a very modest percentage of ethnic and religious minority students," argued Sharif.

"Okay, but it won't be plain sailing," said Khan.

"If they don't accept what we say, we'll withdraw funding and impose the new names by Act of Parliament. If necessary we will drag them kicking and screaming into the Twenty First Century."

Sharif was true to his word and shortly after being appointed Education Minister, he embarked on a campaign to "update" some of the Oxbridge Colleges. He encountered some resistance from graduates and the Press but significant numbers of dons and students supported his actions, leading to the Colleges in question putting up less resistance than had been anticipated.

As a result of his efforts, Christ Church, Oxford

was re-named Red Crescent College; Balliol, Oxford became Jinnah College, named after the founder of Pakistan. In Cambridge, Trinity College became Karl Marx College and St John's became Gandhi College.

Prime Minister Lena Khan folded the newspaper and slotted it into the webbed pouch in front of her knees. She fastened her seatbelt and while the stewards checked the passengers were likewise ready for takeoff, she sat back to reflect. There was still jihadist trouble despite concessions to some Islamic aspirations. It was clear that fundamentalist elements would continue to regard Ibrahim's party as not truly Islamic. MI5 she knew was struggling to contain jihadi threats as illegal immigration from the war-torn Middle East continued to defy renewed efforts at border security.

Having taxied to its takeoff position, the chartered aircraft roared its engines into life and they began their ascent. Watching the airport buildings below dwindle and vanish behind her, she was startled by a touch on her shoulder and the look of concern on the face of Mike Sharrock, her MI5 duty.

"I've been alerted of a threat to the King on his way to open Parliament," he said. "The Director needs your authorisation to postpone proceedings."

"What now?"

A stewardess suddenly appeared as Sharrock was passing his mobile phone to the Prime Minister.

"I must insist you switch off your phone and return to your seat, sir."

"There is a matter of national security that needs immediate attention," he retorted sharply.

"If a mobile phone is not in flight mode, there is a serious risk of interference with the communications from Ground Control." The stewardess looked from one to the other sternly. "You will be endangering the lives of everyone on this plane."

"This will only take a minute." Khan's tone was also firm and authoritative as she put Sharrock's phone to her ear.

"Saladin, Sir Reginald," she replied to the urgent voice demanding her codeword for identification. "Fill me in briefly if you would…"

The plane banked suddenly and the phone was yanked out of her grip. As the stewardess fumbled frantically with the keypad, Khan's attention was diverted by the screams of her fellow passengers, mainly Khan's staff and media people. The fast approaching Sussex countryside dispelled all thoughts of phones, MI5 and the security of His Royal Highness King James.

Grabbing a newspaper as he emerged from the Westminster underground station, Majid Sharif continued walking briskly toward the Houses of Parliament. Impatiently leafing through the Sun as he went, he shook his head.

While the paper exposed and deplored corruption by Treasury officials, and paedophiliac activity in the Church of England, there was insufficient condemnation of the partisan interference by the King on the side of the old Establishment and its financial, military and religious institutions. Sharif expected more of Andy Sheikh. It didn't help mollify social relations in the RUK of course that Queen Clarissa still had not retracted her insults about "khaki coloured scumbags" and Karim being an imposter like Perkin Warbeck. Nor had King James condemned her views or done anything to distance himself from them. The Sun's support for the MDP was hardly going to influence the behaviour of the King and Queen but the majority of people would be hoping for more robust criticism from the paper that prided itself on being anti-establishment. The crowd were in good humour though as they lined Parliament Street waiting for the royal carriage, happy that at last democratic norms had been restored after an election even if there was no longer any United Kingdom.

The Education Minister should have taken his place in the Commons an hour ago but responding to the number of complaints about renaming Christ Church Oxford as Red Crescent College in particular, had delayed his journey. Nevertheless, at 11.10 am, when the Diamond Jubilee State Carriage, resplendent in black and gilt, drawn by four white horses escorted by the Household Cavalry, came into view as it drew level with the Winston Churchill statue on Parliament Square, Sharif stopped to watch the royal couple beaming and waving to the crowds behind the barriers along its course.

Majid Sharif felt stirred by conflicting emotions. The royal carriage was built out of a cornucopia of cultural artefacts, symbolic of what made Britain great not only as a military power but as a civilising force. Since studying the British monarchy as part of his degree course, Sharif had kept abreast of developments. He knew the crown on the roof of the carriage had been carved from Nelson's flagship Victory, its walls and door panels decorated from what had been retrieved from Scott's Antarctic base and Henry VIII's flagship Tudor Rose, and that some part was made from a musket ball from the Battle of Waterloo.

Majid Sharif was surprised at how patriotic he was feeling. His parents felt strongly that the British Empire had robbed their homeland of its resources and he had joined Ibrahim's party at their behest with the intent of burrowing into the heart of the Establishment and changing the UK from within. Uncomfortable in feeling a sense of pride in his adopted country, Sharif tried to rationalise his conflicting emotions. Britain's confidence as a nation was based on its coherent set of values of openness, tolerance and fair play, built upon the significant efforts of its leading lights to do the right thing in the world as well as by its history as the largest empire ever to bestride the globe. While this coach represented conquest, there were elements in its construction that related to Shakespeare, Charles Darwin, Edward Jenner and Florence Nightingale as well as digital copies of the Domesday Book and the precursor of Britain's democratic tradition, the Magna Carta.

Aware he had to be in the Commons chamber before the carriage arrived at the Sovereign's entrance, Sharif turned left and pushed his way through the throngs of people cheering the royal procession. Turning for a last look, he froze. A man was leaping over the barrier in a gap between two policemen. Then running alongside the carriage, the cry 'Allahu Akbar' went up just as the man detonated his suicide vest.

It must have been a huge charge because the explosion was ear-shattering. The ornate crowned roof was immediately ablaze and 2.75 tons of carriage was blasted across the street, dragging the horses with it, to crash into a barrier. Police were immediately visible, several tearing through what remained of the mangled doors of the carriage to attend to the royal occupants, others to help the onlookers crushed under the carriage and barrier.

Amid the smoke, screams and confusion, Sharif ran over to help. A groaning woman was bleeding from her crotch as she tried to get out from under the barrier. Seeing she was pregnant, Sharif looked around for any sign of medical help and saw an ambulance stationed close by. Its paramedics were already busy among the crowd; seeing Sharif's urgent gesticulations, one came to help and together they lifted the bleeding woman into the ambulance.

Looking around for the next victim to help, Sharif's eye fell on a sparkling object lying in the road. In the confusion nobody observed him pick it up and slip it into his pocket. What to do with the diamond-encrusted imperial carriage door handle would be a matter of conscience that the high-flying son of British colonial subjects, hailing from the Empire's jewel in the Crown, would wrestle with when he had a quiet moment later.

At 10 Downing Street, the mood was sombre. By 3pm, the Joint Intelligence Committee (JIC) had

assembled in the Cabinet Room to assess the events of the morning. Being the only minister to witness the monarch's assassination, Sharif had also been invited to join the meeting. From his seat close to Ibrahim, Sharif could read the front page of the afternoon edition of the Evening Standard the Acting Prime Minister had spread out on the oak table in front of him.

While most of it comprised the bold headline '**OUTRAGE**' above pictures of the mangled carriage, the lower part of the page of the paper read:

"PRIME MINISTER KILLED AS PLANE TAKES OFF. TERRORISM SUSPECTED"

"Colleagues, this is an unprecedented moment in British history," said Ibrahim. "Never have we lost both our Sovereign and Prime Minister to terrorists, let alone on the same day. While you would think the odds of such happening again in the future are negligible we must not presume this, nor let our guard slip. We must take immediate steps to identify the perpetrators of these heinous acts, plug the holes in our intelligence responsible for its failure and ensure security is tightened. The situation must not be allowed to deteriorate further."

Ibrahim looked across the table directly at the Director of MI5. "So how do you account for such a massive intelligence failure, Sir Reginald, and what measures will you be taking to assure us nothing like this will ever happen again?" he asked.

"There was no failure of intelligence, Prime Minister," came the unfazed Director's response. "MI5 were aware of the threat to the Royal Family. We contacted your predecessor at once for authorisation to halt the opening of Parliament. With the most tragic of timing, her plane was lost before she could give it. I was actually in conversation with her at the time it went down."

"And what did you deduce as to the cause?"

"I immediately assumed there had been a breach of security but there was no explosion or gunfire before we were cut off, only screams.

The Black Box flight recorder has been recovered but there has not been enough time yet to analyse the data. I am assured that, contrary to popular belief, a phone call to or from a mobile is never enough to cause the loss of control of an aircraft. In the absence of pilot error, we are likely to be left with an electronic systems failure or contaminated fuel, as the likely cause. Be that as it may, due to this fatal incident, I was unable to get authority to call a halt to the proceedings."

Ibrahim's phone vibrated. The Prime Minister glanced down then put it to his ear.

"Your Highness… yes, I am with our security chiefs now." Sharif was aware Ibrahim had spoken to Prince

Richard within minutes of his father's assassination not to only express his deep personal sympathy but to advise him that he should address the nation as soon as he had the composure so to do.

"Their advice is you address the country this evening," Ibrahim advised the new King. He continued to listen in silence to the response before clicking off the call.

"Colleagues and officers, you will understand Prince Richard is in deep shock. He feels he cannot address the country this evening. Indeed, he is planning to leave Britain at the earliest opportunity once the King and Queen are buried."

Silence fell. After what seemed to Sharif an eternity, it was Sir Reginald who broke it.

"With respect, Prime Minister, the nation too is in shock. Somebody with political authority needs to address the public and assure them they are in charge, that the danger has passed and His Majesty's security forces are in full control of the situation."

"Yes, I agree," responded Ibrahim. "As Deputy and now Acting Prime Minister I will address the country this evening."

"It only needs to be a calming 2 or 3 minute session just saying you are in charge and that the emergency services, including the military, are in full control of the situation on the ground," offered the MI5 chief.

"That's not a problem, I will do it," confirmed Ibrahim.

Following the untimely deaths of his father and stepmother, King Richard IV quickly decided to accept an invitation from Julian Muldoon, the Canadian Prime Minister, to take refuge in Canada on an extended holiday with his wife and family.

Three days after James and Clarissa's State funeral, Ibrahim telephoned Richard in Canada.

"Good morning, Prime Minister, or even afternoon, I expect, in your case."

"Good day sir – I will get straight to the point – when do you intend to return here, please?"

"Mr Muldoon has said we can stay here as long as we like and, as you know, we have always been very welcome in Canada and we are really feeling at home, thank you."

"I know the murders of your father and the Queen were a terrible shock for you, as they were for me and your government. We would, however, like you to return here and assume properly your role as Monarch and Head of the Commonwealth based in London."

"To be frank, Prime Minister, I am fed up with London, fed up with Britain, and I honestly fear for the future – I have a young family to consider and it looks like your government is unable and, dare I say it, unwilling in some cases, to guarantee my security."

"I'm very sorry to hear you say that, sir, but we need a fully functioning Head of State – a Monarch as we are not a Republic and you are the rightful heir to your father's kingdom. May I also remind you that all MPs still swear an oath of allegiance to the Monarch before they are allowed to take their seats in the House of Commons."

"That's all very well, but there are clearly undercurrents in British society that don't want the likes of my father and me around any longer…"

"It's only a very small minority, sir."

"People often say that, but if security is not tight enough, then a small minority can do a lot of damage, as we have already seen. My wife wants me to abdicate for the sake of her and the children–"

There was a pause of a few seconds while Ibrahim digested this information.

"I hope that's not a serious proposal, sir."

"I'm thinking about it, and you will be the first to know if I decide that's the way to go…"

"It's not just Britain that's involved, it's the Commonwealth as well, sir. Personally I would very much like you to continue, just so long as you know that."

A few pleasantries were then exchanged and the call ended.

Ibrahim only told the Foreign Secretary, Ross Clarke, about the content of this call, but when two weeks later Richard and his family had still not returned from Canada, popular speculation in the Press and elsewhere suggested that Richard and family would not be returning to London any time soon.

Ibrahim telephoned Richard and discussed the speculation that Richard was already aware of.

After a lengthy discussion, it was eventually agreed that Richard would let Ibrahim have a final decision on whether or not he would abdicate, within the following ten days.

Nine days later, Ibrahim received the call from Richard he had been dreading.

"Prime Minister – I said you would be the first to know – I have decided to abdicate on behalf of myself and my heirs. The only precedent I can think of is that set by my uncle, Edward VIII, in 1936. However, I am sure government lawyers can draw up the necessary documents and I will instruct my own solicitors, Duncan Lithgow, of Chancery Lane to assist where necessary at my expense."

"I am very sorry to hear you say that, sir, but naturally I will respect your decision and do everything possible to promote an orderly transition…"

Ibrahim was struggling to contain his emotions and his concern that he would inevitably be blamed in some quarters for Richard's abdication.

"May I ask a favour, sir?"

"Go ahead."

"I think it would be appropriate for you to broadcast your decision to the nation…"

"Yes, I had thought of that and I will do it – don't worry, I will put in a word for you and confirm that I absolve you from personal responsibility."

"Thank you, sir."

It was sobering for Ibrahim to realise that, over the years, he had morphed from staunch Republican critic of British Imperialism through to admirer of Churchill, and now a sentimental supporter of the Monarchy – hence his personal sadness at Richard's decision.

In the days and weeks following Richard's abdication, left wing and Republican MPs took full advantage of the Monarchy's precarious state and managed to persuade Ibrahim and the Cabinet to declare the RUK a Republic, with Ibrahim as Prime Minister and acting Head of State, such was his personal popularity. The Republic would be known as the British Free State.

Ibrahim later confessed to Karim that he found the dual role extremely stressful and that it detracted from his ability to carry out either role effectively.

◦━━━◦

Meanwhile, a development in the lives of Karim and Kirsty was to give the Press more positive news to write about following recent traumatic events.

"Kirsty, I love you, please will you marry me?"

They had climbed to the top of Arthur's Seat, the 820-foot volcanic hill dominating the centre of Edinburgh, a city they both loved.

"I love you too, Karim, so the answer's of course I will. Why did you have to wait so long to ask me…?"

Karim, encouraged by the positive response, then produced the Cartier engagement ring his father had given his mother on the ski slope in Italy – it was in its original box and Kirsty was suitably impressed.

"Darling Karim, where did you get this from, it's fantastic?"

"It was my mother's, I'm sure she would have wanted you to have it…"

They kissed and embraced for several minutes.

"When and where shall we get married?" asked Karim.

"As soon as possible, please," said Kirsty.

"Okay, and where?"

"Crieff Castle, Perthshire, near where my mum and dad live."

"That didn't take you long to decide!" said Karim.

"Well, I've been dreaming about my wedding since I was six years old – since well before I met you! I just never mentioned it to you."

"That's fine, Darling," said Karim, "I'll go along with anything you say – within reason!"

15

"We're worried about this joint campaign being run by The Times and the Daily Mail, Prime Minister."

The Foreign Secretary, Ross Clarke, and Labour Party Chairman, Steve Bradley, had asked for a special meeting with Ibrahim at Number 10.

"The campaign demands an end to the influence of Republicans and Islamists in the top echelons of government and it looks like the opinion polls are swinging behind it."

"So what are your suggestions?" said Ibrahim.

"Well, the obvious way to water down the so-called Islamic influence is to amalgamate the MDP and the Labour Party," said Bradley.

"It would need a new entity with a new name as some of our people don't want to inherit Labour's baggage, in particular do not wish to be subservient to the will of the Unions," said Ibrahim.

"Fine, so if you can agree in principle, we'll think about a new name."

"Yes, I can agree in principle, subject to there being a majority in favour amongst MPs and Party activists," said Ibrahim.

"Do you have a view on the point about the Republican influence?" said the Foreign Secretary.

"It's probably no secret any more that I am not happy being Head of State and Prime Minister – I'd be quite happy to see the restoration of constitutional monarchy, with the right person as Monarch of course."

"In that case, we could initiate a review of the issue – and promote a public debate, leading perhaps to a Referendum – legally binding this time, not just advisory!" said Bradley.

"This will need a debate and vote in the House of Commons so we will need to inform the speaker," commented Ibrahim.

The subsequent debate in the Commons ten days later was, at times, fractious and heated. Ibrahim had to call upon all his powers of oratory to persuade waiverers that a Republic had been tried – he had been the guinea pig as Prime Minister and Head of State and it wasn't working, and wasn't popular. In his opinion the polls this time were right.

The motion was:-

This House supports in principle the restoration of a constitutional monarchy and the holding of a legally binding Referendum to gauge the will of the people and who should be their Sovereign.

The motion was eventually carried comfortably with 330 in favour, 45 against and 70 abstentions. Most sceptical MPs were reluctant to be seen as anti-democratic by opposing a Referendum.

The motion was then drafted as a Bill – the Restoration of the Monarchy Bill – which passed through the House of Commons and the House of Lords within the next three weeks.

Ibrahim again had to work hard to counter opposition to uniting formally amongst some MDP and Labour Party members and MPs, but the leading lights in both parties were strongly in favour of joining forces and a vote to merge at a special joint party conference was eventually carried, as was a motion to call the merged Party the Free Democrats.

"I'm determined to invite Richard and Sophia to our wedding – Richard is my only potential link with my mother's family, and this would be the best way of breaking the ice."

"Surely your mother had several other blood relatives living," said Kirsty.

"Quite probably, though my gut feeling is that Richard is the most likely to accept me."

Karim and Kirsty were discussing the guest list for their wedding at his grandfather's flat in Cadogan Square.

Though now well into his eighties, Hassan was still on the ball, and Karim bowed to his better judgment on many things.

"Don't forget I'll be funding most of this wedding so you can easily ask 250 if you wish," offered Hassan.

"That's very kind of you Granddad – we have sold the exclusive rights to take Press photos to Hello magazine for £75,000 so we were going to use, say, £50,000 of that towards the wedding and give the rest to charity."

"I think that may look slightly mercenary – it would be better to err on the side of generosity and give it all to charity – I can easily afford £50,000," Hassan commented.

"That is fantastic, I can't thank you enough," said Kirsty, "my parents can only afford around £10,000 max and Karim and I have various friends and contacts who would be offended not to be asked."

The invitation for Richard and Sophia was to be sent to them in Canada by international courier and

Karim, with input from Kirsty, drafted a letter to the (ex) Royal couple which read as follows

Dear Prince Richard and Princess Sophia

I expect you will have read in the Press that we plan to marry at Crieff Castle, Perthshire on 5 July 2018. We are enclosing an invitation to the wedding and would be very honoured and pleased if you would both attend. Karim attaches great importance to working towards a reconciliation with the family of his mother, Caroline, the late Princess of Wales, despite the trials and tribulations of the past.

With very best wishes
Your sincerely
Karim Khaled and Kirsty McShane

The letter was handwritten and two weeks after it was sent, a formal typed response was received at Kirsty's parents' address in Perth.

Prince Richard and Princess Sophia thank Mr and Mrs McShane for their kind invitation to the wedding of their daughter, Kirsty, to Karim Khaled, but regrettably they are unable to accept due to other commitments.

Inside the envelope was a smaller, handwritten envelope addressed to Karim personally. It contained a handwritten letter which read as follows:

Dear Karim Khaled

Many thanks for your letter and for inviting us to your wedding. Despite having abdicated, my diary is very full – the Canadians are still very keen to invite us to their social and charitable functions and seem to be in denial re the point that I'm not their Head of State.

Believe it or not, I would very much like to have attended your wedding and followed it up with a visit to St Andrews, where I spent several happy years as a student. I was advised this was a non-starter, mainly due to the political situation.

It may interest you to know that I have no reason to doubt that you are who you and your family say you are, and one day when things are calmer, I would very much like to meet you.

Please keep the content of this letter confidential – I am sure you understand the reason for this.

With best wishes to you and your bride-to-be.
Richard

Karim was delighted that Richard had taken the trouble to write to him personally.

"Darling, this is fantastic – he has acknowledged my existence and in language that's about as positive and friendly as any I could have hoped for—"

"Don't let it go to your head Darling, there's still a lot of work to do before you can hope to meet him," responded Kirsty.

"But he says he wants to meet me – that's us presumably."

"Maybe, but I expect he still has some stuffy advisers who will see us as a threat."

"On the contrary, I expect the stuffy advisers will have deserted him following his abdication," responded Karim.

"It remains to be seen if that's true or if it's wishful thinking by various journalists – how about reviewing the guest list for our wedding, Darling – we need to get on with it otherwise the Press reports will overtake reality…" commented Kirsty.

"Well it won't be the first time – everyone knows Andy Sheikh will make up news if he's not told anything," said Karim.

"By the way, what's this I hear about his dodgy wedding present to us?" asked Kirsty.

"Oh he's threatening to provide us with a belly dancer specially flown in from Cairo – he's cottoned on to the point that belly dancers often perform in traditional Arab weddings. The ulterior motive is that it will give him something to write about that will appeal to Sun readers. I prefer to just let him get on with it, do you mind?"

"That's typical Sheikh – anything to appeal to the lowest common denominator," said Kirsty.

"He'll call you a snob if you repeat that," warned Karim.

"It's okay, I'll stay out of it, I know you don't want to fall out with him," – Kirsty sighed – "even so, I can't imagine what my mum will think."

"She can think what she likes just so long as she doesn't make a scene – that would play into his hands," said Karim. "And don't forget Sheikh has also offered to pay for the two bagpipers – so you can tell that to your mum – that should keep her quiet."

"Mum couldn't be happier really – she's also very grateful for your granddad's generosity in paying for most of the wedding. Mum and Dad were very worried before about footing the bill for entertaining all these high profile guests AND he's giving us a Discovery 4 x 4 on top…"

"AND paying for a Berber band to be flown in from Marrakesh – we're very lucky…"

"I know that darling" said Kirsty – "I'm very excited – I think it's going to be a great day," she continued.

Several weeks later, on a sunny Saturday in early July, while amongst family and friends, Karim and Kirsty found themselves taking their wedding vows in the Chapel of Crieff Castle, Kirsty having entered the Chapel on the arm of her father while a lone piper played Amazing Grace.

The Service was mainly Christian and included hymns such as 'Jerusalem' and 'Guide Me O Thou Great Redeemer'. In 'Jerusalem', the words were carefully altered to include Scotland instead of England, as the preferred location for a new Jerusalem. Sheikh made a mental note to include reference to this in his write-up of the event for The Sun a couple of days later.

Partway through the Service, a passage was read out from the Koran in Arabic to acknowledge the bridegroom's heritage. An English translation of the passage was printed on the Service sheet. It read:-

God is Bounteous

And they say "Our Lord, let our spouses and children be a source of joy for us, and keep us in the forefront of the righteous."

"Our Lord, admit them into the Gardens of Eden that you promised for them and for the

righteous among their parents, spouses and children. You are the Almighty, Most Wise."

Among His Proofs is that He created for you spouses from among yourselves, in order to have tranquillity and contentment with each other and He placed in your hearts love and care towards your spouses. In this, there are sufficient proofs for people who reflect.

Today, all good food is made lawful for you. The food of the people of the scripture is lawful for you. Also you may marry the chaste women among the believers, as well as the chaste women among the followers of previous scripture. You shall maintain chastity, not committing adultery, nor taking secret lovers.

Anyone who rejects the faith, all his work will be in vain, and in the Hereafter he will be among the losers.

Many of the guests commented after the Service that the bride looked stunning in a cream dress with lace and a veil complementing her red hair.

After much soul searching and consultation with Kirsty, Karim wore a dark jacket with bow tie and trews in the Stuart tartan. He insisted he had a right to wear these as his mother was a direct descendant of Charles II, no doubt via one of his mistresses, but the family tree of his late mother was not something Karim was prepared to question.

When Sheikh heard this he again made a mental note to include such factoid in his piece for The Sun.

At one stage, Karim had intended to wear a ceremonial version of Dubai Dish Dash, but Kirsty had gently reminded him that the Scottish weather could be unkind and soggy Dish Dash would not look very smart, as well as being too cold for the climate.

Following the wedding service, the party continued with a reception in the Castle's impressive baronial dining hall lined with portraits of the current and previous Dukes of Atholl, whose family had owned the Castle and its land, now comprising 145,000 acres and some of the best fishing and deer stalking in the whole of Scotland.

The reception included a feast for 250 at which the guests were offered various canapés, followed by a choice of main course comprising either fresh salmon with green salad and new potatoes, or a Moroccan lamb stew with sweet potatoes, dried apricots and cous cous.

This was followed by locally grown strawberries or Rocky Road pudding. There were generously filled glasses of champagne and large quantities of soft drinks for teetotallers, of which there were several on Karim's side of the family.

During this time the guests were serenaded by a Moroccan Berber Band flown in at the expense of Hassan. This Band was accompanied, discreetly, by an Egyptian belly dancer, as promised. She made a beeline for Karim, who was relatively unmoved, much to Sheikh's disappointment.

Karim had been advised by Hassan to steer clear of religion and politics in his speech, which was generally low key, as were the other speeches, much to the relief of Kirsty and her mum.

There then followed the spectacle of Reeling – Scottish country dancing – serenaded by two pipers and two accordions – the reels attempted included the Duke of Perth, an Eightsome, and the Reel of the Fifty First.

Theo, Karim's best man – a friend from Uni and fellow band member, had recently finished reading a biography of Oscar Wilde. He had picked up a point he decided then and there to share with Karim.

"You may be better off taking Oscar Wilde's advice…"

"What's that?"

"He said he'd try anything once apart from incest and Scottish country dancing!"

"It will disappoint Kirsty if I don't give it a try."

"No really, you may fall over, which would disappoint her even more – it's much more difficult than it looks apparently – that's the dancing I'm talking about not the incest!"

By this time Sheikh was listening in to the conversation.

"Exactly, and you don't want to injure yourself and be off games tonight," he guffawed.

"That's enough – both of you – stop nannying me around," snapped Karim.

He took Theo's advice all the same and confined himself to some safe moves in the disco that followed the reeling.

The party continued til 2.00 am, at which point Karim and Kirsty adjourned gratefully to the marital bed. It was at times like this that Karim thanked his lucky stars he was teetotal – on the night Kirsty had good cause to be grateful he was teetotal as well.

The following morning, Karim and Kirsty had breakfast before most of the other guests and set off in the new Discovery presented to them by Hassan.

For their honeymoon, they spent the next ten days touring the Western Isles, mainly Mull, Iona and Eigg.

They swam from a deserted beach on Iona, complete with white sand – the product of millions of years of erosion by clear salty water.

They sampled the delicious fresh salmon on offer at the best restaurant in Tobermory, arguably the most picturesque harbour with the purest air and cleanest sea water in the whole of Britain.

They visited Duart Castle on the north-eastern tip

of Mull and marvelled at the commanding views over the adjacent sea loch, an ideal location for repelling any seaborne invaders who might decide to mount a challenge to the local supremacy of the MacLean clan.

After an idyllic honeymoon during which they agreed they'd found, in each other, soul mates and not just spouses, they eventually found themselves back in Edinburgh.

Karim was lucky indeed to have Kirsty as his partner, an ideal person to have by his side during the severe test of character and courage that would soon engulf them…

16

"This referendum isn't going to work unless we have at least one genuinely popular candidate to be Monarch, and you are one of the two obvious choices," observed Ibrahim, who had rung Karim the day after he'd arrived back in Edinburgh.

"Who's the other obvious choice?" asked Karim.

"Prince Richard."

"So if I stand against him, what will be his reaction?"

"I don't know yet – I haven't raised the subject with him – but he's got no veto, he's abdicated."

"I'll have to discuss all this with Kirsty."

"Of course, but if you don't stand, you will probably regret it for the rest of your life. You can really make a difference as King – how about mediating in the Middle East for a start?"

"There's no guarantee anyone will listen to me – I'm not even thirty yet."

"Don't write yourself off like that – it may take

time, but once you're elected, that will be it, you won't need to stand again in five years time like a politician."

"It must be a fair contest. Can you give me your word you will encourage Richard to stand?"

"Of course, I'll be telling him it's his patriotic duty to stand."

"Fine, how long can you give me to think about this?"

"Get back to me by this time next week – are you okay with that?"

"If I say yes, what happens then?"

"It's written into the Act that candidates have to be approved by the Government – any alternative could have been farcical – everyone's banking on you and Richard being the only two approved candidates. It's likely there will be two ballot papers in the referendum, one will ask for a decision on the re-introduction of the Monarchy, and the second will ask the voter to decide, hopefully between you and Richard. Obviously if fewer than 50% vote yes to a Monarchy on the first ballot paper, then the second ballot paper will be irrelevant."

"Assuming Karim Khaled is a Government approved candidate, then we need to back him.

Richard represents the old order and his case is weakened obviously by his abdication," said Sheikh.

The editorial conference at The Sun was in full swing and Andy Sheikh was determined to generate maximum enthusiasm amongst his staff and readers for Karim's candidacy.

"Karim's wife, Kirsty, is a super girl as well – I went to their wedding in Scotland."

One of his newsroom editors was more sceptical.

"Isn't it weird to have an elected Monarch – surely you should inherit the Monarchy, not be chosen for it. Besides, Karim is a Muslim."

"Well, he's related to Charles II via his mother's family, so that makes him a Stuart, and so am I a Muslim – less than half the Electorate say they are Christian these days, so what's the problem?"

Harry, the Oxford History graduate, then chipped in:-

"The best precedent for choosing a Monarch is in Sweden in about 1810 where a group of worthy citizens invited Count Bernadotte, one of Napoleon's Generals, to be their King. They were impressed by his humane treatment of some Swedish prisoners of war. He accepted the invitation and became Charles XIV, ruled for at least twenty years and was generally regarded as a very successful Head of State."

"Thanks, Harry, you've just earned next month's

salary with that contribution – convert it into a feature and I'll make that two months' salary!"

"Fine, Andy, it's a deal," said Harry.

A couple of days after his call to Karim, Ibrahim called Prince Richard.

"Sir, I have an important proposal to make…"

"What's that?"

"I expect you've seen in the media we now have a Restoration of the Monarchy Act."

"Yes – if this means restoring me, I reckon you can count me out."

"It's not quite as simple as that, sir – we wish to have a ballot as an add-on to the referendum, with at least two candidates, of which we would like you to be one…"

"Who's likely to be the other candidate – David Beckham, perhaps?"

"No, Karim Khaled."

"I see – but he's a Muslim and could not, therefore, be head of the Anglican Church."

"I reckon we can get round that problem. With less than half the Electorate now calling themselves Christian… believe me, sir, many people will be wanting to see you on the list of candidates – you can promote yourself as the Anglican candidate for a start – I'm sure your mother would have wanted you to stand – it's your patriotic duty, surely?"

"What guarantees can you give me that I won't be assassinated as soon as I set foot in England again?"

"I will give you a special protection squad of twenty SAS regulars – I would add that you wouldn't need to stay here throughout the year – you could spend, say, ten months of the year in Canada with the rest of your family."

"Yes, that would appeal to my wife and kids, I expect – I will talk it through with her and get back to you within four or five days. By the way, I assume you will be supporting Karim Khaled in all of this?"

"No. I've taken the decision not to campaign and not to vote – I see that my patriotic duty to England, my adopted country, is to organise the referendum and election, and be impartial at all times in the public interest."

"I'm sure that's very noble of you."

"Forget about whether I vote or not, please sir – we need you to campaign in this referendum and stand in the election."

"I'll get back to you as soon as I can."

"Thank you sir."

Both Richard and Karim had their work cut out to persuade their wives and families to agree to their putting their names forward to be Monarch – both eventually succeeded, and both got back to Ibrahim within the week to confirm their willingness to stand.

On hearing from each of them that they had decided to stand, Ibrahim gave both of them, separately, the same spiel.

"I need to make clear to you, the Electorate will consist of citizens in all the so-called Commonwealth realms, as well as Britain. So that will include Scotland, Australia, New Zealand, Canada plus Jamaica, Bahamas, Barbados and around six others, mainly in the West Indies. They have all had the English Monarch as their Head of State, so they must be allowed to participate. Assuming the Cabinet will approve both your candidatures, which is almost certain, then I will get back to you with the wording on the two ballot papers, so you can be familiar with what will be involved. My office will also need to liaise with the BBC and ITN about official interviews and who they want to conduct them, and when."

Within four days the Cabinet had approved the two candidates and the draft wording for each ballot paper.

The Voting Form for the referendum was to be on light green paper and was to read:

Do you approve the proposal that a
Constitutional Monarchy be restored for Britain

and the Commonwealth realms as previously
existed in 2016? Yes or no.

There was some debate on the wisdom of using such terms as constitutional Monarchy and Commonwealth realms, but the Treasury Legal Department insisted this was the correct legal position, and it was decided that an impartial publicity campaign would need to explain such terms to the Electorate.

In regard to the light blue ballot paper to decide who would be Monarch in the event of a yes majority, the wording was agreed as:

Place an x next to the name of the person who you
would wish to be your Constitutional Monarch.

☐ *Richard George Charles Windsor*
☐ *Karim Ali Stuart Khaled*

There had been a discussion on whether or not Richard should have his various titles included on the ballot paper, but Ibrahim had requested a level playing field between the candidates, and Richard was easily persuaded that his name should go forward shorn of his various hereditary distinctions.

As soon as the candidates' names became public knowledge, the campaign started in earnest.

The liberal progressive Press were in favour of Karim's candidacy. These papers included The Sun, Guardian, Mirror, Times and New Statesman.

Richard's side included the more conservative traditionalist papers like The Telegraph, Mail, Express and Spectator.

The BBC, still smarting from allegations of bias against Brexit in the EU referendum, tried to be scrupulously impartial, but some seasoned commentators detected a slight bias in favour of Karim.

ITN also attempted to be impartial, but was rumoured to favour Richard.

Eventually the interviewers were selected – each candidate would have one interview with each of two interviewers – Piers Wheatley from the BBC and Hamish Buchanan from ITN.

A list of likely questions would be provided to each candidate as neither candidate was a professional politician, and it was felt that an ability to prepare, maybe with some professional help, would ensure a fairer and more meaningful contest.

After some debate, it was agreed that each candidate would be interviewed alone, firstly for thirty minutes by Wheatley, and then, after a break of an hour, for a second thirty-minute session by Buchanan.

Wheatley would ask about family background, education and leisure pursuits, for example, while

Buchanan would concentrate on political and religious beliefs and ambitions.

All interviews would be shown on both BBC1 and ITV1.

Meanwhile, the campaign on social media quickly went into overdrive.

Anticipation of the interviews sent social media into a spin. Contributions and observations were a mix of popular commentary on the merits of the candidates with the presentability of their wives as much as them. Kirsty always looked striking. She had a creative penchant for re-fashioning clothes she had purchased from charity shops, always stylish and often daring. Sophia, by contrast, was modestly turned out, consistently tasteful and elegant, so reassuring to Facebook users of a more conservative bent. Many tweets resurrected the standard that both women would be compared to, as photos of Princess Caroline were posted, of her for example in 1994 arriving at the Serpentine Gallery in a gown by Christina Stambolian.

Where opinion differed on the political substance of the contest, it broadly split along lines of preference for a resumption of tradition and a more daring strike toward a multi-cultural and apparently classless future. Supporters of Richard tweeted he had a duty to rule and the idea of a popular vote was inconsistent with the principle of monarchy. Richard replied on Twitter he had no more right to rule than his half-brother. This sparked a Twitter storm of constitutional argument. Many pointed out that Karim was not the son of an existing Sovereign but of a liaison between a divorced Princess and a commoner, and a foreigner to boot.

Most supported the democratisation as a healing process after so much conflict, regardless of the result. Both candidates tweeted messages about their respect for each other and how much they were looking forward to an opportunity to meet. This was very popular on social media. Ibrahim anticipated a high turnout would result from the worldwide Electorate which he would publicly interpret as an endorsement of the further democratisation of constitutional monarchy, even if there were a lot of posts and tweets that reflected highly partisan passion for one or the other candidate for the throne.

The TV interviews took place on 20 August 2018 around six weeks before the referendum.

Karim was the first to be interviewed by Piers Wheatley.

"I would like to ask about your adoptive parents and family out in Dubai. Was it a close-knit family?"

"It was a very close and affectionate family – I never felt deprived either materially or emotionally – I was very lucky."

"I know this is a sensitive question, but what was

the personal impact on you when you discovered your natural parents had died in very unfortunate circumstances?"

"I suppose I was about thirteen when I became aware that my father's car crash may not have been accidental – that it may have been orchestrated by someone."

"Who did you suspect?"

"I only had the rumours circulating on the internet to go on and many of those mentioned rogue elements in MI6."

"Do you still believe that?"

"Possibly – it looks like they had a motive – to prevent my father, a Muslim, from getting too close to Prince Richard by becoming his stepfather. And also to prevent him from fathering any children with my mother, who would then be blood relatives of Prince Richard."

"Have you met Prince Richard?"

"No, not yet."

"Do you want to meet him?"

"Yes, very much so."

"Why?"

"Well, blood is thicker than water, as they say – I want to ask him about our mother, among other things, but I don't wish to go into detail on this – it's too personal."

"But by standing against him in this election, are you not inviting him to be hostile towards you?"

"No – he was the one who abdicated, not that I blame him for doing so. By subsequently standing for election, he's accepted the rules of the contest and he's already said that he will accept the voters' decision. I believe he knows he can't be Monarch by divine right – those days have gone."

"What does your wife think about being Queen?"

"To her, it's really a way of being able to make a difference to people's lives by charitable work – we both see that as a continuation of my mother's projects."

There then followed another ten minutes or so of straightforward questions, followed by an hour's break, during which Karim looked at the list of questions to be raised by Hamish Buchanan, ITN's chief political correspondent. The scripted questions seemed manageable, but there were bound to be unscripted questions that could be problematic, and so it proved.

"I see you studied Politics at University – does the role of the Monarch change, or do you think it should stay as it is?"

"Yes, I remember studying British constitution during my first year at SOAS. We were taught that a British Monarch has three rights – the right to be consulted; to encourage and to warn – this was according to Bagehot, the Victorian journalist. This all sounds good stuff to me, but I'd just like to add some obligations. In particular, the obligation to get stuck into some serious charity work and also to mediate, if invited so to do – I am mainly thinking of international disputes here."

"Are you thinking of Commonwealth disputes, as you would be head of the Commonwealth?"

"Yes, but also those in the Middle East, perhaps, where both sides feel they can trust me."

"Would you say that your mother was let down by the Establishment and this explains your reputation for having radical left wing views?"

"Yes, that's part of it, but also I was brought up in Dubai as a Muslim and I became aware of the Western bias against Muslims in history, starting with the Crusades."

"But the fact that you're left wing and a Muslim will both be seen as reasons why you should not be chosen for this role, surely…?"

"Well, if I was a right wing Christian, some would say those are reasons I should not be chosen. I am not a Jihadi – I'm sure everyone knows that, but I understand Islam and I believe moderate law abiding Muslims should be looked after – we should cater for their aspirations on the same basis as other citizens, including Christians."

"But the Monarch is supposed to be Head of the

Anglican Church, so you can't fulfil that role as you are not an Anglican?"

"No, but we can separate Church and State and the Archbishop of Canterbury can have that role, and I can remain as Defender of Faith, not necessarily the Christian faith. The Government can obviously do this by a single Act of Parliament."

"As you are setting out your CV, may we please know about your leisure pursuits?"

"Certainly – I am very keen on skiing and music."

"Do you play an instrument?"

"Guitar and trumpet – enough competence on the former to play in a band – not so good on the latter, but very keen. I acquired an interest in jazz from my dad – my adoptive dad – in Dubai."

There followed a few more basic questions not causing Karim any great difficulty and the interview ended.

Next up was Richard, being interviewed by Piers Wheatley, the arch-enemy of his father and stepmother.

"Good evening sir (it was actually midday, but Wheatley knew the programme would be screened in the evening and had decided to try and con the audience into thinking the interview was live). I'm sorry this must all be a chore from your viewpoint – having to stand for election when you could have been crowned as King earlier without any such fuss."

"Well no – I decided to abdicate for what seemed like good reasons at the time. I've now decided to stand in this election and, if I win, it will reinforce a sense of legitimacy that maybe I wouldn't have otherwise had."

"Fine – but as this is an election, sir, I'm obliged to ask about your qualifications and so on. It's well known you went to St Andrews University – was there any particular reason you chose a red brick University when you could have gone to Oxbridge, presumably?"

"It's not red brick for a start, it's more like grey granite. Most St Andrews students past and present would be horrified to hear St Andrews described as red brick.

I chose it because it's the top University regularly in the top five of all the league tables and I've always been keen on all things Scottish, like many other members of my family."

"I see, sir – please remind me and our viewers what you studied and what class of degree you obtained."

"History of Art and Classical Civilisation, and I obtained an Upper Second."

"Fine, what leisure pursuits did you cultivate at University and since?"

"Skiing and polo mainly, when family commitments permit."

"Of course, and what about politics – would you say you've inherited the reactionary views and desire to interfere which were a hallmark of your father's term as Monarch?"

"I don't have reactionary views and I object to your question – come to think of it, you were the interviewer who failed to edit the unfortunate interview just after my father and stepmother were released by their kidnappers – perhaps you would now like to apologise for being a substantial cause of their assassination!"

Wheatley reddened with a combination of embarrassment and anger.

"That's outrageous – it wasn't my fault the interview didn't get edited."

"It was your responsibility, and you know it – it's people like you who signed my mother's death warrant into the bargain – that's it, this interview is terminated."

At that point Richard rose from his chair, tore off the mike and walked out of the studio.

Richard's planned interview with Hamish Buchanan of ITN then had to be postponed while the repercussions from Richard's walk-out were dealt with and absorbed.

Headlines in the anti-Richard Press the following day like **RICHARD QUITS AGAIN!** in the Mirror didn't help, and it was with great difficulty that Richard's friends and advisers persuaded him to continue his campaign.

A full 48 hours passed before Richard sat down to

the interview by Hamish Buchanan and that was on the condition that no mention was made of his walk-out over Wheatley's comments.

Buchanan had already resolved to stick mainly to the scripted questions so Richard would have no cause to complain.

"It's often said your grandmother would have easily got the job if she'd ever had to apply for it. Does that apply to you – if so, please say why?"

"It's kind of people to say that about her – I'm sure she would have been very flattered to know that's what people thought. As for me, I was brought up knowing that the Crown would be mine one day if I wanted it, and I was also brought up to know about many of the tips and tricks involved in being a popular Royal – as regards whether or not I would get the job, we shall have to wait and see how the Electorate vote. I will, of course, fully accept the result of the vote, whichever way it goes." Such was Richard's measured and diplomatic response.

Buchanan continued.

"I see that you are emphasising you are a Christian and member of the Church of England, in particular. Do you see this as much of an advantage now that only around 44% of the population regard themselves as Christian?"

"It's still the case that the Monarch is Head of the

Church of England, but I would not be worried by a constitutional decision that this role should be adopted by the Archbishop of Canterbury. In my view, there is a debate to be had about the pros and cons of Church and State being entirely separate.

A separation may be the more modern approach – again, I will accept the decision of Parliament and the Government on this."

Much to the relief of Richard's friends, advisers and supporters, the rest of the interview went well enough for Richard to declare himself to have been fairly treated this time.

Piers Wheatley's antagonism to Richard sparked bitter exchanges on social media. While many sympathised with his point that his stepmother was vulnerable to the predations of the Press, which was antagonistic toward her reactionary and prejudiced views, particularly after her recent kidnapping, Richard's reaction to Wheatley's pointed questions reminded others of John Nott. As Minister of Defence during the Falklands War in 1982, he had been so uncomfortable when questioned about his role in the handling of the conflict, he tore off his microphone and stormed out of the interview. It was commented by many on social media that Richard should have shown restraint commensurate with his Royal or ex Royal status.

In its piece about the interview Karim had with Hamish Buchanan, ITN reported the popularity of a tweet suggesting he should back a campaign to make Islam the State religion. Despite Karim declaring his contempt for Jihadism and his commitment to separating Church and State, this tweet attracted over 12,000 likes and replies adding a demand for Sharia to replace English law.

When asked by ITN for his views as a Muslim on this, Prime Minister Ibrahim pointed out that Islamist fundamentalism was a worldwide phenomenon and that it was most unlikely much of this response was from British Muslims.

"Twitter is plagued by a multiplicity of false profiles" he told the Spectator in another interview. "The Home Secretary has made the effort to meet the major social media companies now and been assured they will police the presence of Jihadist platforms and eradicate such abuse. Failing that, my government will be proposing legislation to force them to take action."

Karim was beside himself with excitement as he and Kirsty, both in evening dress, installed themselves in the back seat of the Jaguar XK driven by a specially trained Police driver, accompanied by armed bodyguard, both from the Royalty & Specialist Protection (RASP) division of the Metropolitan Police (known affectionately by the Royals as Raspberries, not just due to their initials, but also due to the red cars they usually drove).

The newlyweds had been invited by Ibrahim to a reception at 10 Downing Street for the referendum candidates and their wives.

"Tell me something Darling…"

"What's that, Honey?" Kirsty gently responded to Karim's plea.

"How in Heaven's name do you plan for a meeting with your long lost half brother?"

"Act natural – don't be stand-offish – it will all be fine," Kirsty wisely advised.

"I hope you're right – I feel I've only got one go at this and I've got to get it right."

As they approached No. 10 it became apparent that the world's media were out in force – there was a large bank of TV cameras and photographers, eager to capitalise on this major event in British and global politics.

There was also a substantial crowd of onlookers, many of whom clapped and cheered when they caught sight of Karim and Kirsty, who arrived before Richard and Sophia.

On the steps of No. 10, Karim and Kirsty turned

towards the media contingent and waved for the cameras.

Someone shouted:

"Are you nervous sir?"

Karim did not respond – he just kept smiling. He was nervous, but wasn't about to admit it in public.

Once safely inside No. 10, they were able to spend a few minutes taking in their surroundings while Karim sipped an orange juice and Kirsty enjoyed a glass of English sparkling wine from a vineyard deep in the Sussex countryside.

The conversation in the room fell silent, which signalled the arrival of Richard and Sophia, both looking immaculate – Richard in a well tailored black tie evening suit and Sophia in an eye-catching royal blue gown.

Protocol demanded that Richard and Sophia be then introduced to the various diplomats first, then the politicians.

Karim and Kirsty were the last to be introduced to Richard and Sophia – by Ibrahim personally.

Karim warmly shook Richard's hand, then, throwing caution and protocol to the wind, proceeded to embrace Richard in a full-on Arabian bear hug – much to the amusement of most of the assembled politicians, diplomats and other prominent worthies, including Richard himself.

Karim disentangled himself.

"I'm sorry, sir, if that greeting seemed over the top, but I've been waiting most of my life for this moment…"

"It's fine old chap – a good way of breaking the ice I'm sure – call me Richard – meet my wife, Sophia; Darling meet Karim."

"Delighted, I'm sure," said Sophia. "We were so sorry we could not go to your wedding, we were advised not to, if the truth were told."

"That's fine," – volunteered Kirsty, "we would have loved to see you, but quite understood when you said you could not accept – Karim has kept Richard's letter – he really treasures it."

Richard laughed. Karim looked slightly embarrassed – the ladies smiled, and chatted together.

"Listen old chap, talking of letters, I have some unfinished business I would like to transact with you."

Richard produced an envelope from his inside pocket and handed it to Karim. Richard continued:

"It's a copy of a letter our mother wrote to me – just wonder if you'd seen it, or knew anything about it, like where it was written?"

Karim quickly re-read the letter his grandfather had had posted to Richard four years ago.

Karim gulped – he knew he should not betray the confidence of his grandfather, and yet he could not bring himself to lie to his blood relative.

"I was aware of the existence of this letter, but would prefer not to say any more right now, except that you're very lucky to have had a letter from her – I wish she'd written to me as well!"

Richard smiled.

"Don't worry, we can perhaps discuss it some other time. When this election is out of the way you must both come and stay at Highgrove."

"That would be marvellous – perhaps you and Sophia would like to stay in our family chalet in Cortina and get down to some serious skiing."

"Yes, that would be very kind of you – all these trips and so on have to be vetted by my security people, but I'm sure a way can be found."

"Can you please assure me of one thing, sir... I mean Richard – that you will not hold the election result against me, win or lose? I would withdraw if you asked me to."

"You really don't need to worry about that either, Karim – as the letter says, our mother wanted us to be friends and that's the way it should be. Besides, I believe an election makes the Monarchy stronger."

"Thank you Richard. I'm relieved to hear you say that – it really puts my mind at rest."

"That's all right, think nothing of it, may the best man win, and good luck!"

"Good luck to you too," said Karim.

At that point a gong sounded signalling that the guests should take their places at the dinner table.

The day after the candidates' dinner at No. 10 saw Sheikh in his office at The Sun discussing the likely election result with his resident history guru, Harry.

"How do you rate Karim's chances?" asked Sheikh.

"The polls show the candidates to be just about evenly matched in most areas."

"What about the Caroline factor; hasn't Karim inherited most of her following?" continued Sheikh.

"Yes, probably, although she was Richard's mother as well – but he does not have her charisma – a nice enough bloke but a little ponderous and self obsessed like his dad.

Karim, on the other hand, does have her charisma in spades" was Harry's response.

"I agree," Sheikh continued, "so he has inherited her legacy – the hearts and minds of a substantial portion of the British public."

17

The Referendum was conducted over 3 days in October 2018 – around 101 years to the day after the accession of the Bolsheviks to power in Russia, as a Guardian editorial helpfully pointed out.

Three days were needed to collate and count the millions of votes cast, not just in Britain but also in the Commonwealth.

Naturally each vote was of equal status, whether cast in Bermuda or Blackburn.

The BBC and Sky News ran round-the-clock coverage of the whole process. Karim did particularly well in Scotland, West Indies, Birmingham and London.

The result of the Referendum was due to be announced by the Chief Returning Officer in the main Banqueting Hall of Windsor Castle at 6.00 pm on Friday 19 October 2018.

Sheikh and the editorial team at The Sun watched the proceedings on the TV monitor in The Sun newsroom.

With regard to the Referendum itself on whether or not the monarchy should be restored, 76% of the Electorate voted for restoration.

Harry, the history guru, joined the editorial group watching the monitor at around 5.00 pm on the day.

"How is Karim doing?"

"Very well, but Canada hasn't declared yet" responded Sheikh.

"The Canadian declaration isn't due until around 5.45 pm" said the TV commentator.

"The Canadian polls indicate that Prince Richard is very likely to do much better than Karim Khaled, but the latter is currently leading overall with 54% of the votes cast. Right now it's too close to call."

As predicted, around 5.45 pm the Canadian result came through.

"… of the 8,400,000 or so votes cast in Canada, around 5,350,000 have gone to Prince Richard… we are now checking through the figures, wait… I have the final result… the winner overall is Karim Khaled with 50.5% of the vote!!"

Sheikh immediately texted Karim, who he knew was sitting in Windsor Castle waiting for the formal declaration.

Congratulations, Karim, you've won. BW Andy S

Karim showed Sheikh's text to Kirsty, who just managed to refrain from shouting "Yes!" in front of the assembled dignitaries, journalists and TV crews.

Following the formal announcement of the results by the Returning Officer, 10 minutes later, Karim immediately sought out Richard and warmly shook his hand.

"This is really the greatest moment. Kirsty and I are so grateful to you for allowing this contest to proceed. Whatever happens, from now on, please stay in touch."

"Congratulations to both of you – I am sure we can rely on you to discharge your duties wisely, and if there's anything I can do to help just say the word," responded Richard.

At that moment the Returning Officer approached.

"Perhaps you would now like to address the Hall sir?"

"Certainly" said Karim. He wasn't about to ad lib a speech at this stage, and extracted his victory speech from his jacket pocket, just double checking it wasn't the other speech he'd prepared which conceded defeat.

"My Lords, ladies and gentlemen
This is really the greatest honour and I am truly humbled by the victory which an international Electorate has bestowed on me

and my wife, Kirsty. Thank you to everyone who participated in this election, whether or not they voted for me, and a special thank you to all those who campaigned for us. I only wish my – I mean our – mother could have been with us today.

I am sure she would have been very proud of both Prince Richard and myself – sorry if that sounds conceited! A special thank you also to my wife, Kirsty, for putting up with me constantly talking about putting the world to rights and for continuing to have faith in me during this campaign.

Finally, it should go without saying, but I will say it anyway, I intend to fulfil my role as your Monarch in the interests of all our people regardless of colour or creed.

Thank you again, and may you all be blessed by the Almighty on this day and always."

"They need to take this seriously, this link between the Anglican Church and the Monarchy has existed in this country for nearly 500 years – since Henry VIII's time," said Harry at The Sun's editorial meeting.

"I'll tell Ibrahim in case he doesn't know it already!" commented Sheikh. "I can't believe the average voter cares much about it these days," he continued.

"It's part of the fabric of our society," said Harry. "Our values, attitude to the law and system of justice are underpinned by Christian values."

"Tell that to the average MP or lawyer – he probably won't understand what the fuss is about."

"That's because people take it for granted."

"What exactly do they take for granted?" asked Sheikh.

"That the Ten Commandments handed down by Moses should be the blueprint for everyone's moral code."

"From what I hear of Anglicanism, you can get appointed as a Bishop without necessarily believing in God, let alone the Ten Commandments," commented Sheikh.

"I reckon there's enough material there for an article – if you write it, I'll make sure Ibrahim sees a copy."

"Okay, you're on" replied Harry.

Following determined opposition from several Anglican Bishops in the House of Lords, the Monarchy (Abolition of Role as Head of Anglican Church) Bill became law on 20 January 2019, paving the way for the Coronation to take place on 25 February 2019.

The location of Karim and Kirsty's Coronation had been the subject of some speculation and debate until Ibrahim and Karim, after consulting various Cabinet members and constitutional experts, settled on Westminster Hall, the oldest building in the Palace of Westminster, and thought to be in keeping with the democratic and non-denominational preferences which both Karim and Kirsty hoped would characterise their new roles.

The Coronation ceremony had to be specially customised to cater for Karim and Kirsty's new style of monarchy. The couple would arrive in the unheated gold plated State coronation coach as used at Queen Elizabeth II's coronation in 1953.

"It's February, make sure you wear a pair of long johns," was Sheikh's advice when he heard about the mode of transport.

The ceremonial dress for both Karim and Kirsty was similar to that applicable to the House of Lords – red robes and ermine.

By this time, Karim and Kirsty were living in a large apartment in Buckingham Palace while the rest of the property was refurbished in readiness for being opened to the public for educational and trade promotional purposes.

By the time the great day arrived, the ceremony had been well rehearsed and everything went like clockwork, fully in keeping with the high standards of the British Monarchy and as expected by the billion strong TV audience worldwide.

Like the location, the Coronation Oath had also been a matter of some conjecture. The Oath was administered by the speaker of the House of Lords and, on the day, the wording was as follows:-

Speaker: *Will you solemnly promise and swear to govern the Peoples of England, Wales and Northern Ireland, Scotland, Canada, Australia, New Zealand and of your Possessions and other Territories to any of them belonging or pertaining, according to their respective laws and customs?*

Monarch: *I solemnly promise so to do.*

Speaker: *Will you in your power cause Law and Justice, in Mercy, to be executed in all your judgments?*

Monarch: *I will.*

There then followed prayers led by firstly the Archbishop of Canterbury, then a senior Imam, who spoke mainly in English but with some quotations in Arabic, and lastly the Chief Rabbi.

"Hedging his bets, I suppose. But why no contributions from a Buddhist or a Marxist?" asked Harry, half jokingly, as The Sun's editorial team watched the ceremony on their main TV monitor.

"They had to draw the line somewhere," was Sheikh's dry response.

Towards the end of the ceremony, Karim and Kirsty walked down the aisle between the onlooking congregation while a choir chanted

Vivat Rex!
Vivat Regina!

"There has to be some Latin content to satisfy the Catholics," commented Harry.

It wasn't immediately apparent but another practical problem had to be surmounted – that was in relation to the crown being too heavy for the Monarch to walk unsupported. The problem was eventually resolved by the use of a more lightweight crown still bejewelled, but enabling greater mobility.

The formalities were concluded by a State banquet in the main dining room at Buckingham Palace populated by the great and the good of British society and public life.

The reign of Karim I was characterised initially by the consolidation of the political power of Ibrahim and the Free Democrats.

"We need now to think about repaying the political debts we incurred on the path to power," remarked Alistair Faulkner, Ibrahim's chief policy adviser. "The Greens, Socialists and Muslim pressure groups, in particular, will now expect something in return for their various contributions."

"I'd like to encourage Islamic banking and Sharia law options in regard to family and criminal law in particular," was Ibrahim's response.

The option of having Sharia law applied in criminal matters was not an unmitigated success.

The option to elect for Sharia law to apply in your case benefited all accused persons, both Muslim and non-Muslim.

Sheikh never missed a trick, and immediately saw an opportunity to exploit the new system for commercial gain.

Sheikh, using an intermediary, proceeded to contact a far right group who happened to support Arsenal Football Club and paid them to chant anti-black slogans, and throw bananas at a black Tottenham player. The Sun then sent a film of the incident to the Metropolitan Police together with a letter of complaint.

Fifteen of the culprits were cautioned and two of the ringleaders prosecuted. The latter opted to be tried under the Sharia system.

The Sharia legal penalty for hooliganism of this type was a heavy fine or a public judicial caning as practised in places like Malaysia. Sheikh, via an intermediary, paid the accused, firstly to plead guilty, and secondly to elect to be subjected to a judicial caning instead of a fine.

From Sheikh's viewpoint, everything went like clockwork. He was even happy with an unplanned twist to the chain of events, which occurred on the day of the caning in Arsenal's Emirates Stadium, prior to the start of an important fixture with Chelsea.

As soon as the culprits dropped their trousers in order to be caned, there was total uproar in the form of cheering and clapping from the 70,000 onlookers.

The causes of this reaction were the icons tattooed on the backsides of the offenders – one had St George's flags – red cross on a white background – on each buttock, the other had left and right palm prints.

The Magistrate supervising the proceedings immediately ordered an additional eight strokes of the Rattan cane to be administered to each offender for showing contempt on top of the basic twelve strokes already ordered by the Court earlier.

Sheikh had paid the offenders £10,000 each and

the following day got his money's worth with 100% sell-out edition containing the never to be repeated headline:

RUMP STEAK 100% ENGLISH BEEF – SPECIALLY PULVERISED FOR TENDERNESS!

There were "before" and "after" photos but only the "before" photos were printed in the paper – the "after" photos were only available online on payment of £5.00.

"Was there by any chance a serious point to this circus?" Harry asked Sheikh at the next editorial conference.

"Kind of – I just have a hunch that there is a strong and substantial element within the English public who are incapable of being humiliated whatever so-called punishment is meted out to them. I reckon my experiment, if you can call it that, proves that point – as well as making us a load of cash."

"Prime Minister, we need to think now about repaying the political debts we owe to the Socialists and the Green Party – do you have any preferences?" asked Faulkner.

"Okay, on socialism let's go for more workers on

Boards and more tax breaks for rewards in the form of shares rather than cash – any related tax reliefs can be cancelled if the shares are sold within 2 years – we can discuss this in Cabinet, but anyway I can't imagine much opposition on those points either in Cabinet or Parliament, after all Smithson promised both in the last Tory Manifesto!"

"In that case they may not be socialistic enough, surely," said Faulkner.

"Just tell them Attlee would have approved, which is probably true, that should shut them up."

"Okay, what about the Greens?"

"Again, tax relief is a possible solution – let's try more tax relief on investment in solar energy and woodlands. We'll discuss it in Cabinet – I don't foresee much opposition as it's just more of the same."

"By the way, where are we on Brexit, is it still a stalemate?"

Faulkner sighed – "We've only got a few more months to play with, Prime Minister, we need to get a grip and start thinking creatively. It looks like business wants a transitional phase, as do most MPs."

"As you know, I was a keen Leave supporter," said Ibrahim. "But, I can see the need for a compromise – how about a Norway style deal lasting for an initial period of 3 years with an option to renew?" Ibrahim suggested.

"The problem with that is that we'd have to keep free movement and contributions to the EU budget," said Faulkner.

"Yes, it would mean being a member of the EEA and single market, but only on a temporary basis, and we'd be able to start making our own trade deals, unlike the Customs Union deal that some people were suggesting," said Ibrahim.

"But free movement is a red line point for most Brexiteers, surely?" said Faulkner.

"Yes, but we can sweeten the pill by beefing up the requirements for EU Nationals and every other would-be immigrant having to have spoken and written English skills before they enter the country. In case anyone questions it, it's already permitted under the public policy exemption within the free movement rules and we've already imposed language requirements on EU Nurses and Doctors."

"But not to apply to seasonal fruit and veg pickers, surely?" asked Faulkner. "It's not what the farmers want."

"Okay, I wouldn't have a problem with that – I'll canvass my Brexit Minister and the Cabinet generally."

Ibrahim's personal and political following and his powers of persuasion were such that he was able to push through most, if not all, of the above policies with some tweaking here and there.

Karim was impressed, and said as much during their numerous meetings. Karim had quietly dropped the term "audience" which he believed to be too archaic a term, in regard to his meetings with his PM.

"May I ask if you are managing to keep busy, sir?" Ibrahim asked Karim at one of their meetings.

"Please don't worry about the sir, just call me Karim. You were mainly responsible for getting me this job, maybe I should be calling you sir," responded Karim. "I'm finding more than enough to do, since you ask – I'm further researching the Arab Israeli conflict so I can be fully qualified to mediate if or when anyone asks me so to do."

"That's certainly a worthy project, well done indeed – have you got anyone helping you?"

"Only my Jewish friend from SOAS, David Rosenthal – he is fluent in Hebrew, which could be useful."

"Well, if you need any other help, just let me know – I could probably arrange for a couple of research assistants from FCO to help you."

"Thanks, I'll bear that in mind – between us, David and I could probably already write a book on the subject, but we may need help later with making contact with the movers and shakers on both sides."

"Have you had any new ideas that could lead to a breakthrough?"

Ibrahim was sceptical, but asked the question out of politeness.

"Yes, in fact we have – keep this under your hat for now – we've been toying with the idea of a neutral city state arrangement for Jerusalem – just the old city, the Temple Mount and the Holy sites – comparable to the Vatican in Rome."

"Interesting, but who would head it up?" Ibrahim was still being sceptical, but polite.

"We were thinking in terms of a rotating Presidency with a change every 2 years."

"Involving who?"

"Senior figures from within the three great religions of the Book – so a Muslim followed by a Christian followed by a Jew, and so on ad infinitum."

"Right – so what about the rest of Jerusalem?"

"West Jerusalem could then be the capital of Israel and East Jerusalem the capital of a new Palestinian State. The stumbling block to Jerusalem being a capital was that it would have involved ceding control of the Temple Mount area, but the neutral city state idea neatly removes the main obstacle, surely?"

"Good, that sounds constructive and original – I've never seen anyone advocating that idea before – well done. Just be prepared for the head bangers on either side to shoot you down – it's just too good an idea for that not to happen!"

Ibrahim decided to be encouraging in his approach, rather than appear negative.

"The problem is we'll all be fair game so far as the paparazzi are concerned," ruminated Karim.

"We'll just have to work round them – we can offer them a half-hour long photo shoot to start with then, provided they leave us alone thereafter, make a few private shots available later to those papers and websites that play the game," responded Kirsty.

"I'm really pleased that Richard and Sophia have accepted our invitation to Cortina – I just want them to have a great time – I'm sure it's what our mother would have wanted. If only Granddad was still with us, he'd have thought of some solution I'm sure."

Hassan had passed away peacefully six months previously but Karim was still having difficulty coming to terms with his loss.

"I heard that our mother used to lose the paparazzi by swapping ski jackets with friends or bodyguards, who would then act as decoys."

"We can't lose them by skiing faster, I'm not a good enough skier," continued Karim, "I've only done a week's skiing in Cortina plus half a dozen trips to the artificial slope in Dubai."

"It's no good running away from them, your grandfather always said that – they will always catch you in the end and punish you. Maybe we could use the point that you're a slower skier than the rest of us to our advantage," said Kirsty.

"How so?"

"I'll let you know later, right now I need to look at these menus for evening meals at the chalet. Everyone needs to be well fed to get the best out of this skiing holiday."

Kirsty knew what she was talking about – in an earlier life she'd had a successful season as a chalet girl in Val D'Isere, having learnt to ski as a child in Aviemore.

Karim, encouraged by Kirsty, had mothballed most of the Royal flight of aircraft in the interests of economy and environmental responsibility.

So, on 10 February 2019, the Royal party flew out of Heathrow to Marco Polo Airport, Venice on a scheduled Alitalia flight.

From Venice, the party progressed to Cortina D'Ampezzo in various 4x4 vehicles including a Range Rover and Jaguar F Pace provided by the Embassy in Rome.

The following day the whole party, including Karim, Kirsty, Richard, Sophia and their 2 children, Edward aged 5 and Grace aged 3, met on the slopes at 10.00am for the pre-arranged photocall.

Karim opened the proceedings thus

"Ladies and gentlemen

I know you have a job to do, and that's why we are having this photocall.

However, I need to warn you, as diplomatically as possible, of two things.

Firstly, if we are bothered later on in this holiday by intrusive and aggressive paparazzi, for want of a better word, any material which is later published will be monitored and that publication, whether a paper or an online publication, will not receive any invitations to photocalls or the like for at least 3 years, and also not receive any of the planned privately taken photos of our holiday, which will be provided to the other publications which have complied with our ground rules.

I am sure I can rely on most of you to respect our privacy. For those that don't, there is always the option of our suing in the Courts for breach of privacy for substantial sums, which we will donate to charity – the option to sue also applies to websites and so on who publish unauthorised photos online.

The second diplomatic warning relates to my lack of skiing expertise."

Karim smiled while his family and some of the Pressmen gently tittered.

"Prince Richard and I have agreed that we will not be skiing together during this holiday as I am still an intermediate. I am pleased to say, however, that my wife, who is an expert skier, has agreed to coach me. The point is that this is likely to be your sole opportunity to photograph all of us together on the slopes as a party, so my advice is to make the most of it and forget about trying to chase us for the rest of the holiday. That's it for now, and I hope you all have a very good day."

Karim wasn't going to publicly admit the point, but this second announcement was Kirsty's idea in an attempt to minimise pursuit by paparazzi trying to secure shots of the whole group together.

On the evening of the third day of the holiday, Karim and Richard found themselves alone, the rest of the party having gone to bed after a tiring, but enjoyable, day on the slopes.

Richard was enjoying a large glass of whisky while Karim sipped at an apple juice.

"There's a photo of our mother I'd like to show you." There was a pause, and then Karim continued. "It was given to me by my grandfather on condition I didn't show it to anyone until after his death, which occurred six months ago."

"Fine, yes, I would very much like to see it," responded Richard.

"It's here," – Karim reached for and opened a slim leather briefcase.

"I don't have it on my laptop in case it might get hacked."

The colour photo was of Caroline by a swimming pool wearing a bikini and clearly pregnant.

She was holding an issue of Paris Match – it was the same photo that Hassan had disclosed to Sheikh at The Sun at least 25 years previously.

The photo had discoloured over time, but was still clear enough to see the well-known French actor whose photo was on the front cover of the magazine.

"So when and where was this taken?" asked Richard.

"As regards when, that would be within a week or so after 21 April 1994, that's nearly four months after the crash in Italy which claimed my father's life."

"How can you be so precise about that date?" asked Richard.

"Because that's the date of that edition of Paris Match – it's written on the back of the photo – you can check it out online if you like—"

"No, it's fine, I'll take your word for it. What about where?"

"At a ranch in Morocco belonging to a good friend of my grandfather – about 50 kilometres from Essaouira – it's a town on the Atlantic coast."

Richard exhaled like he was stressed.

"I'm finding it hard to take in all of this. I knew she was still alive but she didn't want us to tell anyone or try and find her."

"Who is 'us'?" asked Karim.

"Smiffy and me."

"Who's Smiffy?"

"Marigold Smith, my nanny. Mummy sent Smiffy a text saying she was alive but she thought her life was in danger – she said Smiffy could tell me but no-one else."

"So she did not want your father to know she was still alive?"

"Quite so – by that stage their relationship was very acrimonious. There had been stories in the Press confirming that, and they had just got divorced, of course."

As if he was reading Karim's mind, Richard added:

"There may have been a conspiracy to kill our mother and your father, mainly because of your father's religion, but I don't think my father would have been involved – it wasn't his style."

"So who do you think would have been involved?"

"Maybe Special forces, like the SAS or MI6 people freelancing."

There was a pause of a minute or two while the implications of what was being said sunk in.

Richard broke the silence.

"So, can you tell me the background to the letter I showed you at No. 10?"

Karim momentarily hesitated while he marshalled his thoughts.

"Yes – right, the letter. Again, Grandfather didn't want me to discuss it until after his death. He said it was written by our mother at the ranch in Morocco and he promised her he would deliver it to you.

His problem was that he thought somehow the letter might incriminate him and that he might be prosecuted for lying to the Police in Italy during the course of their investigations into the car crash.

Eventually when he thought the dust had settled, he got one of his lawyers to post the letter to you over twenty years after it had been written!

He said that if I ever met you, I was to apologise for the delay!"

"It's okay – I can see things must have got very complicated very early on – at least he kept his word eventually."

Richard continued. "When we heard from her bodyguard she'd died in childbirth, I was naturally devastated – I only had Smiffy to turn to – the text also said the baby had died at the same time, that would have been you."

"Grandfather told me the bodyguard died in the Middle East a year or so later in some kind of shoot-out with kidnappers. Grandfather said he was an ex Marine who was very loyal and had done a great job – he paid him a regular retainer but never had any doubt that he would keep his story under wraps, with or without a retainer." Karim continued. "So what was our mother like as a person – have the journalists and commentators missed anything?"

"She was very loving – a great mum – glamorous but also idealistic, hence the Aids and Landmine campaigns. Also she could be great fun to be with and very funny. But she could be moody and sad, stemming, I think, from an unhappy childhood. Her parents had a very acrimonious divorce when she was very young and it scarred her for life, I reckon.

The rest, as they say, is history."

"Okay Richard, thanks for that – it's been a long day – I'm going to turn in – certainly we've both got a great deal to chew over."

"Fine, Karim – goodnight – see you in the morning."

All things considered, Richard hadn't told Karim much he didn't already know, or half know, but it was still very important to Karim that they'd had the conversation man-to-man.

He would like to get Richard on the payroll of HMG, maybe as an ambassador of some description. He would speak to Ibrahim.

The rest of the holiday was relatively uneventful. A couple of paparazzi tried to get some shots of the King of England falling over on the slopes, but were hustled away by minders with nothing to show for their efforts.

Shortly after his return to London, Karim broached the subject of a role for Richard at one of his weekly meetings with Ibrahim at the Palace.

"I would like to show Richard I recognise his friendship and loyalty and maybe both can be enhanced if we give him a meaningful role – maybe some kind of roving ambassador would be appropriate."

"Yes, that should be manageable – with special responsibility for the Commonwealth, perhaps."

"I may also need him to use his clout to secure meetings for myself and David in Israel and the Palestinian territories. It's obviously going to be very delicate but Richard may be able to arrange some preliminary meetings for us, if he has some kind of official status."

"All right, I'll consult with the Foreign Secretary and we'll see what can be done. In return I'd like your support, please, on a pet project of mine. An all Asian Guards Regiment."

"Sounds fine to me," said Karim.

"We have in mind most of the Officers being either Ghurkhas or Sikhs – both have substantial military traditions already, of course."

"Will, say, Indians and Pakistanis be able to work together?"

"Probably – we'll have to work on that. It will be a British Army Regiment so their allegiance will be to you and not their respective mother countries. Most of them will have been born here anyway so we are hoping sectarianism will be diluted by their being mainly British."

"And once we've got a new Guards Regiment, how about a new Cavalry Regiment with camels instead of horses?!"

Karim was only half joking.

Ibrahim just said:-

"Maybe in 20 years' time, but for now one thing at a time, if you don't mind, sir…"

18

"Darling, they've offered me what Ibrahim's calling roving Ambassador status – with special responsibility for the UN and the Commonwealth – what do you think?" Richard asked.

"How much time will it take up and what will they pay you?"

Sophia was practical in character – as a result, Richard always consulted her when an important decision had to be made, particularly on financial matters.

"Ibrahim reckons between four and six months per year and the salary will be £200K plus all expenses. He says it's about what the PM gets, but less onerous as it's only part-time!"

"Okay, then, go for it if you like, we could certainly use the money."

"Ibrahim says it was Karim's idea – Karim wants me on the payroll."

"That reminds me, when are we having a return match after Cortina?" asked Sophia.

"I was thinking of May – the garden should be looking good then."

They had both already decided to invite Karim and Kirsty to Highgrove, but the timing needed to be finalised.

"Fine – I'll ask Jackie to arrange for the invitations to be sent after checking what dates are available."

Jackie was their private secretary. They'd had to cut down on staff drastically since the abdication, but realised they couldn't live without at least one secretary between them.

"Agreed – by the way, I'll accept Ibrahim's offer…"

As usual Richard let the phone ring a few times before answering.

"Richard? It's Karim here."

"Fine, how are you?"

"Fine, Kirsty's pregnant, so we're both very excited."

"I read about a few rumours in the Press so congratulations."

"Thanks. Have you got a couple of minutes?"

"Yes, sure, how can I help?"

"It's partly about your status as roving Ambassador – by the way, we're really looking forward to seeing you all at Highgrove – I think the arrangements are nearly finalised."

"Yes, I believe so…"

"As I was saying – your role – keep this to yourself obviously – I am studying the Arab- Israeli conflict and thinking about ways of ending the stalemate…"

"Go on."

"I've got a Jewish friend from Uni working on it with me and we seem to be making progress, though people like Ibrahim are very sceptical."

"So where do I fit into this?" asked Richard.

"I would like to discuss informally how you could help when I see you at Highgrove. I need someone to head up fundraising and also probably to make overtures to the movers and shakers on both sides with a view to some kind of conference in, say, Geneva or some other neutral venue."

"I see – I would need to do some research obviously before approaching anyone."

"Yes, of course – perhaps you could have a think about this and we can discuss it further when we meet. I reckon our mother's legacy as a humanitarian gives both of us clout in this kind of area and I, with mixed British and Arab parentage, am probably better placed than most to try and mediate."

"You – we – can but try – I agree we have a responsibility to honour our mother's memory and we have the time and resources to give it our best shot," responded Richard.

"Thanks, that's marvellous – see you at Highgrove."

Over the next 6 weeks, Richard spent time researching the Arab-Israeli conflict as agreed with Karim. Richard had been advised to go back to the Bible as the primary source – he realised it would be no good going back just to the foundation of the State of Israel in 1948 or the Balfour Declaration of 1917. Richard grappled, in particular, with the concepts of the Promised Land and Zionism.

"This is a different world for the likes of you and me though I expect my mother would have felt at home here," said Karim.

"Yes, it's the world of the English upper classes, partially exported in the past to Scotland, India and other far flung corners of the Empire – anyway, here we are at Highgrove, who'd have thought it? I for one am quite ready to enjoy myself, even if it means being a part-time Hooray Henrietta for a few days!" ventured Kirsty.

That evening at dinner, Richard filled them in on what they could expect over the next few days.

"Firstly, there is a tour of the garden created by my father more than 30 years ago – your guide will be the Head Gardener, Frank James."

"Fine, delighted I'm sure," said Karim.

"Then we will need to show our faces at the Badminton Horse Trials taking place a few miles away."

"Is that horse racing?" asked Karim.

"Well, they race against the clock."

"So, will we be betting?"

"No, not officially – there won't be any bookmakers but I suppose you might be able to bet online if you're desperate."

Karim laughed. "No, I'm not desperate. I used to enjoy the racing in Dubai – camels and horses – though a quick way to lose money it has to be said."

"Quite so – by the way, have either of you ridden before?"

"Camels mainly – a horse only a few times" said Karim.

"About a dozen times" said Kirsty.

"That's fine, we'll get you fixed up with a couple of quiet cobs – I can then take you on a guided tour of the farm."

"What's a cob?" asked Karim.

"It's midway between a thoroughbred and a carthorse – solid, dependable, go anywhere – the Land Rover of the horse world," said Richard.

"Good, we'll look forward to that I'm sure – don't you agree Kirsty?"

"Yes, I guess so, so long as the horse really is quiet – don't forget I'm pregnant."

"That's fine, I'll make sure you get the quietest," Richard promised.

The next day saw the King and Queen touring the garden, guided by Mr James.

The visitors were particularly fascinated by the Islamic Garden and the ornamental hen houses.

After dinner, when the others had gone to bed and Richard and he were alone, Karim broached the subject of the Middle East question.

"How did you get on with your research over the last few weeks on Israel and so on?"

"Fine, yes – however, neither side seems willing to compromise much – I can see that the status of Jerusalem and the Palestinian request for a right of return are two of the main stumbling blocks," said Richard.

"Yes, plus Israel's need for security and the problem of the Israeli settlements on the West Bank," said Karim.

"I can help with a charitable fund," said Richard.

"I've not seen any attempt to compensate those Palestinians who fled their homes during the period 1946 to 1949 and this is part of the problem, I reckon," said Karim.

"I daresay many of them are dead," continued Richard.

"Okay, but what about their descendants?" said Karim.

"There would be a problem identifying the right people," said Richard.

"Or simply distribute funds on the basis of need rather than identity," suggested Karim.

"Yes, fair enough I guess," Richard continued, "we need to think about where the cash would come from."

"The sources of the cash will probably need to be the EU, Arab States, the US and the UN," said Karim.

"How much?" asked Richard.

"Maybe, $50 billion from each grouping, creating a total fund of $200 billion?"

"We could collect the money by way of cash and/or pledges for cash," said Richard.

"Yes, that would be fine – the cash would need to be administered, probably via a UN agency in Switzerland. You would have to be seen as international and neutral," said Karim.

The informal conversation continued and took in Karim's proposals for Jerusalem and who Richard should approach to persuade to attend the conference. Prior to the discussion ending, both parties agreed to keep the other informed about all future developments.

The next two days were taken up with the parties' attendance at the Badminton Horse Trials – cross country eventing on the first day and show jumping on the second.

Karim and Kirsty observed cross country from Richard's Range Rover, with Richard giving a knowledgeable commentary.

There was a pavilion provided for the Royal Party to view the next day's show jumping and, during a break, a stallholder was delighted to sell a Barbour jacket to Karim and a Husky gilet to Kirsty.

"They've both got 'By Royal Appointment' labels already, so you are just continuing a long established tradition!" remarked Sophia.

The next day saw Karim and Kirsty riding two grey cobs out of Richard's extensive stables. Karim was put on Yeti, a dappled grey gelding, and Kirsty put on a quiet mare, also grey, called Snow Goose aka Goosey.

"She's about as excitable as a sack of cement," was Richard's pithy comment. This was later put to the test when Yeti became agitated by a barking dog. Goosey remained perfectly calm.

"I think she may also be slightly deaf," was the further dry comment from Richard.

Prior to the party setting off on a tour of the farm,

several photos were taken of the riders by a girl groom at Karim's request, using his phone.

With Richard's permission, Karim later emailed the two best shots to Sheikh at The Sun, who printed one the following day under the headline:-

KIRSTY AND KARIM JOIN THE HORSEY SET!

Karim knew that, despite his discrepancies, Sheikh was fundamentally loyal and Karim was, therefore, prepared to reward him from time to time.

The riding tour party, guided by Richard, took in the herds of Jersey cattle, the Jacob sheep, pheasant pens, woodlands, the entirely organic market garden and last but not least, the specially designed private sewage system.

The following morning Karim and Kirsty departed, after expressing genuine gratitude for Richard and Sophia's generous hospitality and converting them both into fans of the English rural way of life. "Almost as good as the Scottish equivalent", as Kirsty sincerely remarked.

"By the way, David, there's a peerage in it for you if you get this right! They say the House of Lords is still the best club in London – it's even better than the SOAS Student Union!" joked Karim.

"I'll settle for a knighthood if we can get a deal to stick," responded David Rosenthal, Karim's friend from Uni days.

"Let's just recap on where we've got to, David. We've identified the four main areas of conflict."

"That's correct, Karim, the four issues are

- Israeli settlements on the West Bank
- The status of Jerusalem
- Israel's security concerns re terrorism
- Right of return for Palestinian refugees living in the Palestinian Diaspora."

David continued "We were discussing last time we met, the possibility of a four State solution, that's firstly Israel, secondly a Vatican style city State comprising part of the Old City and the Holy sites in Jerusalem. Thirdly the Gaza Strip becoming a self governing province of Egypt and fourthly the West Bank becoming a self governing province of Jordan. A bit like Northern Ireland's status in the UK."

"That's a good analogy," commented Karim.

"It's building on the existing Peace Treaties between Israel and Egypt in 1979 and between Israel and Jordan in 1994", continued David. "The precedent for splitting the Palestinian territories is Pakistan, where we've ended up with Bangladesh instead of East Pakistan and West Pakistan has dropped West from its name."

David then commented further. "These proposals should appeal to the Israelis as it makes it easier for security to be safeguarded, as there would be no dedicated Palestinian Army. However Gaza residents could join the Egyptian military and West Bank residents could join the Jordanian military."

"Fine, the head bangers on both sides will oppose all of this, of course," commented Karim. "But we need to isolate them or buy them out."

"Talking of which, that brings us to the right of return for Palestinians and the status of the Israeli settlers on the West Bank. It seems logical to talk about linkage."

"I take it that's reciprocity?" asked Karim. "Between the number of settlers on the West Bank and the number of Palestinians having the right to return?"

"That's right," responded David. "We can go back to the Oslo Peace Accords in 1993 which were implemented in 1995 – for the first time the Palestinian territories of Gaza and the West Bank got a kind of formal status, so Israeli settlers since 1995 were ignoring the Peace Accords and can now expect to pay the price by vacating the West Bank. The Israeli settlers in Gaza had to vacate in 2005.

Those that are left, say around 200,000 can stay there and that figure, ie 200,000 should be the number of Palestinians allowed to return to Israel."

"So we need to work on how it's decided who gets the right to return," said Karim.

"I'll deal with that in the draft blueprint, probably some kind of lottery," said David.

"Fine, how much longer do you need to prep the blueprint – can you have it ready in ten days?"

"Give me a fortnight and I'll have something for you."

"Okay, agreed," said Karim.

Two weeks later Karim and David met again in Karim's study in the Buckingham Palace apartment.

"I've got the draft blueprint – the full version is forty pages – I've also got a summary."

"Okay, let's see the summary first."

Rosenthal's bullet pointed summary contained the following key points:-

- The four State solution was as previously discussed and included a Vatican-style city state area for the Holy sites and Old City in Jerusalem, with West Jerusalem as the capital of Israel and East Jerusalem as the capital of the West Bank territory, which was to be substantially Palestinian and would be annexed to Jordan. Gaza would be annexed to Egypt.

- The Israeli settlers on the West Bank would be reduced to around 200,000, the 1995 figure. Those who are to vacate to be paid around $60,000 per adult out of the $200 billion compensation fund.
- Reciprocity would involve 200,000 Palestinians having the right of return to Israel to be decided by lottery involving conditional oath of Israeli citizenship prior to being able to participate in such lottery. Unsuccessful lottery participants would also be offered $60,000 compensation per person.
- Three million was the likely number of Israelis and Palestinians needing compensation, so at $60,000 each, the total compensation payable would be $180 billion, leaving a $20 billion contingency fund to be administered by the UN out of Geneva.
- If the Palestinians were to say they wanted more than 200,000 returnees, then any extra would need to be balanced by more Israeli settlers on the West Bank.

"It's all a compromise – everyone gets something, no-one gets all of what they want," was Rosenthal's comment after Karim had been studying the summary of the blueprint for 10 minutes.

"My main worry is how do we sell this to the likes of Hamas in Gaza, who don't accept Israel's right to exist?" asked Karim.

"It'll have to be behind the scenes, softly softly – it's a once in a lifetime opportunity to join or re-join the international community, rather than continue as a pariah," said Rosenthal.

"I like the land ownership restrictions – that will prevent the Palestinian territories being swallowed up by Egyptian and Jordanian settlers," said Karim.

Rosenthal had provided for the ownership of land in Gaza and the West Bank to be restricted to holders of Palestinian authority passports and only one property per citizen. There would be similar restrictions placed on the ownership of land in Israel.

Andy Sheikh had decided to shelve any thoughts of solving global political problems for the time being.

His mind was on one thing – he had decided to practice what he preached and take a second wife. His long-suffering first wife, Faizah, had consented to the idea.

"She's more interested in food than sex these days and has a figure to match," he had confided in Harry.

"So who's the lucky girl who will be her number two?" asked Harry.

"Zara, I met her online – she's a Palestinian and needs a passport – she's very honest about it – that's one of the things I like about her, that and her looks."

"The perfect symbiotic relationship then – you get the sex, and in return she gets a passport plus a hefty meal ticket."

"Don't knock it – if everyone's happy, what's the problem?"

"No, it's fine – if you play your cards right Karim will award you an OBE for services to procreation!"

"I'll be inviting the whole office to a slap-up wedding reception in a couple of months' time – I'm kind of hoping people will have got used to the idea by then."

"Don't bank on it – I know Western guys your age often have mistresses but it's usually fairly discreet – the novelty is someone being totally open about it," said Harry.

Two weeks later Sheikh issued invitations to the wedding reception. Cue much ribaldry from the guys in the office and giggling from the girls.

Everyone was silenced, up to a point, a couple of days later when they were all introduced to the glamorous Zara, who turned out to be intelligent, well educated and charming.

Importantly, she also seemed to like Sheikh – laughing at his jokes and draping an arm round him at opportune moments.

Afterwards Harry, for one, was generous with his plaudits.

"I take back my banter – I think Zara is very nice and you've done well. How does she get on with Faizah?"

"Oh, fine so far – they take great delight in ganging up on me to take the mickey, but I don't mind, I've got what I want and basically everyone's happy."

Three weeks after their discussions at Highgrove, Karim met Richard in Karim's office at Buckingham Palace.

"Here is the draft blueprint of David Rosenthal's and my proposals for a peace settlement. At the front you'll find a summary, so you don't need to read all forty pages right now. When you've had a look at the summary, may I suggest that the next step is to firm up on your fundraising role?"

Richard then spent 15 minutes reading the summary.

"Yes, it seems fine – my knowledge is more limited than yours, but I guess the stumbling blocks will be to get Hamas in Gaza to participate and also to get the Israeli settlers to agree to cities like Jericho and Hebron being permanently part of Jordan."

"I know, we will need to work very hard to persuade them all to compromise – that's where the money will come in useful – any thoughts so far on fundraising?"

"I am waiting for you to tell me to start. I need to know what I can say in any publicity literature and so on."

"Good point – say it's a humanitarian venture with the distribution of funds being partly dependent on the peace process. If the latter process stalls, then after, say, three years you would use the funds mainly for health and education, particularly for Palestinians. I reckon you will need to instruct lawyers to form the charity – as regards when to start, the sooner the better please. Please bear in mind that once you've got funds promised or actual of, say, $15 billion, then we will need to invite the leaders and other interested parties to a conference, probably in Geneva. We can discuss later who precisely should be invited."

"That's fine, I'll get weaving," responded Richard.

With their traditional marriage vows completed, Sheikh and Zara launched themselves full tilt into the "slap-up reception" that Sheikh had promised everyone.

The venue was Claridges. Everyone had special instructions from Sheikh to be especially nice to Faizah so at least three of The Sun office "drones" swarmed round her at any one time, like she was the queen bee. She had her hands full looking after the three children, but seemed to enjoy the drones' attention, much to Sheikh's relief.

Karim and Kirsty sent an original Cartier silver cigarette box with a note that it was sent for purely aesthetic reasons, not intended to encourage them to smoke. They had been invited to the reception but had declined to attend as Sheikh was now considered too partisan politically.

The main dish consisted of a fish curry accompanied by various oriental sweetmeats. To wash down the food, the guests had a choice of Pol Roger champagne or various fruit juices for the teetotallers.

After the food, the guests gravitated to the dance floor, where a live band serenaded them with a selection of mainly 70s and 80s hits. The proceedings were enlivened by the appearance of a belly dancer, who turned out to be Dagenham born and bred, much to the disappointment of some of the guys from Sheikh's office, who had been expecting someone a little more exotic.

When the band finished, the guests were invited to participate in some karaoke and Sheikh nearly brought the house down with a rendition of Sinatra's "My Way."

The happy couple then departed for their honeymoon in Oman.

"Many congratulations on becoming a dad – I can highly recommend it," said Richard. "And how is the mum?"

"Kirsty and the babies are doing fine, thanks, we are very spoilt with two nannies assisting, but we're still very busy – we didn't realise twins were on the way till quite recently."

"That's fine, what are their names again?"

"Suleyman and Jasmine."

"Ah yes, Suleyman the Magnificent – I've heard of him but what was his claim to fame?"

"He was an enlightened ruler of the Ottoman Empire in the 16th Century."

Around three months after their previous meeting, Karim and Richard had met again in Karim's office in the Palace to discuss progress on the charity front.

"How is the fundraising progressing?"

"I've raised $2 billion with pledges from the EU and USA for a further 50 billion within two years."

"What about the Arab States?"

"I'm still working on them – UAE are likely to commit to $20 billion in the near future, probably spread over two or three years."

"And what about the UN?"

"They're very slow to respond to anything, but

I'm ever hopeful. I have to say, if we have a successful conference, the cash should start to flow more quickly."

"Yes, I agree – we therefore now need to contact Israeli and Palestinian leaders to invite them to a conference. Can you please take care of that – in your capacity as a UN rep? Say we will present a new draft blueprint for peace which needs to be debated."

"Who do you recommend I contact?"

"Israel now has a Labour Prime Minister – Shimon Levy – they have previously been more likely to make concessions than their right wing parties like Likud. Then the West Bank leader is Ahmed Said – again, he's reasonably moderate as compared to Hamas in Gaza."

"Who's the leader of Hamas?"

"Abdel Najib – he's a bit of a firebrand – make sure you say Ibrahim and I, fellow Muslims, are supporting you in regard to this new initiative. Say also there is a compensatory financial package being put together. If he says compensation for what, say he'd better come to the conference, then he'll find out!"

Richard struggled to get himself heard by the three main leaders Karim wanted to invite to the conference. They were all difficult and played hard to get. They also all wanted to know what was in the blueprint.

Richard confined himself to saying that his interest was humanitarian rather than political and he was just carrying on from where his mother left off. He said the blueprint offered a fair compromise – some would be disappointed – some Palestinians would be offered a right to return and those that were not would get financial compensation. The same would apply to any Israeli settlers required to vacate the West Bank.

The full text of the blueprint would be released nearer the date of the conference. It would be a draft to be discussed and debated.

After several phone calls, Levy and Said agreed to attend. Najib said Hamas would send two "observers" – he had no mandate to agree to attend any conference that might involve recognition of Israel.

Richard reported all the above back to Karim two weeks later.

"Some time we'll have to get Ibrahim to speak to Najib. Ibrahim understands how to deal with this kind of impasse – he's also a devout Muslim so Najib will listen to him," Karim commented.

The next three months were taken up with organising the conference, fundraising and finalising the draft peace blueprint.

When approached on the Hamas issue, Ibrahim

declined to speak to Najib prior to the conference.

"We know where Najib stands, and what his problem is – if the conference is a success, I'll approach him with a view to persuading him that it's worth his while to get involved and that he needs to explain to his people Israel is here to stay."

19

The draft blueprint for peace was published by H M Government on 20th October 2019. The blueprint had essentially been written by David Rosenthal with Karim's assistance and approval.

The peace conference was due to take place a month later in Geneva.

Most of the Western media welcomed the blueprint as, in the words of The London Times editorial, "imaginative, realistic and fair."

The blueprint was, however, immediately condemned by Israeli settler organisations on the West Bank and Hamas in Gaza. Both said it was biased against them.

"They can't both be right," was Sheikh's pithy comment.

While the majority of postings on social media were in favour of the blueprint after so many years of false dawns on a settlement, the extreme positions were in evidence too. While Israelis 4 Palestine, Jewish Voice for Peace and the National Committee of the global Palestinian Boycott, Divestment & Sanctions (BDS) Movement all endorsed it, others persisted with a hard line. A poetic rallying call appeared on Facebook:

DEFY, DISSENT, DISPUTE!
Heaving sighs of soul-deep misery
I felt the weight of truth
And will not buckle.
I cannot tolerate this false face of freedom,
Never bend to this lie of peace.
Defy, dissent, dispute.
Defy this artificial truce.
In defiance of their presence,
Raise your voices and your flags.
Bid them gone from this our Palestine, our home!
Defy this theft of hearth and heart,
Turn our lives toward this purpose;
Defy, dissent, dispute.
Dispute their claim.
Though written words feign authority,
They are no more than dust,
When measured with sovereignty of soul.
Let no charter of indignity and submission,
Alter your conviction to the cause of justice.

Defy, dissent, dispute!
Defy this occupation.
Do not give weight to fearful thoughts,
Or puppets who pedal them in these Palestinian
    streets.
Do not be sold a myth of peace and freedom
To incarcerate your soul.
Find strength within and continue where many
    endured before,
Defy, dissent, dispute!
Defy their right to remain.
Their methods are shameful and villainous.
Do not submit to artifice,
When deeds belie their words.
Make a ritual of your defiance,
In the name of those who died uttering;
"Defy, dissent, dispute!"
Defy, dissent, dispute!

In response, Israeli hardliners vilified the Palestinian leadership, Hamas and the PLO equally, as terrorists who praised suicide bombers and mass murderers as heroes, naming streets, squares and sports stadiums after brutal murderers who target civilians. "They dance in the streets and hand out sweets when Jews are killed. They indoctrinate their children to grow up to become martyrs. Their hate speech against Jews is as disgusting and bigoted as anything from the Third Reich."

Israel by contrast with the Palestinian Authority had already tried to provide for its Palestinian population when it installed very expensive infrastructure in Gaza, to build the economy. Within 2 days, it had been trashed and destroyed for good. "The Gazans complain of poverty while their Hamas leaders drive around in Mercedes and Porsches and live in penthouses in Doha, Abu Dhabi and Paris."

The peace conference was chaired by the British Foreign Secretary, Ross Clarke.

There were a total of 125 delegates plus 2 observers from Hamas. Israel, the West Bank, Jordan and Egypt accounted for around a quarter each of the attendees.

Various problems were highlighted during the debates at the conference, in particular defining the area of Jerusalem which was to be under the jurisdiction of the neutral City State arrangement.

It was agreed more work would be needed on defining the boundaries, but the majority of Israeli and West Bank delegates approved the idea in principle.

Some of the Palestinian delegates questioned why any Israeli settlers on the West Bank should be compensated for vacating the territory, particularly as they would be getting a fair price for the properties they were vacating, on a market value basis.

The Foreign Secretary offered the following comment:-

"To get any to vacate it must be either a carrot or stick approach, or a combination of both. We prefer primarily to use incentives as too much stick is likely to lead to substantial bloodshed. Besides, it's not Palestinian money that's going to be used to compensate them, it's other people's money."

Another problem was identified by some of the Egyptian and Jordanian delegates. Why should the ownership of land in Gaza and the West Bank be confined to holders of Palestinian passports, which would be a sub-set of Egyptian and Jordanian passports respectively.

Again, the Chairman intervened.

"The land has been in dispute for decades and is not a large area. It's only right that the refugees in relation to the conflict, ie the Palestinians, should have privileged status in relation to the limited area available. If at a later date the citizens of Gaza and the West Bank vote to extend the ability to own land to other people, that will have to be their democratic decision, and not made by anyone else. However, to allow a free for all now over land ownership would make a mockery of the peace process and the lives the conflict has claimed over so many years."

Both Levy and Said broadly welcomed the blueprint in their final conference speeches. Levy quoted Rabin as follows:-

"We who have fought against you, the Palestinians, we say to you today, in a loud and clear voice, enough of blood and tears… enough!"

This drew rousing applause from most of the delegates in the hall.

The final vote to approve the blueprint in principle was carried by 90 votes in favour to 20 against, with 15 abstentions.

"Yes, the conference was a success, but much work still needs to be done," said the Foreign Secretary.

Karim had called a meeting in his office at Buckingham Palace – those present with him were David Rosenthal, Richard, Ross Clarke and Ibrahim.

"Richard, please update us on the fundraising," requested Karim.

"The good news is that, on the back of the conference, two large charitable Foundations have each donated $25 billion, so on the basis of 200 billion being the global target, then everyone else can reduce their targets and commitments by 25 per cent."

"Is there now a consensus that $60,000 in compensation for three million disappointed refugees and Israeli settlers will be enough?" asked Ibrahim.

"Obviously it won't go as far in Israel as elsewhere due to property prices and so on, but it's really the best deal that can reasonably be expected." David Rosenthal continued "There should be at least 20 billion balance not yet allocated, that can be used additionally to help deserving cases."

"Decided by who?" asked Ibrahim.

"Ultimately the UN Agencies based in Geneva," said Richard. "They will have reps on the ground to assess need."

"Another issue is Hamas in Gaza – Ibrahim, when can you speak to Najib?" asked Karim.

"Sometime within the next month or so – initial contact needs to be made by the FCO and that's the Foreign Secretary's area, obviously."

"Agreed, I'll get my people to start working on it," said Ross Clarke.

A month later, Ibrahim found himself on a direct skype link from No. 10 to Abdel Najib in the Hamas HQ in Gaza.

"Good morning, Prime Minister, how can I help you?" asked Najib in accented but otherwise perfect English.

Ibrahim was surprised by the affable tone of this so-called firebrand, but quickly recovered his composure.

"Thank you for offering your co-operation, my friend.

To get straight to the point, there are many people hoping and praying that you will see fit to approve, at least in principle, the peace deal that was welcomed by most delegates at the Geneva conference."

"I've got no mandate to agree it, even if I wanted to, and I'm not convinced I do want to either," replied Najib.

"Please allow me to try and convince you and we'll think about the mandate later."

"Fine, go ahead."

"Firstly, there's to be a right of return to Israel for about 10 per cent of your people, to be decided by lottery, with compensation to be paid to those who are unlucky in the lottery."

"How much compensation?"

"$60,000 per person – a fund has been started with a target of $200 billion. To participate in the lottery and either have a right of return or compensation, then all participants must recognise the State of Israel's right to exist in accordance with UN resolutions."

"So many will be expected to part with their birthright for filthy lucre," countered Najib.

"Israel is here to stay; it's got nuclear weapons and the unconditional backing of the USA. At the moment, Gaza has neither."

"It may have both if it gets annexed to Egypt as proposed at the conference."

"Maybe, but I reckon the need to safeguard the existence of Israel trumps just about everything else in US foreign policy. Also, Egypt already has a peace treaty with Israel, signed in 1979."

"Let me touch on the emotional content of our politics. My ancestors tended their flocks of sheep for generations on pasture that is now occupied by Israel. When this point was mentioned to one of Levy's predecessors, Navon – Moshe Navon, all he could say was that Israel had built villas with swimming pools on the land as though it was self evidently a better use of the land. Have you any idea how enraged that makes us feel?"

There were a few seconds silence while Ibrahim digested this latest salvo.

"My friend, if it's any consolation, I would feel the same way as you, but we are where we are. By the way, Navon is awaiting trial for alleged corruption, so not every Israeli politician thinks or acts the same way as him. Another Israeli politician said the problem is that Palestinians never missed an opportunity to miss an opportunity – I suspect that statement may also enrage you?"

"Kind of, but what is your point please?"

"This offer, in principle, approved at Geneva represents a once-in-a-lifetime opportunity to get part of what your people want – peacefully – without bloodshed."

"But it's mainly just money – we've been struggling for more than just money for decades."

"It's more than just money – it's a way of no longer being an international pariah – you can re-join the international community with dignity."

"And if we turn this down?"

"Then, none of you will have the right of return and the money allocated for your people will all go to the West Bank Palestinians. My friend – believe me – you would be held up for ridicule – even if not by your own people, certainly by most of the media globally."

There was a pause of maybe twenty seconds while Najib digested what Ibrahim was saying.

"I will consult with my colleagues – we will think about it."

"Good, I will contact you again in a couple of weeks' time."

"Agreed."

Over the next year, progress was made though it was, unsurprisingly, much slower than Karim would have liked.

Sometimes it was a case of two steps forward and one step back, as when a Government in financial difficulty went back on the pledge it had made to Richard.

"We need to tour the areas affected, to meet and greet the people and generate goodwill," said Karim at a meeting at Buckingham Palace to review progress a year after Ibrahim's first talk with Najib.

"Who is 'we' in this context?" asked Richard.

"You, David Rosenthal and myself, plus Kirsty probably – we need a female presence to chat to the leaders' wives."

"I agree – my staff at the FCO can arrange the tour for you," Ross Clarke continued "may I suggest you take in Cairo, Amman, Gaza, the West Bank, Jerusalem and Tel Aviv, probably in that order. I reckon one day each in Cairo and Amman plus two days each in the other locations, so that makes it a ten-day trip minimum."

"If Kirsty goes I expect Sophia will want to go," said Richard.

"No problem," said Karim. "I expect Kirsty would

welcome some moral support by way of additional female company.

"Where does the fund stand at present by the way?"

"We have around $160 billion in cash and pledges for cash."

"That's marvellous. Ibrahim, what progress if any with Najib?" asked Karim.

"We've spoken maybe twenty times over the last year – it's all been done on skype and I feel I know the guy quite well – we've swapped our life stories and so on. I've told him the current draft deal is the only game in town, and I think he now just about accepts that what I say is correct and realistic. It's still about 50/50 whether or not he can sell the deal to his colleagues and Electorate."

"Will he give his Electorate a chance to vote on the deal?" asked Karim.

"This is what I was getting to – there's an election in about 3 months' time in Gaza – he has implied his colleagues are split into hawks and doves – he's not yet taken sides as he is seeking unity. If he's neutral or sides with the doves, then I think we're in with a chance…"

"That's probably the best we could have expected at this stage, so many thanks for your efforts. Foreign Secretary, what feedback have you got on the direct talks between Levy and Said?"

"The talks are mainly in secret, so not much to

report right now, but their spokesmen say they've made progress – the boundaries in Jerusalem have been difficult to get to grips with, as you would expect. The same applies to some of the West Bank boundaries, or at least that's what I've heard on the grapevine," responded Ross Clarke.

"Our tour should give some momentum to the talks – how quickly can it be arranged?"

"Probably four to five months time minimum – I'll treat it as a priority, but people's diaries often fill up a year in advance – don't worry, we'll emphasise the urgency – as if they didn't know it already!"

In a downmarket suburb of Tel Aviv, two Israeli friends were discussing the recently publicised plans of Karim to visit Israel to promote his peace plan.

"I don't care if he's King of England and married to the Queen of Sheba, he's still just another goy," remarked Uzi Eshkol.

"Apparently he's got a Hebrew speaking Jewish adviser called Rosenthal," commented Baruch Shazar.

"That's right – David Rosenthal," Eshkol continued. "I've done some research on him and he publicly condemned the IDF's Gaza campaign when he was a student in London. You can bet your life they'll be keen to shaft the likes of you and me – like Rabin did – they're no better than Nazis," said Eshkol.

"I agree," Shazar continued, "the draft peace plan talks about getting 200K settlers to vacate the West Bank and then expects us to take in 200K Palestinians exercising a so-called right of return."

"Anyone would think we lost the 1967 war the way some of these arseholes go on," remarked Eshkol.

"Can't we get the settlers to take a stand against the plan and stop Khaled and Rosenthal in their tracks?" Shazar asked.

"They're too timid and image conscious. This is a test for us – for our beliefs – don't you see it?"

"What do you mean?"

"We're true believers – remember what that Rabbi said – who wrote that book – how a violent act can be evidence of devotion to God – it's authentic self expression, that's what he said," said Eshkol.

"What do you propose then?" asked his companion.

"Deal with them – that's what – deal with them like Rabin was dealt with – the two of us can do it if we work together."

"I was neutral during the election on the peace plan issue," said Najib.

"Remind me, what percentage did the pro peace plan candidates get?" asked Ibrahim.

"Around 70 per cent – it seems like the Electorate has grown tired of conflict – I've offered to continue as President, which I wanted to do whichever way the vote went."

"That's fine – it was always a key part of the jigsaw to have Gaza on board. The King is delighted and he asked me to say he looks forward to meeting you on his tour in a couple of months time."

"I'm sure he will be welcome here," said Najib.

"As you know, the main objective now is to build up the momentum towards having final peace talks in London, with a view to the signing of a Treaty." Karim was talking privately to Richard in the RUK Embassy in Cairo on the first leg of their tour.

"With regard to the funding, we need to have the cash in place or pledged by the time the final talks take place, so a complete package is on the table."

"Quite so," said Richard. "The total cash fund now stands at $100 billion with 80 billion pledged if a Treaty is signed, so we are 90 per cent there."

"That's marvellous, thanks for all your hard work," said Karim.

Karim's charm offensive went down well in Cairo and Amman, but it was not until the party arrived in Gaza that public enthusiasm went into overdrive.

"Will we get such a warm welcome as this in Israel? That's the $60,000 question," commented Karim.

"We'll find out soon enough," responded David Rosenthal.

The warm welcome continued on the West Bank – a couple of red carpet receptions, a TV interview and crowds of children waving Palestinian and Cross of St George flags en route from one venue to the next.

Then came the first of several tests in Israel. First up was Karim's speech to the Knesset – a virtually unprecedented event – the only foreigners previously to address the Knesset were US Presidents and that was rare enough.

The text of Karim's address was as follows:

I am truly honoured that I am being permitted to address you today.

This peace initiative would not have happened had it not been for the contributions made by three people in particular. Firstly, my mother, Princess Caroline, whose legacy to me involved my having her example to follow when considering humanitarian problems sometimes thought insoluble by conventional politicians.

Her campaign on the landmine issue is the best example of her determination and charismatic ability to persuade people to take action.

Secondly, my half-brother, Prince Richard, who has tirelessly worked over many months to build a fund comprising billions of dollars to compensate those on both sides of the divide whose aspirations cannot be met.

Lastly, my University friend, David Rosenthal, who has been the main architect of the blueprint for peace that was approved not least by your representatives and diplomats at the Geneva conference.

Politically, David and I have at least one thing in common – in particular we admire the contribution to peace made by your Prime Minister, Yitzhak Rabin, who was felled by an assassin's bullets just when the world thought we were on the brink of a lasting peace settlement.

I like to think he would have fully approved of our efforts. I also hope you agree that myself and my team are carrying on conscientiously from where he left off and also that this peace process has the support of most of the ordinary people on both sides of the conflict. May I say, the views of ordinary people are ignored by politicians at their peril.

It was once said by an Israeli politician that Israel's problems only concern Israel and can only be solved by Israel.

I beg to differ – the problems of Israel, possibly more than any other country on earth, have had truly global repercussions and have been used as an excuse, a pretext or a reason, depending on your viewpoint, by extremists and activists with a global reach to justify their actions.

Let us finally draw out the sting, let the wound heal and pray for peace.

Many thanks for your attention, and I wish you well.

Karim's speech was intentionally short on detail and it was left to David Rosenthal to be interviewed on the main Israeli TV news channel, in Hebrew. He was asked point blank about his opposition to the IDF Gaza campaign. He justified his view on the basis of humanitarian and world opinion and the statement that bombing someone doesn't make them agree with you.

Uzi Eshkol and Baruch Shazar watched Karim's speech and David Rosenthal's interview that evening on TV at home in Tel Aviv. Eshkol cradled his namesake, an Uzi sub-machine gun, in his lap while Shazar practised reloading a Berreta of the same type that had been used to kill Rabin. The weapons had been "liberated" from an Army store several months previously while both were training as Army reservists.

"That guy just spouts platitudes – he's hardly said anything and what God does he think he's praying to – not my God that's for sure," said Eshkol.

"That Rosenthal's a traitor – he's a mealy mouthed London liberal and he's come here to lecture to us – it makes me want to puke," was Shazar's contribution.

"Still there's no point in getting steamed up right now – we're on a mission to deal with them – like – tomorrow," said Eshkol.

"You can't take that with you, it's too bulky," said Shazar, gesturing at the machine gun.

"I know, it's Berettas for both of us plus the car bomb."

"The car's fully primed and ready to go. I checked it an hour ago."

The car bomb exploded at 4.37 pm local time, sixty metres away from the Rothschild Boulevard in Tel Aviv while the convoy of Volvo stretch limos was conveying

Karim and his party to a reception in Independence Hall.

The perpetrators could not have parked the car any closer due to the tight security. Their initial objective was to cause chaos and distract the attention of the Police.

Fifteen people were killed instantly, all Israelis, including five children.

The limos ground to a halt.

The second Volvo contained Karim, Kirsty and David Rosenthal. Their bodyguard made the mistake of winding down the bullet proof window to get a better take on what was happening. He was immediately shot dead by Eshkol, who had run out of the crowd, Beretta in hand. Eshkol fired three more shots through the window of the stationary car. One hit Karim in the shoulder, the second hit Kirsty in the abdomen. The final shot hit David Rosenthal in the neck – he died almost instantaneously.

Meanwhile, from the other side of the road, Shazar had approached the third Volvo containing Richard and Sophia. He also had a Beretta in hand – his first shot shattered the rear side window but did not go through it. He was then felled by a shot from a nearby policeman who then turned his attention and gun on Eshkol, who was trying to re-load. The latter sustained two shots to the shoulder but survived. Shazar died in hospital two hours later from loss of blood.

After what seemed like an age, but in fact was only a few minutes, ambulances started arriving, sirens wailing. Priority was given to Karim and Kirsty – by this time Kirsty was unconscious and Karim, who was less badly hurt, was attempting to revive her. She and Karim were put on saline drips and taken at speed to the main hospital, the Sourasky, in the city, where both had blood transfusions.

Both had operations to remove bullets. In Kirsty's case the op lasted three hours while her guts were repaired, apart from her womb that the surgeons had to remove.

After his op, Karim was soon sitting up in bed enquiring after Kirsty.

"I'm told she will pull through but she's weak right now due to loss of blood – she's sedated in Intensive Care, but stable and improving," his doctor said.

"Thank God for that, I thought I'd lost her. What about David?"

"I'm sorry – he didn't make it…"

There was a pause – Karim welled up.

"I feel terrible and responsible – I asked him to get involved in the first place."

The doctor shrugged and then hurried away to his next patient, leaving Karim alone with his thoughts.

329

A couple of days later Eshkol was deemed well enough to be questioned.

"I stopped that Rosenthal creep – it's just a shame I didn't stop Khaled. Someone else will have to do that for us."

The detective interviewing him winced.

"So what was your motive?"

"To save the Promised Land – cities like Hebron and Jericho – it's God's will."

"So what about the fifteen innocent people you killed with the car bomb?"

"They were in the wrong place at the wrong time – shit happens."

"Are you going to apologise?"

"It's Khaled and Rosenthal who need to apologise – they brought this upon us."

The assassination attempt made Karim a hero overnight. The outpouring of sympathy was global, as was the revulsion in respect of Shazar and Eshkol's crimes, particularly the callous disregard for the fifteen killed by the car bomb – and the brutal assassination of David Rosenthal.

Karim's heroic status merited a personal visit in hospital by the Israeli Prime Minister, Shimon Levy, who delivered the welcome news that his son, Ben, a recently elected member of the Knesset, had expressed a willingness to take the place of David Rosenthal to carry forward the peace process.

"That's truly marvellous news – when can we meet?" asked Karim.

"When you feel well enough," Levy responded.

"If the medics permit it, later this week should be fine – please thank Ben for his interest."

"I certainly will. By the way, we're the ones who should be thanking you – it's taken creative outsiders to think the unthinkable about solutions to our problems and you've risked your life for us into the bargain…"

Jews for Peace on Facebook were the first off the mark to congratulate Karim for brokering the peace agreement.

A Daily Mirror journalist tweeted this was the best outcome anyone could have imagined. As hope for a genuine two-state solution had realistically died with PM Yitzhak Rabin's assassination by an Israeli right-wing extremist in 1995, it was all the more surprising a blueprint such as Karim and David Rosenthal had produced would be agreed at conference.

Most of the commentary was an outpouring of sympathy for Karim and Kirsty, wishing them well for a full recovery, then sadness Kirsty could no longer bear children when details of her wounds and operation were broadcast. The hard-line positions taken when the blueprint first appeared were now less in evidence as most Jewish contributors expressed appreciation that a Muslim peace-broker was able to show imagination and flexibility where it had not been shown before by the Palestinian leadership in negotiation. The speculation was that this was because Karim was outside the cauldron of Middle East politics and held a status above the fray.

There was much debate about the Israeli electoral system which gave extremist parties such as Likud disproportionate influence in government. Ben Levy himself tweeted that this had to change. It was purely good fortune that the Labour Party was in power. The peace agreement would not have happened if his father had not shown a statesmanlike breadth of vision unthinkable if his rise to power had been through Likud, like his predecessor as Prime Minister.

Others on social media responded to Ben Levy by pointing out that Menachem Begin, a prominent right winger, had signed the Camp David peace agreement with Egyptian President Anwar El Sadat in 1978, guaranteeing that Israel's most powerful military opponent recognised its right to exist. Begin had been the preeminent Middle Eastern terrorist of his day (or patriotic freedom fighter, depending on your viewpoint) as leader of Irgun in 1940s, responsible for planning the destruction of the King David Hotel (91 deaths) and the massacre of Deir Yassin (100 to 260 deaths, including women and children).

Ben Levy used the debate to reinforce his plea on Twitter for electoral reform. He pointed out that such a recurrence of an extremist becoming statesman, of seeing the light on the road to Damascus as it were, could not be guaranteed in future to foster a peace settlement.

As well as taking the heat out of the social media debate, Ben Levy's number of followers increased tenfold as his tweets were re-tweeted and liked more than 40000 times.

"It's not the first time a Jewish martyr's been created by one or more of his own people murdering him," said Harry pointedly.

"I know, it's probably to do with spending too much time reading the Old Testament and not getting out more," Sheikh continued – "What news of Kirsty?"

"She's making progress but they've had to give her a hysterectomy."

"Rendered barren in a violent attack – that sounds like something out of the Old Testament as well," commented Sheikh.

"At least they've already got two kids" said Harry.

"I know, but it's still upsetting, to put it mildly."

"The most likely outcome of this episode is to increase support for Karim's peace initiative – he's already achieved hero status in the Middle East, and probably globally," said Harry.

"How about running a feature on the blueprint for peace and where it's got to so far?" suggested Sheikh.

"Can do – I'll reduce it to bullet points and put in a few maps and photos. We can't assume our average reader has any prior knowledge," replied Harry.

"That may be true, but he or she won't want to be patronised."

"I know – leave it to me – I'll pitch it right – don't worry," replied Harry.

Ben Levy and Karim hit it off soon after meeting. Ben was progressive in his politics, ebullient and humorous.

"Are you prejudiced against Arabs?" This was one of the first questions Karim put to him.

"Well, you and they are family, in effect – we're all related with Abraham as a common ancestor. I know some of them can be a pain in the backside, but so can any relative!"

"Good, I like your attitude – I can work with you I'm sure. Have you got any criticisms of the blueprint for peace?"

"In theory most of it seems fair. In practice, there may well be problems – the Jewish settlers who are left on the West Bank need to be fully safeguarded by the Jordanian government with a full set of human rights – citizenship, freedom of religion and so on. Also there may be problems with the 200,000 Palestinians in Israel who've won the right to return. Many of them will have no money, so it looks like the State of Israel will have to house them."

"We expect to have $20 billion to help people in need – apart from that, the US is likely to help more provided the transition is peaceful," responded Karim.

"The other point is that I reckoned the Israeli Electorate would be generally sceptical, but after this assassination attempt, most people here think you can do no wrong!"

"I am truly flattered if that's what people think. In that case, let's preserve the momentum and move to final peace talks within a few months – what do you think?" asked Karim.

"Agreed, let's go for it."

Three months after Karim's Middle East tour, final peace talks started in Lancaster House, London. The talks were presided over by Foreign Secretary Clarke again.

Most of the spadework had been done before the talks started in that the blueprint had, by now morphed into a 220-page Treaty complete with maps, plans, detailed clauses as to how the lottery was to be organised, provisions for compensation and so on.

It was recognised that the re-location would take time, so a two-year implementation period was included. Those present included the Egyptian and Jordanian Foreign Ministers, the Israeli PM, Levy, plus Said representing the West Bank and Najib representing Gaza. These five were expected to be the signatories of the Treaty.

The agenda included receptions at the Egyptian, Jordanian and Israeli Embassies, speeches by each of the five signatories, the signing ceremony, Press conferences and finally a State dinner in the Great Hall, Windsor Castle for all participants in the talks.

Mainly due to substantial prepping by the likes

of Ben Levy and Ibrahim, and much to the surprise of the sceptics, the proceedings progressed without any major upsets. Opponents of the Treaty were to be found in demonstrations supervised by the Police outside the building. They made themselves heard, but were otherwise substantially sidelined.

With the signing ceremony and Press conferences out of the way, Karim and Kirsty were delighted to host a lavish State dinner. Both had by now substantially recovered from their ordeal in Israel. The following day, the Press and global media generally acknowledged that the Treaty of London 2021 represented a major achievement for English diplomacy in general, and Karim in particular.

Three months later, while relaxing in the gardens at Buckingham Palace with Kirsty and their children, a call was put through to Karim from the RUK Ambassador in Norway.

"Good afternoon, sir. I'm sorry to disturb your weekend, but I have some excellent news for you."

"Fine – please continue."

"I've been asked by the Nobel Prize Committee to inform you that they wish to award this year's Peace Prize to you and Prince Richard jointly on account of the work you have both done to secure the signing of the Treaty of London this year. May I be the first to congratulate you, sir... it goes without saying there surely cannot be a higher honour..."

There was a pause of several seconds while Karim digested this information. Then he managed to blurt out a few phrases like "Fantastic news... totally unexpected... it was a team effort...," before finally landing on his feet with a practical question.

"When and where will the award ceremony be?"

"In about four months in Oslo, hosted by King Harald."

"Fine, marvellous, thanks very much for letting me know – I take it you will be contacting Prince Richard?"

"Yes, sir, as soon as I can locate him."

"Good – thanks."

"Goodbye, sir."

"Goodbye, Ambassador."

In the glittering Nobel Awards Ceremony in Oslo, Karim included the following in his acceptance speech:

I dedicate this award to my friend, David Rosenthal, who not only worked very hard over several months drafting the peace plan, but ultimately gave his life for his people and his humanitarian beliefs.

I believe ultimately he will be seen as a martyr and folk hero like Michael Collins in Ireland, who also gave his life after promoting a peace plan, almost exactly 100 years ago.

Richard, in his acceptance speech, followed suit, up to a point, by dedicating his prize to their mother, Princess Caroline, whose charisma and legacy had helped them so much in their quest for peace.

The following day, the Daily Mail ran the headline:

KARIM TRIUMPHANT!

With the sub-heading:

The two sons their mother would have been proud of.

Karim reckoned that such praise from The Mail, a paper that had originally opposed him, meant that he had truly arrived – at last!

ACKNOWLEDGEMENTS

I started putting this book together at least 7 years ago. During that time I have received help and encouragement, for which I am deeply grateful, from the following people in particular:-

Pete Gaskell, who has made a substantial creative contribution, particularly to the "action" scenes; Sarah Joy, who wrote the song lyrics on page 1 and also the poem in Chapter 19; Luiza Pearson, who has been my "phantom literary agent" and explained to me how to get started; Veronica Boult, who has patiently typed my sometimes garbled dictation and amendments; Sophia Bellamy plus Claire and Ian Curry, who have proof read and edited out, hopefully, the worst of my errors; Hannah Dakin and colleagues at Matador plus Ian Churchward for helping me with the publishing and printing phase of the project; Lawrence Harrison of Swan Turton, media lawyers, for advice; Richard Tranter and Ahmed Rajab for information on Islam plus Simon Cohen and Alan Rodgers for information on the Middle East generally, derived from first-hand experience acquired over many years in each case; Prestel Publishing (represented by Will Westall) and

Boris Friedewald (author of "Picasso's Animals") for permission to use Paloma Picasso's quote at the start of Chapter 3.

Many thanks to all of the above for enabling me to put this book together, grammatically, literally, legally and physically.

ABOUT THE AUTHOR

Baz Wade made his living variously as a farmer, insurance salesman, lawyer and diplomat, after obtaining a degree in History and Politics, and before becoming a writer.

His leisure interests include skiing, classic cars, karaoke and walking the dog.

He lives in the West of England, where he is kept entertained and busy by his family and extended family.